with me in seattle book 8

Forever
with me

KRISTEN PROBY

Dear Reader,

Writing this series has been an incredible journey for me. And to think, when I began writing Come Away With Me, I didn't intend to write a series. That book was intended to be a stand-alone. But once I met Jules and all of her brothers, how could I resist giving everyone their own love story?

I couldn't.

And I'm so happy that I didn't. Many of you have sent me letters and notes telling me that the Montgomery clan has become a part of your own inner circle. Your family. This moves me more than I can ever tell you. It's the same for me! I've lived with these people for more than two years, and they are very dear to me. I can't imagine my life without them. It's been a joy and a privilege to watch this family grow. To watch the friendships form, the babies be born. And I admit, saying goodbye is hard.

I struggled with ending the series with Forever With Me. But I truly believe that I've given each of our couples the best happy ever after possible. The Montgomerys will always hold a very special place in my heart, and the best thing about books is we can always revisit them.

So get comfortable, grab a steaming cup of coffee or perhaps a glass of wine, and settle in. I have a story to tell you . . .

Kristen

This book is dedicated to the Montgomery, Williams, McKenna, Nash and Salvatore families. Thank you for this wild ride. I'll never forget you.

books by
KRISTEN PROBY

WITH ME IN SEATTLE SERIES:
Come Away With Me
Under The Mistletoe With Me
Fight With Me
Play With Me
Rock With Me
Safe With Me
Tied With Me
Breathe With Me
Forever With Me

LOVE UNDER THE BIG SKY SERIES,
available through Pocket Books:
Loving Cara
Seducing Lauren
Falling for Jillian

THE BOUDREAUX SERIES:
Easy Love
Easy for Keeps: 1001 Dark Nights Novella

Easy Charm

Easy Melody

Easy Kisses

THE FUSION SERIES:

Listen to Me

Close to You

Blush For Me ~ Coming Soon

prologue

"**W**ake up, sweetheart."

What the—?

Soft lips skim down my neck to my collarbone, making me moan and arch my back. A strong hand pulls me from my side to my back and those lips slide back up my neck to that spot right behind my ear that makes every nerve in my body come alive.

"What are you doing?" My fingers find their way into his thick, dark hair as I feel him grin against my skin. My nipples pucker almost painfully. His body is deliciously firm and warm next to me. I manage to open my heavy eyes to find Dominic smiling down at me, those ice blue eyes of his glowing in the moonlight.

"I think it's pretty obvious what I'm doing, *bella*." He cups my face in his large hands and lowers his lips to mine, kissing me gently at first, his lips sliding back and forth across mine, and then he settles against me, one leg planted between both of my thighs, his hard thigh pressing against the center of my universe with just enough pressure to make my hips tilt up against him, and he lays the sexiest kiss I've ever had on me. He tastes like wine and mint and sexy man. He's devouring me in the most delicious way.

I knew Dominic Salvatore would be an excellent kisser.

My hands roam from his soft hair down to his shoulders and arms . . . his impossibly chiseled, strong arms.

"Don't tell me no, *bella*." His voice is rough as he kisses his way down my chest to one breast where he pulls my nipple into his mouth and tugs gently, making me rub my core against his naked thigh again.

"Please. I need you."

"This is crazy." But I don't push him away. Instead I plunge my fingers into his hair again and drag him up for another long, deep, hungry kiss. God, I can't get enough of his mouth.

He shifts, settling his pelvis against mine. His cock is long and thick and moves easily between my slick folds, the head massaging my clit in a mind-numbing staccato.

"You're so wet," he whispers harshly. "Open your eyes."

It's not a request.

He's staring down at me with an intensity I've never seen from anyone before. God, he feels so good. I drag my hands down his back to his ass and grip him firmly as I raise my knees high against his sides, opening myself up to him.

"I wasn't going to do this with you."

He clenches his eyes shut and tilts his forehead against mine.

"I can't stay away from you. I've tried, *bella*."

I can hear Italy in his voice. His body is tight with yearning, but he's holding himself steady, waiting for my decision. Every muscle is pulled tight. He's trembling.

How can I say no to this?

I don't want to say no to this!

"Dom?"

"Anything. Anything you want."

I circle my hips. A slow smile spreads over my lips, as his jaw clenches and he mutters an Italian curse word through gritted teeth.

"Yes." I whisper.

His hand palms my breast; his thumb circles my tight nipple.

"Are you sure?" His hand glides down my side and around to my ass, pulling me more tightly against him.

"Yes."

"You're *so* damn wet, Alecia."

"I know."

He grins down at me, pulls his hips back, and then slides inside me in one smooth motion, filling me completely.

We both gasp, eyes locked, as he stills, buried inside me, and I swear to God, buried in the very heart of me.

Except, I don't do hearts and flowers.

"Don't make me fall in love with you," I plead. His eyes soften, but he doesn't reply, he just pulls out all the way, looks down between us and pushes back inside me and repeats the motion twice more.

"Faster," I beg.

"No."

I glare up at him, but he simply smiles back at me before kissing my forehead, linking his fingers with mine and pinning my hand above my head. And then he begins to really move those hips, setting up a punishing rhythm. His pubis nudges my clit with every thrust of his hips, pushing me closer to the edge.

"Do you know how badly I've wanted you, Alecia?" he whispers against my ear as his free hand continues to cup my ass and he controls the speed and depth of his thrusts.

"No."

He kisses my ear, my cheek, my nose, and finally my lips as he picks up speed, fucking me harder, faster, making me squirm and moan and pant.

Jesus fucking Christ I can't take it.

My hand grips his harder and my toes curl.

"You're going to come, bella."

"Yes."

"Let go. Do it."

I'm almost there. I'm just on the edge. Fuck me, if he keeps hitting my clit just like *that* . . .

BEEP BEEP BEEP!!

I sit up, sweaty, panting, and every nerve in my body on fire, eyes wildly searching my bedroom. Everything is normal. Except all of the covers have been pushed onto the floor, my tank and panties are gone, and I'm on the brink of the most explosive orgasm of my life.

And very alone.

I slap my hand on the snooze button, swearing long and loud.

Seriously?

Seriously?!

He's in every daydream I have, and now he's invading my sleep too? And I'm about to come without him even touching me.

Son. Of. A. Bitch.

one

I'm late. I'm *never* late. I don't do late.

It's Dominic Salvatore's fault.

Okay, maybe that's far-fetched, even to me, but seriously, does he have to infiltrate every thought? Even my dreams? Dreams that leave me sweaty and panting and . . . and . . . *damn it.*

I stare at myself in the mirror and shake my head.

Get it together.

I don't have time for this. I don't have time for *him*. I have a day packed full of meetings and appointments with potential clients. No time to dwell on the hot Italian that I can't seem to shake from my subconscious.

My hair doesn't want to cooperate as I twist it up into its usual knot and secure it with bobby pins. What's up with my hair today? I do my best to smooth it out and try again, but at just past 7:30 in the morning, my day seems to already be in the crapper.

I blow a wayward lock of hair off my forehead with a deep sigh and prop my hands on my hips, glaring at my hair. I wear it up every day. Every. Day. It's professional.

I'm not wearing it down today.

So I do my best, then dress in my favorite pink summer suit—maybe it'll improve my luck today—with pink Jimmy Choo heels and turn back to brush on my makeup and dash out the door. But just after I finish with my mascara, I sneeze, leaving black marks on my cheeks from the wet makeup.

Seriously? If this is the way my day is going to go, I should just go back to bed.

My phone rings just as I wipe away the black marks and am heading for the door.

"This is Alecia."

"Hey, boss lady. I'm already here. Where are you?"

"Wishing I were back in bed," I reply dryly, and press the call button for the elevator. "This day sucks. Is the client there?"

"Not yet. You're just now leaving your condo?" Emily, my assistant, sounds shocked. And for good reason.

I don't do late.

The elevator arrives and as I step on, the heel of my shoe catches in the rail of the door and snaps right off.

"Son of a bitch!"

"What's wrong?"

"I just broke my favorite Choo heel." I throw my arm out to stop the doors from closing, pluck my precious heel out of the track and walk back to my door, up, down, up, down, swearing ripely the whole way.

"Wow, that's some language you have going there."

"Eight hundred dollar heels, Em."

"You can probably have them fixed," she says.

"I can hear you laughing at me."

"I'm not. I swear. I think the client just got here, and you're still thirty minutes out?"

"That's if I don't hit traffic. Damn it. Start without me. Buy her coffee. Chat her up. I'll get there in twenty."

"A speeding ticket won't help."

I hang up without responding and take a precious two minutes to mourn the loss of my shoes. The break on the heel isn't fixable.

So much for my favorite suit turning my luck around today.

THE SPEEDING TICKET I got on Interstate 5 held me up by an additional fifteen minutes, putting me almost forty-five minutes behind.

Emily jinxed me.

Damn her.

"I'm so sorry," I begin, as I walk briskly to the table Emily and a potential client, Summer James and her fiancé, Robert, are sitting at. I hold my hand out to shake theirs and smile brightly. "Traffic this time of day is horrific."

"I would think you would have planned for the traffic," Robert replies and glances down at his phone, checking the time. Summer scowls at him and then smiles at me.

"I understand. Emily has already given us a lot of great information."

"Perfect." I grin at Emily, who is eyeing my hair like it's a three-toed sloth, and I turn my attention back to the couple. "I'm sure you've already discussed some of your thoughts and plans with Emily, but I'd appreciate it if you'd quickly fill me in."

As I ask the couple about their date and go over some of their preferences on bridal party size and guest count, Emily fetches me a much-needed coffee.

Thirty minutes later, after we've covered the basics and I've gone over the prices for my services, Robert looks mildly sick to his stomach from information overload and sticker shock, and Summer is beaming.

Typical.

"I think . . ." Robert begins, but Summer interrupts him.

"I think we should hire her too!"

"No, babe, I was gonna say I think we can do this ourselves."

Her jaw drops and she blinks rapidly. "Really? When will we have time?"

"You have weekends off," he reminds her.

"So do you. But this is a full time job. I can't do this alone!" She's becoming very shrill, making the pounding at my temples even worse, so I do what I do. I step in to avoid a crisis.

"I understand," I begin calmly and lay my hand over Summer's arm. "This can be overwhelming, and it's a big financial commitment. Take the weekend to think it over and call us next week."

"Absolutely," Emily agrees with a wide smile. "You don't have to decide today."

"Really?" Summer looks like she's on the verge of tears, and Robert now looks mildly panicked.

"Yep." I nod and pat her arm, then pass her a file full of the information I've just gone over with her. "Have a wonderful weekend. Enjoy your engagement party."

"Thank you," Robert replies and leads Summer out of the coffee shop.

"I'll bet you a thousand bucks he talks her out of it," Emily says, when they're out of earshot and we're gathering our things to leave.

"I'll take that bet. I need new Choos."

"You think she'll talk him into it?"

"She will." I sigh and take one more sip of my now-cold coffee. "I don't think I grabbed my bottle of Advil this morning."

"You okay?"

"I got a speeding ticket, thanks to you jinxing me." I turn and glare at her, but she giggles. "I don't find it particularly funny."

"You don't look great today." Em tilts her head and watches me thoughtfully. "Did you go on a bender last night?"

I laugh and shake my head. "I wish. No, didn't sleep well." I can't very well tell her that I had wild sex dreams about the sexiest man I've ever seen.

"Insomnia." She nods wisely. "You should take melatonin. It works wonders."

"I'll remember that," I murmur and check the time on my phone. "I have to be in Olympia by noon."

"Are you meeting with Will Montgomery?" she asks. She smiles softly and sighs.

"Yes."

"Can I—"

"No, I don't need you to come along for this."

She pouts, making me laugh. Emily has never made it a secret that she has a crush on the handsome football star.

Hell, we all have crushes on the whole Montgomery family. They're all fine specimens of men, and their women are sweet and funny. What's not to like? They're also my best clients, and are the reason I can afford my condo and my shoe fetish.

And I like to think that they've become friends as well.

"You get to have all the fun," Emily says.

"I do. And I also get to handle all of the bridecrazies and complaints. I believe it falls in my 'owner' job description."

"Yeah, you can keep those. I'll meet you back at your place later this afternoon?"

"Yes. You're meeting with the Peterson couple to go over their flowers, right?"

"Yep. The MOB is a pain in the ass."

"The mother of the bride is paying for a one hundred thousand dollar wedding. She's paid for the right to be a pain in the ass."

"True." Emily holds her fist out to bump mine and grins. "Have a good time with the hot Will Montgomery."

"I will. I'll have my cell on me if you need me."

"Back at ya."

With that, Emily climbs into her Honda Civic and drives away. I pause and take a deep breath before I jump into my SUV and head toward Olympia. It's still early, but that's okay.

I should be early for *something* today.

"YOU LOOK . . . interesting." Blake, the caterer and my best friend, cocks his head to the side and watches me with humor-filled eyes as I walk into his office and sit on the edge of the chair across from his with as much dignity as I can muster.

"Fuck you." I smile sweetly and pull my iPad out of my handbag.

"We've been there, done that. I think you still have some of my T-shirts."

"I sleep in them," I remind him, and bring my iPad to life, thumbing through client files until I find McBride-Montgomery Wedding.

"But if you want them back, you can have them."

"I don't give a shit about the shirts." I glance up to find his chocolate brown gaze watching me. Blake is a looker. He's no Dominic Salvatore, but then, few are. Blake is tall and thin. His arms are muscular, thanks to all of those hours in the kitchen. He has a solid, square jaw and short dark blond hair. He's the only person I've ever allowed myself to fully trust in my life.

"Are you ready for Will and Meg?" I ask, hoping to change the subject.

"I'm ready for you to tell me what's up with you today. And what's up with your hair?"

"It's not that bad." I roll my eyes, but Blake smirks.

"It's not your usual perfect. Which means you were flustered this morning."

"It's just been a shitty day. Bad hair day. Broke the heel of my shoe." I pout, making Blake grin.

"The expensive ones?"

"They're all expensive."

He smirks again. Blake is good at smirking. He can be an arrogant ass. "Is that all?"

"Got a speeding ticket and I was almost an hour late meeting a client."

"Wow." The humor leaves his face and he quirks a brow. "Bad day."

"Yeah." I clear my throat and glance back down at my iPad.

"Been happening a lot lately."

I ignore him and stare blindly at the words on the pad in my lap. He's right. I've been off my game for the past few months, and I don't know why. Life is good. My business is thriving. I love it. I have a beautiful condo right on the water of the Puget Sound and good friends.

But something feels . . . *off.*

"Wanna talk about it?"

"I really just want to talk about Will and Meg, Blake. They'll be here in a few minutes."

"I have the staff in the kitchen putting the finishing touches on the dishes we already talked about. The wine is corked and ready. We're ready."

"Great."

"Hello?"

Megan McBride's voice calls out from the lobby of Blake's offices. I jump up, happy to see her, and grateful for the change in subject. I join her and Will, with Blake on my heels.

"Hi guys." I smile and hug Meg and offer Will my hand to shake, but he just laughs and pulls me in for a big hug too. He's surprisingly gentle for such a big man. Standing at least six foot four, he's nothing but pure muscle and mischievous bright blue eyes. Will is my favorite of the brothers because of his fun-loving attitude and sense of humor.

Meg is a lucky woman.

"Sorry we're early," Meg says with a shrug.

"I'm always early when food is involved," Will adds, and rubs his hands together. "Bring it on."

"He's so classy." Meg shakes her head and slips her arm through Will's and kisses his bicep.

"We're almost ready," Blake says, and motions for Meg and Will to follow us into the dining room. Blake's staff has set it up to look exactly like the tables that Meg has chosen for her reception, complete with the centerpiece of her flowers of choice.

"Oh, babe! Look how pretty it is." Meg grins and reaches out to touch an orange tiger lily.

"Have a seat." I sit and lay the linen napkin in my lap and grin at the happy couple. Meg is oohing and ahing over the flowers, the china, even the party favors at each place, and Will is watching her with soft, love-filled eyes.

The Montgomery family almost makes me believe that true love really exists.

"Okay, first we have the Dungeness crab cakes with Washington apple slaw paired with Dominic's Riesling." The servers take their place to each of our left, and then in perfect synchronization, lower our plates before us.

"Wow, this looks amazing." Meg grins and raises her fork, then laughs when she glances up at Will, only to find he's already eaten one whole crab cake. "Good?"

"Mm . . ." He rolls his eyes and digs into the next one. "Good call on going with the Pacific Northwest menu, babe."

"But we added the steak for those who don't like fish," she adds, looking to Blake for confirmation.

"Yes, you'll get to taste both the salmon and the filet mignon today as well."

"Oh, God, I won't be able to eat it all. I have to fit into my wedding dress in two weeks."

"Just take a bite or two of each," I suggest with a smile. "Blake won't be offended. That way you can taste everything and approve it for your guests."

"Good idea."

"I'll be eating it all," Will informs us and sips his wine. "I don't have to fit into a dress. Damn, this wine is good."

"Crab cakes and slaw are a thumbs up," Meg agrees and sips her wine.

"Ready for what comes next?" Blake asks, and Meg and Will both nod. Blake signals the servers to return with the salad course. "Okay, here we have a grilled chicken salad with mandarin orange vinaigrette." The servers again go through the ritual of setting our plates before us in perfect synchronization.

"Oh, yum," Meg whispers, and digs in to her salad. "So good." Will nods, his mouth too full to speak. Blake and I wink at each other. Blake is a master in the kitchen and my caterer of choice, especially for big events like this one.

Will Montgomery's wedding is going to be all over the news and in every major magazine there is. This is a huge deal for all of the vendors involved, including me. It's important that I only work with established vendors who are at the top of their game.

And no one is better than Blake.

"The wine pairing with this is the pinot gris?" I ask and sip the delicious wine.

"It is." Blake nods and takes a few bites of the salad, seemingly satisfied with the outcome.

"I love it all so far," Meg says with a grin and looks up to Will. "What about you?"

"I love it too." He grins and leans down to kiss her lips softly. "Whatever you want, babe. You know that."

"Now we begin with the entrée. First we'll try the salmon." Blake nods at the lead server. "This is a grilled copper king salmon with tomatoes, balsamic marinated mushrooms and pancetta salad, paired with Dom's merlot."

We all cut into the flakey salmon and moan in elation. Blake does food so well.

"Oh my God," Meg mutters with a moan and braces her hand on her chest. The rock on her finger sparkles.

"Keep moaning like that, Megan, and we'll leave before the next course." Will doesn't look down at Meg, but she blushes furiously and squirms in her seat. I have to bite my lips to keep from laughing out loud. I love how the Montgomery and Williams men aren't afraid to make it clear that they not only love their women, they can't get enough of them physically.

They are in a league all their own.

"And now the filet," Blake says, his eyes also full of humor. "I had these prepared medium. It's served with a blackberry cabernet sauce and baked potato."

The beef cuts like butter, making us all sigh in pleasure.

"And the wine?" Meg asks.

"Dom's cabernet sauvignon."

Meg takes a few bites of the beef and potato and closes her eyes as she raises her wine glass to her lips. "This was so good."

Will has managed, of course, to clear every plate presented before him. He's only sipped the wine though, choosing to drink water instead.

"We have a surprise," I reply with a grin as the servers clear our plates.

"There's more?" Meg asks with wide hazel eyes. "My belly is full."

"I think you'll have room for this." The waiters return and set plates before each of us with four mini cupcakes on each one.

"You got Nic to make our cupcakes?" Meg asks, referring to Nic Dalton, the owner of Succulent Sweets, and Will's brother, Matt's, girlfriend.

"Yes, she made mini ones for the tasting today, so you could taste them after you've had the meal. All four of the flavors you chose are there. Lemon raspberry," I point to each flavor as I name it. "Tiramisu, Death by Chocolate and vanilla with vanilla frosting."

"And Dom has paired them with a late harvest Riesling," Blake adds. "It's sweet and will go nicely with any of these flavors."

"Wow," Meg mutters and she takes a bite of the raspberry lemon and sips her wine. "That's amazing."

"Megan," Will sighs and clenches his eyes shut. Meg giggles and licks the frosting off the chocolate cupcake, looking up at Will with wide, innocent eyes, clearly just egging him on.

"What did I do?"

Will laughs and eats the remaining cupcakes on his plate, then wipes his mouth. "I think I'll take you home and show you what you've done."

Meg raises a brow. "Sounds fun."

"Oh, it's gonna be more than fun." Will turns hot blue eyes on me and I can't help but bite my lip. The Montgomery men are hot, but add turned on and they're just . . . *wow.* "Do we have anything else we need to discuss today?"

"I take it you both approve of the menu?" I ask, and sip my Riesling, as I look through the catering contract on my iPad.

"I love it," Meg confirms.

"We're still waiting on some of the RSVP's," I inform them with a shrug. "But that's not uncommon. Most people hold onto them past the due date."

"How many do you have so far?"

"We have 232 confirmed yes," I reply, and Meg gasps as Will shrugs.

"That's a *lot* of people." Meg glances nervously at Will. "This is going to be really expensive."

Will chuckles and kisses Meg's forehead softly. "It won't break us."

"I can cut back on the flowers."

Blake and I share a glance, thinking we should leave and let them talk, but Will just laughs and leans in to whisper in Meg's ear. Her worried face relaxes and she bites her lip and nods as Will kisses her temple and pulls away, shaking his head as though he finds her adorable.

"We're good. I keep having moments of panic," she admits. "And then Will has to talk me down from the ledge."

"Perfectly normal," I reply with a smile. "This is a big deal."

"Yeah." Meg nods and takes another sip of wine. "Emphasis on *big*. But Will's team is big, we have a big family and lots of friends. I have so many colleagues and friends from the hospital. I don't want to leave anyone out."

"Hey, you should celebrate with everyone you love." Blake smiles kindly at Meg, and I remember why I love him so much. He's a *nice* guy.

"Thank you." She smiles back at him and then glances up at Will who has continued to watch her. "So, we're meeting on Wednesday out at the vineyard?"

"Yes. We'll walk through and talk about the set up and all of the final details. But you don't have anything to worry about. All of the vendors are ready and the food is now approved and ready to go. The hard part is over."

Meg's smile is wide and happy. "Okay. We're getting married."

"Thank God. This has been the longest engagement on record." Will scowls down at Meg, who just laughs and rubs her hand along his rock-hard arm.

"It's almost over, football star."

"Let's go home."

Hugs and handshakes are exchanged, and as Will and Meg turn to leave, I return to my seat, sip my wine, and ask Blake to look over the final contract with me.

He steps behind me and rubs my shoulders as we read through it together and I melt back against him. "So, this price point should work up to 250 guests. But I need you to work up the additional price, should it go as high as 300."

"There are still that many RSVP's out there?"

"Unfortunately."

"Hey, what are you doing here, man?" I hear Will say as he and Meg reach the lobby.

"I have a meeting with Blake." Dominic's voice.

"You should see if they have any of the food we just tried left over. It's awesome."

"I'm fine, but thanks. Did you like the wine pairings?"

"They're perfect. Thank you, Dom." Meg replies. "I wish you'd let us pay for the wine."

"No, *bella*. It's a gift. Have a good day. I'll see you this weekend."

A chill runs down my spine as Blake leans over me to point at something on the contract. He's still kneading my shoulder with the other hand. I have no idea what he's just said, so I just nod.

"I'm sorry you're having a rough day," he murmurs and kisses the top of my head. "Headache better?"

"Yeah," I lie, and offer him a small grateful smile, then look over my shoulder to see Dom watching us. His hands are shoved in the pockets of his slacks. He discarded his suit jacket long ago and rolled the sleeves of his white button-down up his forearms, showing off his tanned skin. His tie is loose. His dark hair is messy, as if he's run his fingers through it in frustration.

And his jaw is clenched and his deep blue eyes are full of heat and anger.

My thighs involuntarily clench at the sight of him, and my mind immediately goes to my dream this morning. Those hands and his mouth on my skin.

What would it really feel like?

I turn away and take a deep, calming breath as Blake crosses the room to Dom and shakes his hand.

"We're just wrapping up here."

"No problem. I'm a little early. I'm meeting my sisters for lunch in a few hours, so I thought I'd see if you could squeeze me in."

"Absolutely."

"We're done here," I hear myself say, as I power the iPad down and stand, preparing myself for Dom's usual flirtatious come-ons and charming smile. I can stay professional.

I *will* stay professional.

I smile at both of the handsome men, but instead of offering me a cocky smile, Dom simply nods at me and turns to leave the room.

"I'll meet you in your office," he says to Blake, who turns a questioning look to me. I just shrug.

"Who knows? But I need my bag from your office." I march with my head held high into Blake's office and retrieve my handbag, shove my iPad inside and turn to Dominic. "The wines you chose are perfect. Thank you."

He nods. "My pleasure."

I don't know what else to say, so I fumble through with, "Enjoy your sisters. Thanks again, Blake."

Before I can turn to leave, Blake pulls me into his arms and gives me a big hug, rocking me back and forth.

"I'll call you later. Take something for the headache."

I pull away and again Dom is watching me with hot blue eyes. He rubs his hands over his mouth and looks like he wants to say something, but he doesn't.

And I can't figure out why I *want* him to. It's good that he's not asking me out or flirting with me.

I'd just turn him down like I always do.

"I will." I nod and walk out of Blake's office and wonder what in the hell *that* was all about.

Dominic

Alecia sends me one last long look and then walks out of Blake's office, head held high and hair pulled up in a smooth twist at the back of her head, if a bit unruly today. She's wearing a pink suit that fits her like a glove, molded to her amazing figure, and the sexiest heels I've ever seen. The confusion in her brown eyes sends an unexpected pain through my chest, but I quickly dismiss it.

I can understand that for the sake of professionalism she's turned down my advances over the past year, but she never once mentioned that she was in a relationship.

Had I known, I would have backed off long ago. I don't poach on another man's territory.

Ever.

Certainly not on a man that I consider my friend and a respected colleague.

"So, like Alecia said, the wines were a hit with your brother and Meg," Blake says, as he sits behind his desk.

"I'm happy to hear it," I reply and smile to myself. It's still a bit of a surprise to hear the words *your brother.*

I have four of them, and despite knowing them now for more than a year, there are moments that it still knocks me back a step. I've grown to love the Montgomery family, and to my utter shock, they've welcomed me into the family as if I'd been with them since birth.

But I wasn't.

"How many bottles will I need to order?" Blake asks, bringing me from my thoughts.

"None. My staff will take care of it. We have plenty on hand."

Blake cocks a brow in surprise. "It's a lot of wine."

"I have a lot of wine," I reply with a smirk.

"Okay, one less thing for me to worry about." He shrugs and taps some keys on his computer. "So, we need to talk about the family reunion event late next month."

"Yes." I lace my fingers and cross my legs. "Did they decide on a menu?"

"They can't come to an agreement." He rolls his eyes. "Some are vegetarians. Some aren't. Blah, blah, blah."

I laugh and shake my head. "You'll figure it out. I can choose a red and a white that will compliment almost anything and call it a day."

"That works." He nods. "You know, you should hire someone to handle all this stuff for you."

"I don't mind."

"Seriously. Alecia does this stuff. You should hire her to organize your events."

No. Way. "I'm quite sure Alecia is busy enough with her own business and her relationship."

His eyes jerk up to mine and his hands still on his keyboard. "Alecia's in a relationship?"

I cock my head to the side and narrow my gaze on my friend. "You're going to tell me you're not sleeping with her?"

Blake blinks and then laughs, clapping his hands as if I've just told the best joke all year.

I don't find it particularly funny.

"No." He shakes his head and goes back to typing on the computer. "That ship has sailed, man."

"Meaning?"

"Meaning that she and I started out as fuck buddies and discovered that we actually *liked* each other, but weren't in love with each other. God, I haven't slept with Leash in . . . almost two years." He shakes his head again and chuckles.

"You're very affectionate for a friend."

He stops typing again and watches me for a moment before answering. I don't drop my gaze.

"I love her like a sister. I know her, inside and out, and would do just about anything for her. She's probably one of the best people I know. She had a shit day, and needed a hug. So I gave her one."

She had a shit day. And I added to it, no doubt.

"I'm sorry that I misunderstood."

Blake leans back in his chair and steeples his fingers together. "You're interested."

"I've been interested for a long while," I admit, and rub my hand over my mouth in agitation. "She's made it clear that she doesn't return the sentiment."

"Hmm." He focuses on something over my shoulder, briefly lost in thought. "It's not a bad idea."

"What?"

"You and Alecia."

"Did you not just hear what I said?" I shake my head and turn my attention to my phone, pulling up my notes for the family reunion. "So, a white and a red—"

"Alecia says no to everyone," he interrupts. "She's not quick to trust. But I think you would be good together."

"Thank you so much for your approval," I reply dryly.

"Oh, you'll need it," he says perfectly calmly. "Because without it, you'd be fucked."

I simply stare at him, waiting for him to continue.

"Alecia doesn't have contact with her family. I'm it. If I didn't like you, it would be a no-go."

"It's a no-go anyway. She's. Not. Interested."

He shrugs and returns to his computer. "Seems to me a girl like Alecia might be worth a little extra effort."

The anger and frustration is swift. Extra effort? I've tried to get her to go out with me for a fucking year. The answer is always the same:

thank you, but no.

I hate hearing that fucking word. No.

"HEY, HANDSOME BROTHER!" Jules grins, her blonde hair loose around her pretty face. She's wearing a flowy, red sundress and looks amazing.

"*Ciao, bella,*" I reply and kiss her cheek.

"Me too!" Natalie says and leans in to kiss me, then presses herself against me for a long hug.

Along with four brothers and all of their beautiful women, I gained two beautiful sisters as well. Natalie, like me, was brought into the fold later in life, after her own parents were killed in an accident. It seems the Montgomerys enjoy adding to their brood.

"*Ciao, cara,*" I whisper into her ear. Her dark hair has been braided down her back. She's in jeans and a tank top, looking happy and beautiful. "To what do I owe the honor of being invited to lunch with you two?"

"We just wanted to see you," Natalie replies innocently.

"What she means is," Jules begins as she gives the menu a quick look, tosses it on the table, and then leans toward me, her elbows planted on the wrought iron. "We need dirt."

"*Dirt?*" I chuckle, and set my menu aside as well.

"We don't know you well enough."

"You've known me for more than a year, *bella.* We've spent quite a lot of time together."

"You're going to scare him off," Natalie says in a sing-songy voice, glaring at Jules, making me chuckle. These two are funny.

"Oh, for fuck's sake." Jules rolls her eyes. "I'm not going to scare him off."

"Depends on where this is going," I reply dryly, but can't keep the smile from my face.

"You're so handsome," Natalie says, and smiles softly as she watches me. "I love your dimple."

"Now you just want something."

"He's gotten good at the brother thing," Jules says to Natalie, making my heart stop.

I hope so.

"So, we're your sisters," Natalie says as Jules nods. "And we love you."

"I love you, too," I murmur, already softening. My God, if I'd grown up with them, I would have been wrapped around their fingers from the moment I laid eyes on them.

Who am I kidding? I *have* been wrapped around their fingers since I laid eyes on them. Both of them, along with all of the women in this amazing family.

"You know that anything you need is yours. Just say it."

"Oh, you're sweet," Jules says, as the waitress sets waters on the table.

"Yes, he is," the waitress says and winks at me. "Is he available?"

"Well—" Nat begins, but I interrupt her.

"No."

"Too bad. Sorry it took me a minute, the patio is always busy when it's nice out like this. What can I getcha?"

We order drinks and when she's gone, I gaze back and forth between the girls.

"We really did just want to chat and see you," Natalie says, and lays her small hand over my arm. "We don't get much alone time with you."

"And we need dirt."

"Jules!" Natalie laughs in frustration.

"What kind of dirt do you want?"

I sip my water and choke when Jules replies with, "Are you fucking anyone?"

"Are you trying to kill him?" Natalie demands, and pats me hard on the back as I cough.

"What the hell?" I ask, and push the water far away from me. I think I need something much stronger and reach for the wine list, satisfied when I see Mama Salvatore wines listed.

"Well, you've always been very hush-hush about your sex life, and I know you're not celibate, so I want to know." Jules shrugs as if this is the most normal conversation in the world, and Natalie offers me a smile, but doesn't try to deter Jules from her line of questioning.

"I don't think I'm going to have this conversation with you," I reply slowly. *No way, no how.*

"Why?" Jules asks with a tilt to the head.

"Because you're my *sisters.*"

"Yes, but we're adults. We have sex. We both have babies, for the love of baby Jesus."

Natalie nods and thanks the waitress when she delivers our drinks. I order a glass of the merlot from my vineyard and we order our entrees as well.

"Let's change the subject," I suggest.

"Killjoy," Jules mutters, making me laugh.

"How are things with Alecia?" Natalie asks.

I'm just going to be reminded of Alecia everywhere I go today.

"There are no things with Alecia," I reply.

"Oh, there are things," Jules replies smugly. "I've seen the way you look at her."

I frown, but before I can reply, Natalie says, "And we know you've asked her out."

"Which she's declined," I reply.

"So?"

Why doesn't everyone understand that no means no?

"I was taught to politely retreat when a lady says no," I say and sip my wine.

"But you only asked her out for, what, dinner?" Jules asks, clearly confused.

"Yes, I believe I asked her to dinner. Three times." I cringe and shake my head. "A man can only take so much rejection from one woman."

"But what else did you do?" Natalie asks.

I pause and frown at her. "What do you mean?"

"What did you do to show her that it wasn't just a matter of wanting to get in her pants?"

What am I missing?

"Dinner doesn't necessarily mean *get in her pants*."

"Sure it does," Jules says with a wave of her hand.

"For example," Natalie continues, "back in the day, Luke would have my coffee delivered to me. He still does sometimes."

"Oh, and remember when he left all those flowers on our front porch after he screwed up that time?" Jules says with a laugh.

"Yep," Nat says with a smile.

"For me, it was the chocolate cheesecake," Jules says. "Nate always had chocolate cheesecake in his apartment—our apartment now—because he knew I loved it."

"Really? Coffee and cheesecake were the ways to your hearts?" I laugh, but Jules punches me in the shoulder. "Ow!"

"You're not listening! It's not about the coffee and the cheesecake."

"It's the fact that they paid attention to the little things," Natalie agrees. "They didn't just say, 'Hey, baby, wanna go to dinner and then go to my place and fuck like rabbits?'"

"Even though we totally fuck like rabbits," Jules adds.

"They *showed* us that they were interested in *us*."

"And this worked for you." My voice is full of sarcasm, but what they say makes sense. All I've done is ask Alecia out when we were both at a family function, usually while she was working. I've never taken the time to make an effort.

Not that I'll admit that to these two.

"So, what are you going to do?" Natalie asks.

"Who says I'm going to do anything?"

Jules punches me in the arm again.

"Do that again, *sorellina*, and I'll take you over my knee."

"Don't think you can charm me with your fancy Italian words," Jules replies, clearly not afraid of me.

"But what did you say?" Nat asks, leaning toward me. It makes me laugh that whenever I use Italian words they want to know what they mean.

"I said *little sister*."

"Aww," Nat says. "I love that."

"Yeah, yeah, it's sweet," Jules says impatiently. "But what are you going to *do*?"

"I'm going to pay for lunch and go home."

"We've failed you," Jules says, and her lip quivers as if she's going to cry.

She's not fooling me.

I laugh as the waitress delivers our sandwiches and Jules wipes imaginary tears off her perfectly dry cheeks.

"Do the other brothers fall for that?"

"They did when we were kids," she replies and grins as she pops a French fry in her mouth. "I used to produce real tears too."

"We just want you to be happy," Natalie says. "Honestly, we do. We love you."

"And we love Alecia. We see how you look at each other." Jules, perfectly serious now, cups my face in her hand. "Give it some thought. Alecia isn't the kind of girl you can just ask out for dinner while she's working a baby shower."

Natalie slides a card across the table at me with a small smile. "Just in case you need her phone number and address." She winks and exchanges a look with Jules.

"She puts her address on her business cards?" I scowl down at the card. If so, she and I are going to have a talk.

"No, I wrote it on the back," Nat replies.

"So, do you like the Mariners?" Jules asks.

"Changing the subject now, are we?"

They both grin while chewing their food.

"Yes, I like the Mariners."

"Good. We're all going to a game in a few weeks."

"We are?"

"Yep," Jules replies. "Adult night out. No kids."

"You should invite Alecia." Natalie suggests. "How do I say *big brother* in Italian?"

Dio, they make me smile.

"Grande fratello."

She smiles and repeats it back, butchering it, but I don't care. Nothing ever sounded so sweet.

I DROVE ALL the way home and paced around my office for an hour before leaving again, plugging Alecia's address into the GPS and heading toward her place, making a stop on the way. With the horrendous Friday traffic, it takes me two hours to reach Ruston Way, the street she lives on. She lives on the water with an incredible view of the Puget Sound and Mount Rainer, with miles and miles of walking paths that meander past restaurants and piers leading to her building.

I park and sit for a moment, second-guessing this decision. But I can't shake the look in her eyes right before she left Blake's office today, or the knowledge that she had a shitty day.

She had a headache.

It may not be welcome, but I'd like to help her feel better.

When I reach her door, I ring her doorbell and wait. Just when I'm beginning to think she's not home yet, her door opens and she frowns up at me, confusion filling her amazing brown eyes.

"Dominic?"

"Natalie gave me your address," I reply softly. She shed her suit jacket and heels, but she's still in her skirt. Her white blouse is tucked into it, molded around her full breasts and showing off her small waist and round hips.

My cock stirs in my trousers, but I take a deep breath and focus on the task at hand.

"How are you feeling?"

"Oh, I'm fine—" she begins, but she winces and presses two fingers to her temple. The headache is still hurting her. "I have a bitch of a headache," she admits.

"I have provisions." I hold up the bag in my hand and offer her a smile.

"Why?"

Good question.

"Because I didn't like seeing you in pain earlier today, and I have a feeling I was a part of that."

She smirks and backs away from the doorjamb, allowing me inside. "That's awfully presumptuous of you."

"Am I wrong?"

She shrugs and leads me past a small, clean kitchen into her living area. Her unit faces the water, and the view is breathtaking.

"Have you taken anything for it?"

She sits on the couch and closes her eyes. "I forgot that I'm out of Advil, and I just didn't have it in me to go out and buy some."

Poor bambino.

"Where is your linen closet?"

She points to the hallway and I go in search of a washcloth. When I find one, I return to the kitchen and soak it in cold water, fill a glass, shake out the Advil I brought with me, just in case, and return to her. Her eyes are still closed. Her hair is still up.

My fingers have been itching to mess her hair up for months.

Instead, I sit next to her.

"Here, take these."

"Do you have to yell at me?" she asks with a scowl.

"I'm whispering, *cara.*" I offer her a smile and the Advil, along with the water.

"Why are you holding leaves?"

"They're lilac leaves." I line the folded cloth with the leaves and take the glass from her. "Lean your head back on the cushion and close your eyes, please."

"Why do you have lilac leaves?"

"It's going to help. It's an old Italian remedy for headaches."

She does as I ask, leaning back against the soft cushions of her sofa and closes her eyes. I lay the cold cloth, leaves against her skin, over her forehead and eyes and press firmly.

"Ohhh," she breathes. I can't resist touching her, so I brush my knuckles down her cheek and murmur to her.

"This will help, *cara*."

"My name isn't Cara," she whispers, making me chuckle.

"*Cara* is Italian for dear or darling," I reply with a smile.

"Oh, that's nice," she says. "We have an appointment on Monday, right?"

"Yes. But don't think about work right now. Just relax."

We sit in silence for a long while as I continue to press the cloth against her head and skim my fingers along the skin of her face, her neck, tucking strands of hair that have dared to come loose behind her ear. She relaxes, the tension leaving her body visibly. When the cloth warms from her body heat, I return to the kitchen to run it under the cold water again and then sit with her once again, pressing it to her head.

"How do you feel?" I whisper. She shivers. "Are you cold?"

"No," she replies softly. "I think the headache is going away."

"There are more fresh leaves on the kitchen counter, along with more Advil and soup."

"Soup?"

"You have to eat, Alecia."

Her lips tip up into a smile as she raises her hand and covers mine, pulling it and the cloth away from her head. "Thank you."

"*Prego*," I reply. "You're welcome."

She glances over at the kitchen counter and then returns her gaze to mine.

"Pink tulips?"

"I think you like pink."

She blinks quickly and before she can back away, I skim my knuckles down her cheek one last time, push a strand of hair behind her hair, and lean in to kiss her cheek.

Merda, she smells like lilacs and her soap and simply amazing.

"Eat the soup, *cara*. Use the leaves if you need them." I stand to leave and she moves to follow me. "Stay there, I can see my way out."

"Dom?"

I stop and look back at her, one brow raised.

"I do like pink. Very much."

I grin and nod and leave while I still can.

Because every instinct in me is screaming for me to scoop her up and find her bedroom and stay there with her for the rest of the weekend.

three

Alecia

He made me feel better.

And he brought me flowers. Pink tulips. Not the stereotypical red roses or whatever was available in the grocery store. Tulips are out of season. He had to *find* them.

The sun is out this morning, but it's not hot yet here on the Tacoma waterfront near my condo. I'm walking briskly—okay, I'm sauntering—just fast enough to feel my heart move.

Or maybe those are thoughts of Dominic Salvatore doing that to me.

And isn't that just ridiculous? So, he was nice. I can't believe that I let my Advil supply run dry, both at home *and* my emergency kit that I carry with me everywhere.

That'll be the first order of business today after my walk: replenish the pain killer supply.

As I adjust my earbuds in my ears and switch to a Plain White T's song, a bald eagle soars majestically over the quiet water of the sound. The tide is out, revealing all kinds of delicacies for the wildlife, and sure enough, within moments the eagle dives down and picks something up in its talons. Probably a crab.

The eagle flies off with his breakfast and my stomach growls as I reach the pier at a restaurant roughly two miles from the condo.

I turn around and head back and try not to think about Dom.

Not gonna think about the sexy Italian who can cure headaches and make me ache in other more interesting places instead.

Nope, not going there.

Shit. I always seem to go there these days. Even through the pain of a headache rated an eleven on a scale of one to ten, his fingers skimming over my skin and his whispered voice in my ear made my girlie parts sit up and take notice.

And then he had to go and put his lips on me, and it was all over.

I haven't been this physically attracted to a man in . . .

Years.

I don't remember the last time. Maybe never. And isn't that just my luck? Because Dominic isn't the kind of guy you have as a *friend with benefits* and not fall for him. It's simply not possible.

And there's no way in hell I'm going to fall for him.

I don't fall. Love isn't real. Affection. Lust. Those are real.

And in my line of business, I see how quickly they fade.

Fuck, I've lived it.

My neighbor from one floor down—*Ray? Ralph? Rob?*—drives past and waves out of the top of his flashy convertible. He's made it perfectly clear that he'd like to give the friends with benefits thing a try. He's good looking. But he's not memorable, and it seems to me that if I can't even remember the man's name, I wouldn't be terribly impressed with what he can do in the bedroom either.

I wave back and breathe a deep sigh of relief when I turn the corner into my complex. I hate exercising. I hate wearing sneakers. I hate sweating.

And I have the ass and hips to show for it.

I mentally shrug and press the button for the elevator as Train's "Hey Soul Sister" beats in my ears.

Now, this I like. I could dance all day. Since I'm alone in the elevator, I cut a rug of my own and boogie around the inside of the car, then come to a complete stop and school my features just as the door opens, in case someone is standing on the other side waiting to get in.

My dance moves are best enjoyed in private. I'm no Meredith Summers.

"There you are!" Emily exclaims and shoves her phone in her hand-bag. She's leaning against my door.

"Why are you at my condo at the ass crack of dawn?" I ask, as I un-lock the door and step inside, Emily on my heels.

"We have two baby showers and an old lady party today."

"Red Hat Society party," I reply, and toe off my sneakers as soon as humanly possible. "How can people wear those?"

"The sister of the mom-to-be at party number one has already called me three times this morning," Emily continues. "The MTB is al-lergic to watermelon."

"We're not serving watermelon." I roll my eyes and strip out of my yoga pants and Blake's old Mariners T-shirt and walk past Emily to my shower. "It's going to be fine. All of the details are in place for all three parties."

"I know, I just figured that if I'm getting calls at the butt crack of dawn, I might as well be with you when I get them."

"That's kind of you," I mutter, and step into the shower.

"How was Will yesterday?" Emily yells out from my vanity where she's primping her hair.

"He was hungry, as usual," I reply with a laugh.

"And Dominic?"

I pause mid-shave on my leg and frown at the foggy shower door. "How did you know I saw Dominic?"

"Because you're almost chipper this morning. Blake doesn't do that to you."

"I'm always chipper," I lie, and return to shaving my legs.

"No, you're not. I love this eye shadow! So? Was Dominic sexy or what?"

Sexy like you wouldn't even believe.

"He's okay, if you like that sort of thing."

Emily busts up laughing, and I can't help but smile with her.

Who doesn't like that sort of thing?

"OLD LADIES ARE better than emotional pregnant women any day of the week," Emily whispers to me as she passes by, refilling the ladies' teacups with fresh hot water.

We are at our third and final event of the day, a late tea with a local Red Hat Society chapter. Eight women are in attendance today, ranging in age from roughly fifty-five to one hundred and five.

And Wilma, the one-oh-five year old is a spitfire.

"I pinched his rear!" she crows and cackles with glee, her wide-brimmed hat shading her happy face. The party is under a tent to keep the heat off the women, and the hostess, Miss Kitty, also rented portable air conditioners for the event.

"Oh, my goodness, Wilma, he's at least twenty years younger than you!" Betty, Wilma's younger sister, laughs and sips her tea daintily.

"You get to be my age, they're *all* twenty years younger than me. I've gotta get my fun where I can."

I smile as I place a fresh plate of scones on the table.

"These scones are delicious," Wilma comments and takes my hand in hers, holding on tight. "You're a doll to bring them for us, Alecia."

"It's my pleasure," I reply with a smile and rub her delicate shoulder with my free hand. "Are you all having fun, ladies?"

"Oh, yes!" All of the women, in their pretty red hats and purple dresses nod and smile, and if I'm being honest, this is the kind of party I like the very best.

"Well, we have surprises for you this month." I nod at Emily who rolls out a cart full of pretty purple gift bags with red tissue paper as the women all gasp in excitement.

"Oh, you didn't have to do that," Leona, a sweet seventy-something woman with mocha skin, perfectly coifed hair, and bright red lipstick smiles like a kid on Christmas morning.

"I know that, but you are my favorite ladies, so I thought we'd bring you something extra special."

"Is it that *Fifty Shades* book?" Miss Kitty asks eagerly.

"Uh, no," I reply, and bite my lip to keep from laughing as Emily and I pass out the bags.

"I've been listening to that on audio," Miss Kitty informs her guests. "That Christian Grey is something to write home about."

"My kids bought me one of those e-readers for Christmas," a lady named Beth adds. "I love it. This way I can read all of those naughty books and no one is any the wiser." She nods conspiratorially with Miss Kitty, then all the ladies turn their attention to their bags.

"Go ahead and open them."

The women dig in and come out with beautiful, hand-dyed red and purple silk scarves.

"I know it's summer, so you probably won't get to wear them for a little while, but I just couldn't resist."

"Oh honey, they're gorgeous!" Wilma exclaims, immediately wrapping hers around her neck. "I'm always cold. I have poor circulation." She winks at me and then gestures for me to lean in and give her a hug.

"I have a date tonight!" Leona announces. "I'll wear my lovely new scarf."

"Who's the lucky guy?" Emily asks.

"Ed Brenner," she replies. "He volunteers at the historical society with me, and after making him wait for a while, I finally said yes to dinner."

"Good for you," I tell her happily.

"How about you, honey?" Wilma asks. "Do you have a date tonight?"

I turn wide eyes on Emily, who just smiles and waits for me to answer with the others.

"No, ma'am."

"I have a very handsome grandson," Wilma replies. "He's sixty, though, so that might be a bit too old for you."

"Just a bit," I reply with a laugh.

"My grandson is thirty," Miss Kitty says with a thoughtful look on her face. "He's going through a messy divorce and has three kids, but I think you two would get along wonderfully."

Not even if it were Armageddon and he was the last man on Earth.

"Oh, no thank you."

"So, you're just going to go home alone tonight?" Wilma asks with a sad face.

"Well, no, I'll be spending the evening with Ben and Jerry," I reply.

"She reads the naughty books too," Miss Kitty says behind her hand to her sister, not bothering to be quiet.

If only my sex life were really that interesting.

HE'S GOING TO be late.

I check the time on my phone for the fifteenth time in the past twenty minutes and scowl.

I hate late.

The front door of the Starbucks near my condo swings open and I glance up. My jaw drops and my mouth goes dry at the sight of Dominic as he pulls his sunglasses off his face and scans the small coffee shop for me, his blue eyes heating when they rest on me.

He's in a black T-shirt and jeans. The kind of jeans that mold around firm thighs and a tight ass and make a girl forget how to think.

Damn, what this man does to a pair of jeans. I rarely see him in jeans.

It's a sight to behold.

"You're almost late," I inform him, as he approaches my table, making his lips twitch.

"But not quite," he replies, and leans in to kiss my cheek, then places a bag on the floor by his chair. "Do you mind if I order a quick coffee?"

"Not at all," I reply, and fist my hands in my lap so I don't reach up and cover my cheek where his lips just were. I'm like a freaking lovesick teenager.

Check that. Horny teenager.

It's disgusting.

I pull my notes up on my iPad and read through them while Dom orders his coffee and returns to me, carrying two cups, and places one next to me.

"What's this?"

"Your tea," he replies and sips his coffee.

"How did you know what I drink?"

"I asked the barista," he replies with a smile. "Not a coffee drinker?"

"I hate it," I reply with a shrug. "I prefer strong tea with honey."

"So noted," he replies softly. "How's your head?"

I tilt my head and watch him for a moment. "Headache's all gone. Your magical leaves worked."

He laughs and shakes his head. "There's no magic. My grandmother used to do that for us."

"Us?" I ask before I can catch myself. What happened to keeping this strictly professional?

"My two cousins and myself. We all lived on my grandparent's vineyard."

"In Tuscany."

"In Tuscany." He nods and takes my hand in his, as if it's the most natural thing in the world and laces his fingers with mine.

"I'm sure it's beautiful there." My eyes are locked on our hands.

Pull away, Alecia Marie. Right now.

"Mm."

My eyes find his again and I have to blink and shake my head to pull myself out of his trance.

This man is potent.

I pull away and return to my iPad. "So, we need to go over the vendors for the wedding."

"I'd like a list of the vendor's employees as well," he replies without missing a step.

"Why?"

"I want my security team to run background checks."

"That's not necessary—"

"Yes. It is." He holds my gaze firmly. "This is my family, Alecia. My very public, wealthy, celebrity family. I have hired security, and they will run background checks on all of the vendors. Even you."

"Me?!" I toss my head back and laugh. "I've been working with the

Montgomery and Williams families for two years."

"Why is that?" he asks and the smile immediately leaves my face.

"Excuse me?"

"I think it's a valid question."

"I think it's an asshole question."

He quirks a brow. "If you like."

I lean back in my chair and cross my arms over my chest, all warm and fuzzy feelings toward Dom out the damn window.

"I work for them because I do a damn good job of it. I know their preferences, and I have a good relationship with them, especially the girls. I'm not star struck by them and I don't allow my staff to be. I *like* them, damn it, so if you think I'd hire vendors that would put any of them at risk—"

"I didn't say you would."

"But you think I continue to work for them because, what, it gives me a rush to work with celebrities? Let me fill you in, Mr. Salvatore, I plan weddings and events for politicians, professional athletes, actors, and owners of Fortune 500 companies you can't even pronounce the names of."

"I'm quite good with languages, actually."

"Screw you. Do you think they'd continue hiring me if I wasn't excellent at what I do?"

"No."

He's perfectly calm, sipping his coffee while I rail at him, pissed and offended, and it occurs to me that it was a test.

I deflate and brace my head in my hands.

"I passed that test, I take it?"

"With flying colors, yes."

I glance through my fingers to find him grinning at me.

"You're not funny."

"I enjoyed that." He shrugs, his muscles straining under his T-shirt. His arms are tanned and strong, his hands long-fingered and I can't help but wonder if he plays the piano.

"Do you play the piano?"

"Yes. Why?"

"You have hands for it."

"That's not all my hands are good at."

I bite my lip and continue to stare at his hands as he runs the very tips of his fingers up and down his coffee mug.

I bet those hands are good at lots of things.

"Did you also hire your own security?" he asks.

"Mm."

"Excuse me?" He chuckles, and I blush furiously.

"Yes, I did."

"I'll have the head of my security contact them so they can coordinate."

"I'm going to want to meet with both teams next Friday on the site and go through the choreography of it all. Nothing can fuck this up."

"Agreed." He pulls a muffin out of a brown paper bag and peels the paper off the bottom, then passes me half of it. "Here."

"I'm fine."

"Did you have breakfast?"

"No."

"Here."

I sigh and take the muffin from him, knowing that arguing is futile. "Thanks."

"I hope you like chocolate."

"I'm female." I chuckle and take a bite of the delicious pastry. "It's in my DNA to enjoy chocolate."

"I have a wine that goes perfectly with a nice dark chocolate."

"I know. The late harvest Cabernet Sauvignon. You don't bottle much of it."

He narrows his eyes and takes a sip of his coffee before responding. "You know your wine."

"I do. I love wine, but it's also part of my job. I can't serve bad wine at events."

He reaches down and pulls the bag onto the table and sets it before me.

"For you."

Inside is the limited edition white wine that I covet every summer.

"Oh," I breathe, stunned. "I love this."

"I know."

I glance up in surprise.

"When I brought it to Brynna and Caleb's wedding last summer you practically drooled over it."

"It's so great. I try to order some every summer. I'll share this with Emily."

"Who's Emily?"

"My assistant. This is her favorite too."

He runs his forefinger over his bottom lip. "I'm sure I can find a bottle for her as well."

"Thank you." How am I supposed to resist a man who brings me my favorite wine and is generous enough to offer the same to my staff?

"When are you going to come out to the vineyard to work?" he asks quietly.

I've been avoiding this. I love his vineyard. And I'm attracted to *him*. And that's just not a combination that makes me comfortable.

But he's right. I have to go out there.

"Does Wednesday work? You don't have to show me around. I'm sure you have staff who can help me out."

"I'll make sure you're well taken care of," he replies noncommittally.

"Thanks. Well, I have another meeting in Seattle in an hour, so I should go."

"Of course." He stands and holds his hand out for mine, helping me to my feet. "Do you need directions to the vineyard?"

"No, I know where it is."

He nods and holds the door open for me.

"Where are you parked?"

"Oh, there wasn't any parking when I got here, so I'm a block over. You don't have to walk me."

"I'll walk you."

"You're rather stubborn, aren't you?" I ask, as we walk toward my SUV.

"That's what mama always said," he replies with a laugh. "But she also taught me to make sure a woman reached her destination safely."

And, queue the butterflies.

"Chivalry isn't dead after all," I mutter.

"It shouldn't be."

I unlock the doors and he opens the driver's side for me, leans in to lay the wine on the passenger seat, and takes in the back of my packed vehicle.

"What do you have in there, *cara*? It's packed."

"Decorations, samples. Stuff. I never know when I might need something."

He turns back to me with a smile, but when his eyes catch mine, his face sobers. He reaches toward me and tucks a lock of hair behind my ear, then gently cups my jaw in his palm and lightly traces circles on my cheek. My nipples pucker, my breathing increases, and he licks his lips as his eyes drop to my mouth.

He's going to kiss me. I lean in, just an inch, craving his lips on mine, yet knowing this is *such* a bad idea.

The worst idea ever.

I don't want him to kiss me.

I so want him to fucking kiss me.

But rather than tip his face down to mine, he backs away, takes a deep breath, and gently pulls his fingers away from my face, leaving me yearning for him.

"I'll see you Wednesday, *cara*."

I bite my lip in disappointment, but offer him a quick grin.

"Wednesday."

And with that, he turns and walks back the way we came, his hands in his pockets, those jeans moving deliciously over his ass and his black T-shirt showing off every muscle in his back and shoulders and every part of me is screaming for him.

Such a bad idea.

four

"**G**ood morning," I say with a smile as I answer my phone via the bluetooth on my car.

"Hi Alecia, it's Meg."

"How are you today?" I ask and change lanes. The traffic on Interstate 5 is surprisingly light this morning heading south. I'm just passing by Fort Lewis, and with each passing mile, I keep getting more nervous.

This is a welcome distraction.

"I'm stressed out. Why didn't anyone tell me that getting married was such a pain in the ass? I should have just followed Leo's lead and gotten married in Vegas."

"Getting married in Vegas suited Leo and Sam, but I don't think that's your style." Meg's mega rock star brother, Leo, married his long-time girlfriend Samantha Williams just last month in Las Vegas when the whole crew, all of the Montgomery and Williams siblings and their significant others, were there for a combined bachelor/bachelorette party for Will and Meg.

I was supposed to join them, and was looking forward to it, but I ended up picking up a last minute wedding and had to bow out.

Then Leo and Sam go and get married on me, and I missed it! Damn them.

"Well it would have been much less stress, let me tell you."

"Okay, talk to me. The stress is *my* job. What's up?"

Meg takes a deep breath. "Twenty-eight new RSVP's since I saw you last week."

"Okay."

"*Okay?* What is wrong with people? All of the RSVP's were supposed to be returned six weeks ago! That's twenty-eight more people that we need to find seating for, Blake has to cook food for. Party favors! Oh, my God, twenty-eight more party favors!"

"Take a deep breath, Meg." My voice is crisp now and all business. "This is what you've hired me for, remember? I have this covered."

"It's twenty-eight more people to pay for, Alecia. I know Will says that he doesn't care about the money, but this wedding has turned into this enormously expensive affair with celebrities and so many people, and it's costing him a fortune!"

I nod, knowing she can't see me. It's costing a fortune.

"Meg, Will *wants* to give you this wedding. He loves you *big*. Anyone can see it."

"He does everything big," she whispers, and I can hear the tears in her voice. All brides are nervous and worry about their day, and few handle the stress of an affair of this size this well.

"It's a lot of people. Celebrities and wealthy people, yes, but Meg, they're your friends. You know every single person you've invited."

"I know. I made sure of that. We're not turning this into a media circus. Only guests we know and care about will be there."

"Exactly."

I hear her take another deep breath.

"I'm being ridiculous."

"You're being a bride," I reply with a chuckle. "It's okay. There will be several more moments like this between now and next Saturday, but seriously, don't sweat it. Everything is under control. We have wiggle room for extra people. This doesn't concern me at all."

That's not entirely true, but she'll never know it.

"Okay. I feel better."

"Good. I'm actually about to turn into Dom's winery right now. I'm going to go over the plans for the set up and start to get things underway."

"Oh, my God! It's happening! The butterflies are back."

"Why do you have butterflies, sweetheart?" Will asks her. He must be hugging her because his voice is very close to the phone.

"Alecia is going to the winery today to start on things."

"Hi, Alecia," he says into the phone."

"Tell him hello. Go attack him or something to take your mind off things. I have this handled. I promise."

"Yes, go attack him," Will agrees. "Bye, Alecia."

"Bye guys." I chuckle and end the call as I park in the circular drive in front of the large villa before me. Meg gets to go have sex with Will Montgomery.

Lucky bitch.

I turn the engine off and stare at the villa for a moment, take a deep breath, and pray that Dom's assistant will be showing me around. He's a distraction I don't need today.

And he *does* distract me.

But luck isn't running in my favor when the door to the villa opens and Dom steps outside and saunters to my door, opening it for me.

You can do this! You're a professional!

"Good morning," he murmurs and holds his hand out for mine.

"Good morning," I reply. I place my hand in his and allow him to help me out of the car, and immediately curse myself when the zing of awareness travels up my arm and lands squarely in my belly, making me warm all over.

Damn sexy Italian.

"You're earlier than I expected."

"There's a lot to be done, and I have some vendors coming this afternoon to drop off supplies. I wanted to get a head start."

He nods and leads me along the sidewalk, away from the front door of the villa.

"Let's look around outside first, then I'll show you the house."

"Sounds fine," I reply and pull my hand from his to turn on my iPad and bring up my notes.

"Would you like to change your shoes?" he asks, making me stop in my tracks. I blink up at him in confusion and then look down at my black heels.

"Why?"

"We'll be walking quite a bit, and those can't be terribly comfortable. Sexy as fuck, but not exactly practical."

I smirk. Yes, my shoes are sexy as fuck.

"These *are* sneakers for me, Dom. I'm fine."

"As you wish," he replies with a half-smile, showing off the dimple in his cheek and making my nipples pucker.

Damn nipples.

He's in dark grey slacks today. I've decided that his ass looks fantastic in *anything*. Jeans, slacks, it doesn't matter. And he's wearing another white button-down, this one has grey pinstripes, the sleeves rolled, and the top button undone.

I want to lean in and breathe him in.

Down, girl.

"Where are we headed first?" I ask, staring down at my iPad.

"Where would you prefer?"

"Let's look at where the dance floor and stage are going. That's the biggest project for construction, and I want to get a feel for it first." I glance up to find him smiling down at me with warm eyes. "What?"

"I like it when you put on your business side."

"I'm so relieved," I reply dryly. *Stop flirting with me!*

He just laughs and leads me around the building. There are sidewalk paths that meander through beautiful, lush green grass and gardens and water gardens. The grounds of the winery are simply gorgeous.

It's still early in the day, so it's not too warm, but I'm glad I wore a light linen shift dress rather than a suit, since I'll be outside the majority of the day.

"You live so far away from the city," I say, needing to cut through the silence that he seems to be perfectly at ease in. He glances down at me with an easy grin.

"Wait until you see why."

"Well, I can see that it's beautiful here."

"Oh, you haven't even seen the best parts."

"Lead on, sir."

The back of the villa is as beautiful as the front. There are wide windows, opening the inside up to the amazing views of the vines and gardens. About fifty yards away, sitting perpendicular to the main villa is a smaller, one-story building with wide barn doors, currently pushed open.

"That's going to be the store," Dom says. "I have a crew in there setting it up. I'd like to have it up and running the week after the wedding."

"That's a great idea," I reply. "It looks different since we were here briefly last year, when Meg and I came out to look around."

He nods. "I've been renovating. I added onto the back of the villa, expanding my private quarters. This is my wing," he points to the section of the house we're walking past now. "And that side is going to be for guests. I might start using it as a bed and breakfast."

"You could even host concerts and events here. There's plenty of space."

His eyes fall to mine.

"Maybe, eventually. The guest wing is finished, and I'll take you in there later to show you where the groom and bride suites are."

"Great. What's over there?" I point over behind the new building housing the store.

"The vines run over on that side of the property. It's hilly, and perfect growing conditions. The reception tent is going over here." He leads me to the left, where the sidewalk ends, and down a long dirt path to a grassy field, at least two square acres big.

"This is perfect." The land is level, so people won't be trying to dance on uneven ground, falling after having too many drinks. "I'll have them set up the stage on this end." I walk all the way to the left, cursing when one of my heels sinks into the grass and kick my shoes off so I don't ruin them.

"I knew you'd shed the shoes."

"My feet don't hurt, they're just too expensive to ruin in the grass," I reply absentmindedly, and keep my eyes on the meadow, mentally measuring the space. "Yes, the stage will fit perfectly here. And with the sound equipment facing the villa, everyone will be able to hear the music, even if they choose to wander through the gardens and such." I bite my lip and turn to gaze at the rest of the space. "This is a perfect place to set up a dance floor. There is plenty of room for tables around the perimeter."

"Did you say there will be a tent?" Dom asks from behind me, startling me.

"Yes. It protects the guests from the sun and the rain, and around here, you never know what you'll get."

"It's going to be a big tent."

"That's why they're coming tomorrow to begin setting up," I reply and fetch my shoes. "This is plenty of space for both a formal sit-down dinner and dancing. I love it. Okay, let's move on to the ceremony site."

I begin to walk away, and then realize he's not beside me. I turn to find him standing, hands in pockets, watching me.

"What?"

"You're good at this."

"Of course I am."

His lips twitch as he approaches me. "It looks good on you."

"I'm working."

"Meaning?"

"No flirting."

"Is that what I was doing?"

"Weren't you?"

He chuckles and reaches over to drag his fingertip down my neck, from just below my ear to my collarbone.

"Yes, but not on purpose."

"Well, stop it." I turn and begin walking again, ignoring the way my skin sizzles where his fingertip was. "Ceremony site?"

"Over here," he replies, and leads me back onto a sidewalk path for about a hundred yards, passing a large, dark brown barn. "The barrels are in there, along with the bottling equipment."

"Oh, that's cool. I'd love to check that out."

"I'll show you," he says, and leads me into a field just past the barn, where vines of grapes are standing in perfect rows.

"Oh, this is beautiful."

He grins and nods. "Meg wanted to get married *in* the vineyard. So, she will. As you can see, there is a wide space in the middle of the vines where we set up harvesting supplies. I think it'll be a good place to set up for the ceremony."

My eyes are raking over the gorgeous green-leafed vines, heavy with purple grapes, and my heart yearns. I wish I could hold *every* wedding right here.

It's amazing.

In the background, there's a steep hill with more vines climbing up it and the Cascade Mountains are the backdrop, providing a glorious painting of color.

"This is beautiful," I whisper. "Where does the sun set?" I shade my eyes and look around for the sun.

"Behind us. So, the guests won't be looking into the sun."

"Perfect." I grin and tap notes into the iPad, doing the happy dance inside. "With the colors of the vines and the mountains, we don't need many flowers out here. I'm going to have my construction crew build a simple arbor at that far end and I'll have the florist weave some flowers into that."

We go over the chair placement and then turn to walk back toward the villa.

"When will you pick the grapes?" I ask.

"The harvest usually begins in late August and goes through September," he replies. "It's a busy time for me."

"Why?"

"I'm harvesting grapes?"

"Alone?" I ask incredulously.

"No," he laughs. "I hire about fifty people to come help. But I love it, so I work right alongside them."

"What do you love about it?" I ask.

"The feel of the grapes in my hands. They're heavier than you'd think. Watching the buckets fill. Getting my hands dirty. I don't even mind the blisters."

"It's hard work," I remark softly.

"Very. But rewarding." His voice is like smooth chocolate, full of affection and passion for this life that he loves. And what's not to love? This place is simply breathtaking.

"Okay, I think we can go inside now and take a look at the bridal suites."

Dom nods and gestures for me to walk with him back to the villa.

"I'll take you through the back."

"I love this patio." The back patio is covered, with a beautiful outdoor kitchen and sitting area. Tuscan tile is laid on the ground and runs up the outside wall, framing a wide gas fireplace. "You could make a few s'mores in that fireplace."

"I haven't even lit it yet." He chuckles. "But I think that's a great idea. I don't believe I've had s'mores before."

He opens the back door and guides me into a wide, open sunroom, furnished with deep furniture in earth tones. A small fountain gurgles in the corner.

It's the perfect space to curl up and read a book.

Not that I have time to read books.

This leads into the kitchen. I'm sure Blake cries tears of pure joy when he works in here. It's industrial and huge, but manages to still be inviting and homey.

"Would you like something to drink?" Dom asks.

"I'd love some water, please."

He fetches a bottle from the refrigerator and twists the top off for me, then hands it to me. "Anything else?"

"No thanks."

"Okay. The guest suites are this way." I follow Dom past a dining room that sits twelve to a staircase that leads to the second floor.

"This banister and hallway separate the two wings up here," Dom says, gesturing to the dark oak banister that opens the hall up to the foyer below. "My personal wing is down there," he points to the right, "and the guest wing is this way."

Six heavy doors stand open to six fully furnished bedroom suites, each decorated in Tuscan colors, but in its own style. Some have king beds, some two twin beds, and a smaller one has a cozy-looking queen sized bed with an over-stuffed chair and ottoman that is just begging to be curled up in.

Another reading spot.

"These rooms are beautiful, Dom."

"Thank you." He grins and leads me to the room at the very end. "This will be the bride's suite."

I gasp when I step inside. The windows are floor-to-ceiling and run the length of the room, filling the space with light. Just inside is a sitting area with a fireplace. There are two doors, one on either end of the room.

"The bathroom is through there," Dom points to the left, and I immediately open the door and gasp again at the ornate fixtures. You could swim laps in the soaking tub. "And the bedroom through that door, but I didn't have the bed delivered. Instead, I had couches, chairs and tables put in there so between these two rooms, there should be plenty of room for all of the girls to do whatever it is that girls do on wedding days."

I smirk, but my heart just melted, and if I was that kind of girl, I would let out a loud, "Awwww!" He's done perfectly, and put so much thought and love into it for his family.

"It's perfect, Dom."

"You think?"

"I know."

He nods once and gazes around the room in satisfaction.

"Where will the boys be?"

"We will be downstairs in the entertainment room."

I let out a loud laugh. "Well, that's appropriate."

"I couldn't very well put us next door or across the hall. I'd never be able to keep Will out of here."

"You're absolutely right," I agree. "Lead on, then."

Once downstairs, Dom leads me to the opposite side of the house and opens a door to a large entertainment room, with two pool tables, movie theater seats facing a wide screen, and a wet bar.

"This is the boy room." The words are out of my mouth before I can stop them, and I immediately feel my cheeks flush. "I'm sorry—"

"No, you're right," Dom says with a laugh. "I've had my brothers over a time or two to help me break it in."

"It's also perfect for the guys on wedding day. I'll have the wet bar stocked with snacks and drinks, and I'll do the same upstairs." I add the notes to my iPad. "Starting tomorrow, I'll be here at six in the morning until late into the evening every day until the day after the wedding."

"Why will you be here the day after?"

"To oversee the cleanup. An event of this size makes a mess, trust me."

"That's quite a commute every day," he says and shoves his hands in his pockets.

"It's fine." I glance back to the iPad.

"Stay here."

My head whips up and I frown at him. "Why?"

"It's more convenient. I have plenty of space. There's no need for you to drive back and forth."

"Dominic, I'm fine with it. It's part of the job."

"Let me put it like this," he replies and steps closer to me. He cups my cheek in his palm, and his bright blue eyes are intense as they stare into mine. "I would prefer you stay with me. It's safer."

"Excuse me, Mr. Salvatore?"

We both turn at the voice in the doorway. A petite woman, in her early forties, wearing a sharp black suit and her jet black hair in a pixie cut, smiles at Dom.

"Celeste," Dom says, and lays a hand on the small of my back. "This is Alecia. From this moment on, anything she needs is number one priority."

"Of course," she replies with a smile and a nod. "I'm sorry to interrupt, but you have a call from Italy, sir."

"I'll take it in my office." Dom turns to me and grins. "Don't leave yet."

"I'm here for a few more hours."

"Good." He saunters out quickly, and Celeste smiles at me.

"Can I get you anything, Alecia?"

"No, thank you. I'm going to walk outside."

"Just let me know if you need anything." She winks and follows the way Dom left. I walk slowly through the house and back out through the sun room, the outdoor eating space, and past the wine store to see the grape vines that I didn't see earlier.

When I turn around the end of the building, my breath catches in my throat. The terrain is certainly hilly, but for as far as the eye can see, it's covered in perfectly straight lines of grape vines. The sun is bouncing off the green leaves as they sway in the light breeze. Heavy purple and green grapes hang from the vines.

The colors are spectacular. The breeze is light and refreshing. I can smell the earth and the pure clean of it all, and in this moment, I know why Dom chose this property, so far from the city.

It's pure heaven.

Suddenly, the air shifts, and I can feel the heat from him at my back. He runs a fingertip along the nape of my neck as he steps closer, and just like that, my entire body is in tune with him, begging to give into the pull that I feel when I'm near him.

"This is the most beautiful view I've ever seen."

He cups my shoulder in his hand, gives it a reassuring squeeze, and then nudges me around to face him. I keep my eyes pinned to his chest until he tips my chin up with his finger. His eyes are bright and warm with affection, which throws me.

How can he know me well enough to look at me with so much damn affection?

"Stay this week, *cara*."

Say no. The commute isn't that big of a deal. But instead, I feel myself nod and his eyes drop to my lips. His hands both cradle my jaw, his fingertips graze my hair, and he inhales deeply before tipping his face to mine. His lips brush over my mouth softly, barely touching my skin. He nuzzles my nose before returning to my lips, kissing me tenderly, as if we can stand here and kiss all day long. His tongue crosses my lips and just barely touches mine before retreating again, and rather than take the kiss deeper, he pulls away, presses his damp lips to my forehead, and then smiles down at me.

"Thank you," he whispers.

For what? I want to ask. Agreeing to stay? Returning his kiss? My body is humming with anticipation. His warmth, his strength, his scent surrounds me, and I have to pull away before I do something really embarrassing, like jump him.

Suddenly, there is a loud truck honking from the front of the villa.

"The contractor is here." My voice sounds strained, even to my own ears.

"We'd better get to work then." He flashes me a quick smile, that sexy dimple winking at me, as he pulls away and simply laces his fingers through mine and leads me away from the breathtaking view.

five

"This is a great start," I say to Scott, the foreman of my construction crew the next morning. He's one of Isaac Montgomery's men, and given that Isaac is Will Montgomery's oldest brother, I know that the whole crew will be paying extra special attention to this project. "The stage is fancy."

"It's sturdy," he corrects me with a grin. "Knowing the Montgomery family, there will be a lot of people coming and going off this stage, and dancing too. We can't have it falling in on them."

"No, we can't." I laugh, knowing he's right. "Also, some of Will's teammates weigh a good three hundred pounds. Each."

"I'm gonna add more support," he says as his face pales, making me laugh again.

"It'll be great. Thanks, Scott. I'll see you in the morning."

Scott waves and moves over to speak with his crew, and I turn toward the house, smiling when I see Dominic.

"How was the first day?" he asks as he approaches, coming from the way I'm headed.

"Busy, but productive." I pinch my neck in my palm and stretch my head from side to side. I'm exhausted, and I'm secretly relieved that he talked me into staying here. Driving all the way home this tired probably isn't the safest thing to do.

"Are you finished?"

"Yes." I grin and take a deep breath. I love the way it smells here. "How was your day?"

"Busy as well." He reaches over and brushes his finger down my neck, making me shiver.

Jesus, all he has to do is touch me with one finger and I want to jump him.

"What did you do?" I ask, trying to keep my voice steady.

"Do you ever wear your hair down?" he asks, rather than answering my question.

"Not on work days," I reply with a frown.

"Why?"

"Because it's more professional and easier to wear it up."

He offers me a mischievous half smile and leans in like he's going to tell me a secret. "I can't wait to mess it up."

My jaw drops, and before I can respond, he smirks and takes my hand in his, gesturing for me to walk with him.

"I'd like for you to have dinner with me on the patio tonight."

"I don't expect you to eat with me every night, Dom."

"I think I just *asked* you to join me."

No thanks, Dom. I'll just head up to my room now. I glance up to find his jaw ticking and his lips pressed in a line, as if he's bracing himself for another rejection. But if I'm being honest, I am dying to eat on that patio. The sun is going to set soon, and the view is going to be awesome.

I'm here for a whole week. I might as well take advantage of it.

"I'd like that."

His jaw and lips loosen, and he glances down at me with a smile. "Excellent."

"So, what did you do today?" I ask again, as he holds a chair out for me at the table on the patio.

"I arranged for Cuppa di Vita wines to be available in a new liquor store chain coming to Washington, Oregon, and Idaho, listened to my cousin, Gianna, complain for about an hour about her brother, Marco, about what, I'm not entirely sure, because I tuned her out. Then Jules called and wanted to know if I was being nice to you," he cocks a brow at me as he sits across from me and begins to uncork a bottle of wine. His hands look amazing, and he works with a quick efficiency, having the bottle open in seconds.

"What did you tell her?" I ask with a laugh.

"That I'd hardly seen you since you arrived this morning."

"I got the same phone call." He passes me a glass of the wine, and I smell it with appreciation. "Mm, smells good."

"From Jules or my cousin Gianna?" Dom winks at me as I chuckle.

"Jules. But she wanted to know if *I* was being nice to *you*."

"What did you tell her?"

"That you're a big boy and can take care of yourself."

"I bet she didn't like that answer."

"I think she might have threatened to come out here tomorrow to check on us, but I pretended that I was being called by a crew member and hung up on her." I wink at him and sip my wine.

"My family is . . . tenacious." Dominic begins uncovering silver-domed plates, and my stomach growls loudly. "Hungry?"

"Oh, God, yes. I just realized I haven't had anything since this morning."

"Well, there's plenty." He scoops large helpings of pasta and red sauce onto plates and passes me one. "This is my mama's recipe."

"You cooked this?"

"It's not hard." He shrugs and offers me bread, watching me with humor-filled blue eyes. His hair is a bit messy today, as if he ran his fingers through it over and over again. I take a bite of the pasta and lean back in my chair, eyes closed, and savor the flavors and seasonings hitting my tongue.

"Damn, that's good."

I hear Dom inhale sharply and open my eyes to find him watching me with his heated gaze.

"I think I love watching you eat," he murmurs.

"I am good at it," I reply with a laugh, and sip my wine. "This wine is excellent with the sauce."

"I know." His smile is smug.

"So, your family was a pain in the ass today," I say, encouraging him to keep talking. I love the sound of his voice.

He stops twirling pasta on his fork and stares at me with a frown.

"No. My family is never a pain in the ass. They can be challenging, frustrating even, but never a pain in my ass." He sets his fork down and takes a sip of his wine. "My family is the best part of my life."

"Better than the vineyard?"

"Better than anything."

"That must be nice," I murmur, and take a bite of pasta to give my hands something to do. I suddenly feel self-conscious and *jealous,* and that's just ridiculous. Not everyone has a tight family.

"Tell me about your family."

"Oh, trust me, you don't want that story."

"I do trust you, and I do want that story."

I take a deep breath and another sip of wine. This man is good with words.

"We're not close."

"Why?"

I shrug and keep my gaze on my dinner. "There wasn't a specific reason, we just never were terribly close. I don't speak to them now. Why did you wait so long to find Steven?" I ask, and immediately want to call the words back. "I'm sorry. You don't have to answer that."

"I don't mind." He uses his bread to soak up any remaining sauce on his plate, pops it in his mouth, and sits back in his chair. He pushes his fingers through his hair, while he gives my question some thought.

Steven Montgomery is the patriarch of the Montgomery family, and it came to light only about a year ago that Dominic was the son that Steven never knew about.

"When my mother was alive, it felt like a betrayal to her to want to find him," he confesses, and swirls the wine in his glass absentmindedly. "She gave me a great life, Alecia. She was so young."

Finished with my own meal, I push my plate away, lift my glass, and stand. "Let's go sit by the fireplace for story time."

"Good idea." He grins and follows me to the fireplace, flipping a switch that makes the flames come to life, before sitting next to me on a cozy loveseat. He shifts toward me, with one knee up on the cushion, so he can look me in the eye.

"She was young," I prompt him.

"Very. She was twenty-two when I was born. She was here in the States on a scholarship for college, and intended to always stay here. She didn't want to move back to Italy. But, she didn't have family here, and being a single parent is tough, so when I was about five, we went back to live with her family in Tuscany.

"My grandmother and grandfather welcomed us and loved us. We lived on their vineyard, which is where I learned to love the lifestyle." He reaches over and pushes a strand of my hair behind my ear and rubs my earlobe between his thumb and forefinger.

The man is forever touching me.

And I don't seem to mind.

"Mama worked as a personal assistant for a high-powered hotelier based in Florence, which was about twenty minutes from our home. When I was sixteen, the hotelier decided to come to the States to build a new resort, and he of course expected Mama to come with him, so we both came."

"What did you think of that?" I ask. I can't take my eyes off of him. He's so expressive as he talks; his accent more pronounced when he speaks of his family and the home of his childhood.

"I didn't want to come. I was horrible to her. I had suspicions that she was having an affair with him, and that's why he wanted her to come with him."

My eyebrows climb into my hairline. "Was she?"

"Probably. But if they were, it was discreet. I do know that they had a great deal of affection and respect for each other."

"That's nice," I murmur.

"So, we came to California. Mama's boss, Arturo Baldovini, was building a big resort near Sonoma."

"Wine country," I murmur with a grin, as Dom refills both our glasses, emptying the bottle.

"Exactly. Once we settled in, I did well. I took jobs with the vineyards during the harvest, earned my own money. I graduated from high school there and then went to college at Sonoma State University."

"Why there?"

"I didn't want to be far from my mom, just in case she needed me." He shrugs. "But then the resort was finished in my sophomore year, and Arturo and Mama returned to Italy."

"And you stayed."

"I stayed. I love it here. I worked my way through vineyards all over California, learning everything I could, so I could one day own one of my own."

"You don't really even have much of an accent unless you speak Italian."

"I've lived here a long time. Well, until Mama got sick about five years ago. I was thirty, and I got a call from Gianna that Mama was sick with cancer, and that I should go home. So I did." He sips his wine and cringes. "She passed less than six months later."

"I'm sorry."

"Well, the point of all of this is, while she was living, it never really occurred to me to look for my biological father. My life was happy and full, and I had a wonderful family. And during the few moments that I did wonder, it felt like I was being disloyal to her.

"About a month after she passed, I was going through some of her things and I found a box full of journals. I set them aside, intending to read them one day, but I wasn't ready yet.

"Arturo came to see me, and said that Mama had asked him to help her invest her money, which he had, and to my utter shock, had done it well. She left me millions, Alecia."

My jaw drops as I watch his face, the awe and the love crossing his face.

"Arturo said, 'Your one dream has always been to own your own vineyard. This is your chance to own it anywhere in the world you want.'"

"And you chose here."

"I chose this land before I knew about Steven."

"No way! That's too big of a coincidence."

"It's true." He lifts a bottle off the floor at his feet and deftly uncorks it, then pours us each a fresh glass. "I'd owned this place for about two years when I came across that box of journals again. I pulled one out of the box, and a letter addressed to me fell out of it. She said that she was sorry for not telling me sooner about my father, but that she didn't know how it could affect *him*. She didn't give me all of the details, and Steven has filled me in on what she didn't say since then, but he was on a business trip and picked her up in a bar. It was a one night stand thing, and after they had sex, he confessed that he was separated from his wife, and that he missed her and his children."

"Wow."

"Yeah. He'd left her his business card, so she knew how to reach him, and when she found out she was pregnant, she did call the number on the card, but his wife answered."

"They'd reconciled," I guess.

"Yes, and Mama couldn't bear the thought of ripping his family apart. So, she didn't tell him.

"I almost didn't look for him, knowing about his family. I didn't want them to think that I was trying to start some drama, or interrupt their lives. But I admit, I was curious."

"I would be too," I add. This wine is going to my head.

"So, I hired a private investigator, and within about a month, he found him."

"And all that time, you were less than an hour away."

He nods thoughtfully and then shakes his head. "I was so fucking nervous. We went through the blood tests to verify paternity, but that wasn't the hardest part."

"What was?" I ask, expecting him to say meeting his siblings.

"Meeting Gail."

"Really? Gail's great!"

"I know that now, but Alecia, how do you say hello to a woman, knowing that her husband had an affair with your own mother well over thirty years ago that *you* are the product of?"

"You tell me."

He shakes his head again and sips his wine. "She hugged me." His gaze turns to mine and he frowns in wonder. "Took one look at me and just wrapped her little arms around me and said, 'I'm so sorry that you lost your mama, sweet boy.'"

"Oh my." Tears fill my eyes at the thought.

"Yeah." He takes my hand in his and threads our fingers together. His hand feels cool and smooth against mine. "I know it had to hurt her, Alecia. But she has never once treated me with any kind of malice."

"She never would."

"The second hardest part was meeting the siblings." He laughs now, and brushes his knuckle down my cheek. "That was not easy. But over the past year, we've come to know each other, and most importantly, trust each other."

"It's a big, overwhelming, amazing family." I smile, as I think of the whole family. "They are the funnest people I know."

"Me too." He chuckles. "I'm lucky to have them. They'll never be a pain in my ass."

"They're lucky to have *you*," I whisper. "Natalie's baby shower for Olivia was my first job with them. That was more than two years ago now. I've helped with every wedding, shower, birthday party, and major event since then. I think you're all lucky."

"Who's lucky to have you, *cara?*"

I blink at him, and just then my phone beeps with an incoming text. *Saved by the bell.*

I glance down and then laugh.

"What is it?"

"One of my brides. She's changed her flower choices four times already, and her wedding is in three months. I don't even know why she's bothering. The marriage will be over inside of eighteen months."

"That's a cynical attitude for a wedding planner," Dom says dryly.

"Just because I plan a good party, doesn't mean I believe in love." I glance up to see him cock a brow and wait for me to continue. "Let's just say that I'm not a firm believer in happily ever after, and yes, I'm speaking from experience, and no, I'm not telling you that story tonight."

"A story for another night, then."

"Or a story for never." I take a deep breath and stretch, and as I look around, I realize that night has fallen and the stars are twinkling brightly around us. "It's late. I have to be up early."

Dom stands and helps me to my feet, then escorts me inside and up to my room, just down the hall from his own room.

I hope I don't pick now to start sleep walking, because he has me so tied up in knots I'll most likely end up in his room, crawling into bed with him.

"Thanks for walking me up," I say, when we reach my door. "And thanks for the story. I enjoyed it."

"Much to my surprise, so did I. I haven't told that story before." I'm facing him, but not touching him. I can smell his body wash and that scent that's simply Dominic, and my whole body tightens.

What is up with the chemistry between us?

Before I can turn away, he gently glides his knuckles down my cheek, then lifts the other hand and cups my neck and jaw, and the air around us is shimmering with longing and lust. He leans down and sweeps his lips lightly over mine and then, just like yesterday, kisses me tenderly, nipping at my lips gently. Finally, he pulls back just an inch to catch his breath and tips his forehead against my own.

"Sleep well, *cara*," he whispers, as he pulls me against him for a long, firm hug. Even in my heels, I fit just under his chin, and being pressed against his chest is the best feeling *ever*. He's hard and warm and . . . *comfortable*.

I could stay here all night.

So I do the only thing that makes sense and I pull slowly away, not even trying to mask the confusion and longing that must be on my face.

"Sleep well, Dominic."

He watches me with heated blue eyes as I turn away and close the door to my room behind me, then lean my back against the smooth wood.

How can a man kiss me like it's the first time . . . *again?*

Six

I wipe the fog off the mirror in my larger than life bathroom and stare at my bloodshot eyes.

Damn sexy Italian.

I slept like shit because all I could think about was the way his lips feel on mine, how standing in his arms is the safest I've ever felt, and that sexy accent of his when he speaks Italian is enough to melt a girl's panties at twenty paces.

I have too much to do today to have him on my mind. I have to keep my head in the game. My eyes on the prize. My . . . crap, what's that metaphor about the target?

Either way, I don't have time to get all moony over Dominic Salvatore.

Just as I begin to rub lotion into my still-wet legs, there's a knock on my door.

While shrugging into a robe, I pad across the bedroom and open the door to find a smiling Celeste holding a breakfast tray.

"Mr. Salvatore asked me to bring you something to eat. Can I set this inside for you?"

"You didn't have to do that," I reply, and reach out to take the tray from her. "Thank you, I'll take it."

"It's no problem. And just between you and me?" She laughs and crosses her arms over her chest. "He chose everything on that tray. It was actually very . . . surprising."

"Surprising?"

"I've never seen him take so much interest in breakfast before. Have a good day."

She waves and leaves, and I carry the tray to the seating area before the window. The silver tray is covered in a cream colored cloth, and boasts a small vase with a single pink tulip, making me grin and my heart soften, just a bit.

Under the silver dome lid, I find scrambled eggs, bacon and yogurt. And he even remembered how I take my tea.

He's not just a sexy Italian. He's a *sweet* sexy Italian.

As I nibble a piece of bacon and sniff at the soft pink petals of the tulip, I notice a small white card with my name written in bold handwriting.

Inside is a note.

Alecia,

Good morning. I hope you slept more soundly than I did. Couldn't stop thinking about how badly I wanted to keep kissing you, and mess up your gorgeous hair. Thank you for listening last night.

Dom

I read it three more times with a silly grin on my face, and feel my belly fill with gigantic butterflies.

Oh boy. What in the hell am I going to do with him?

"I DON'T GIVE a shit if every hole has been dug, you're going to fill them and re-dig them."

Isaac Montgomery, the eldest of the Montgomery clan, is pissed, and for good reason. The person in charge of digging holes for the tent measured incorrectly.

"You got it, boss."

"Mark," he calls over to Mark Williams, another member of the huge family, and a part of Isaac's crew. "How is the arbor coming?"

Mark cringes and joins us. "Hey, Alecia."

"Hi, Mark. What are you doing here today?"

"Scott's kid came down with appendicitis, so I'm taking over this job." He turns to Isaac. "We don't have enough supplies. One of the guys forgot to restock his truck last night."

"What the fuck?" Isaac asks, and props his hands on his hips. "Since when did this become an amateur operation?"

"He's headed back to town to get what we need, but we'll lose two hours."

That means we'll *all* be working an extra two hours today.

"Okay, it is what it is." I consult my iPad and make notes. "Mark, do you know when the outdoor restrooms will be delivered?"

"My brother just had to order the hoity-toity toilets," Isaac laughs.

"I'm sorry, but I refuse to put a Honey Bucket out for the guests to use," I reply, and shake my head.

"Hell, the men could find a bush," Mark says with a smirk, and then laughs when he sees the scowl on my face. "I'm just kidding."

"This isn't a frat party, you know."

"Wait until the music and liquor start." Isaac pats my shoulder almost apologetically. "And it's not the boys you have to worry about."

"Our girls know how to have a good time," Mark adds with a smile.

"Oh, I'm aware, and I'm looking forward to it," I reply. The girls are a blast, if a bit of a handful. "You know you love it."

"We wouldn't have it any other way," Isaac confirms with a half-smile. "I'm going to go check on other details before I leave you in Mark's capable hands."

"Let me know if you need anything." I nod at the guys and turn away just as my phone begins ringing. "Hello, Tonya."

"What the fuck, Alecia? I've texted you *nine times* today!"

"I'm aware. I haven't had a chance to respond."

"I need more attention than this! This is ridiculous! I need to feel like I'm your only client!"

I roll my eyes and rub the back of my neck. "Your business is appreciated and important, Tonya, but you're not my only client. What's going on today?"

"If you would have read my texts, you would know. My fiancé's sister is a bitch. I don't want her in my wedding."

"Okay." I take a deep breath and mentally think, *hello pot, meet ket-tle*. Tonya is my most challenging client. If you look *bridezilla* up in the dictionary, her photo is right there. "Have you informed her that she's not going to be in the wedding party?"

"That's *your* job."

"No, Tonya, it's not my job. This is a family matter."

"What did I hire you for?"

I take another deep breath and count to ten.

"You know what, if you're not going to do your job, I don't fucking need you! I don't need this stress! You're fucking fired!"

She hangs up on me, and I exhale. That commission was *huge*, but sweet Jesus, it wasn't worth the shit that girl can sling.

"What's wrong?"

My head whips up and I find Dominic standing ten feet away, hands in his pockets, watching me quietly.

"I'm fine."

His jaw ticks, and the next thing I know, he takes my hand in his and leads me across the grass, into the back of the villa, and into the sunroom, shutting the door behind us.

"You're not fine." He stalks to me, all tall muscle and intense blue gaze, and just like that, my breathing increases and I can't remember why I'm frustrated and pissed off. I back up as he advances, until my back is against the wall. He braces one hand on the wall beside my head and cups my cheek with the other. "You're not fine," he whispers, just before his lips meet mine in a slow, lazy kiss, just like the last two.

But I'm not feeling slow or lazy.

I moan and bury my fingers in his hair, grip it in my fists and press myself against him, taking the kiss from easy to hot in one-point-three seconds. I bite his lip, then devour his mouth, sucking and biting, and I just can't get fucking close enough to him.

He growls as he leans into me, pressing me between his hard body and the hard wall at my back. His hands travel from my shoulders, over my breasts and down my sides, and then he gathers my skirt in his hands, pulling it up around my waist. I slide one leg up his, hook my leg around his hip, and moan in delight when his hand cups my ass firmly, tilting me against his hard erection.

"*Cazzo, cara,*" he whispers, as he kisses his way down my jawline to my neck.

Oh, God, my neck! It's my sweet spot.

I'm not responsible for my actions if he kisses my fucking neck.

Suddenly, from somewhere behind him, someone clears their throat loudly, making us both come to a halt. Dom catches my gaze in his molten blue one and slightly shakes his head, warning me not to move.

Thank God he's shielding me from the view of the person behind him.

"Yes, Celeste."

"You're needed out in the barn, sir."

"Thank you."

We hear her walk away and he lets my leg lower to the floor. We're both panting hard, my nipples are hard nubs, stabbing his chest, and dear God, I've never ached for anyone the way I'm aching for him right now.

"Are you okay?" he asks.

"We didn't even hear her," I mutter with frustration. What am I *doing?* Thank God the sun shades are pulled on the windows of this room; otherwise, the entire crew would have had an eyeful.

"Are you okay?" he asks again.

"Fine." *Fuck, I'm not fine.*

He watches me for a heartbeat, then presses his lips to my forehead. "That was a lie. You're only allowed one, *cara.*"

"I'm not—"

"We'll talk tonight." He steps back, makes sure I am steady on my feet, and then drags his fingertips down my cheek. "Don't ever let anyone speak to you the way that woman did again."

I raise a brow in question.

"She was loud. I could hear her as if I had my own ear to the phone.

You don't have to be abused like that by your clients."

I blush and smooth my skirt down my legs. "It doesn't matter. I'm not working for her anymore."

"Good." He tilts my chin up and I'm caught in his bold blue gaze. Damn it, I *like* him.

"Thank you for breakfast."

"You're welcome." He smiles now, a bright, full on, infectious smile that lights the room before leaning in and pressing one more light kiss to my lips. "Tonight."

He winks and then walks back outside toward the barn. I have to take a moment to catch my breath.

What the hell was *that*?

I can't control myself around the man. He barely kissed me and I *climbed* him like a tree.

And, God help me, I want to do it again.

I shake my head and walk into the kitchen. I need a cold bottle of water STAT, and then I need to get back to work.

I stop short when I see Blake in the kitchen bustling about and whistling happily.

"I wasn't expecting you here today."

"I needed to check in with Dom on a few things and decided to start organizing things in here the way I want them." He tilts his head and narrows his eyes at me, and then a slow, sly grin spreads over his lips. "You're getting some."

"Shut up." I roll my eyes and stomp to the fridge to retrieve a water.

"Is this why you've been avoiding me?" he asks, and makes a note on his notepad.

"I'm not avoiding you." *Exactly.*

"Called you twice," he murmurs, and avoids my gaze as he pulls open a cabinet door to count cookware.

"I've been busy. You know this is my biggest event this year."

He nods and purses his lips.

"What, are your *feelings* hurt?" I smirk and take a long pull on the water.

"Well, given that in the last three years you've never not called me back, I might be a bit pissed."

"I'm not at your fucking beck and call," I reply hotly, and immediately hate myself.

What the fuck is wrong with me?

I'm damn sexually frustrated and having a shit day.

"So, what crawled up your ass today, Leash? Because whatever it is, can we pull it out, so you can stop with the crabby-ass attitude?"

Dominic Salvatore is my issue.

So not telling him that.

"I'm sorry." I sigh and round the island to give Blake a hug, and sigh when his strong arms circle around me and hold me tight. "I'm a bitch."

"You're not a bitch. But you're not yourself."

"It's a big event," I say again.

"You never used to lie to me." I cringe and think of Dom's words about lying in the sunroom.

"It's just a bad day. Honest." I plaster a smile on my face and look up into his big brown eyes. "And I'm sorry I didn't call you back. I was distracted last night."

He quirks a brow.

"Not like that." I pull away and reclaim my water before heading for the door and away from Blake's all-knowing gaze. "I'll call you later."

"Be careful, Leash."

"I'm *fine.*" I roll my eyes to make him smirk and head back outside to work.

I CAN'T FREAKING sleep.

Again.

There were no more issues with the construction crew this afternoon, but we were set back long enough that we all worked through dinner, and by the time I was done for the day, I just didn't have it in me to face the sexual frustration that comes from being with Dom. I made a hasty retreat up to my room to return calls, check my email, and get ready for tomorrow.

And now my work is all caught up, it's late, and I should be fast asleep.

Instead, all I can think about is the sexy Italian most likely asleep just a two-minute walk away.

I blow out a gusty sigh and toss the covers aside, throw my hair up into a messy knot on the top of my head, and pull on a pair of yoga shorts with my plain white tank before opening the door to my room and sticking my head out to make sure no one is walking down the hallway.

No one, meaning Dominic.

Assuring myself that the coast is clear, I pad down the hall to the linen closet and almost jump with joy when I find cleaning supplies. I load my arms with sponges and cleaners and pad back to my room, close the door, and march into the bathroom.

When I'm stressed out, I clean. It's soothing, and I do my best thinking when I'm scrubbing the hell out of something.

I pull my travel speakers out of my computer bag and connect the Bluetooth on my iPhone to them, then set my music to my *angry cleaning playlist.*

Eminem and Rhianna begin singing about Monsters and away I go, swinging my hips with the blaring music.

It's a good thing I'm the only one on this side of the villa. No one will be able to hear my music.

Half an hour later, I've scrubbed the sink, the toilet and the shower and I'm on my hands and knees, cleaning the floor around the sunken tub.

Where does Dominic get off, always coming on to me anyway? I've said no to his advances in the past. You'd think the man would take a hint, for crying in the night!

And what's up with his arms? Why do they have to be so . . . *defined?* I bet he doesn't even have to try to look like that.

He just *looks like that.*

I scoot backwards toward the door and scowl.

"And what's up with his secret Italian home remedies?" I ask the room at large, just able to hear myself over the sound of Lady Gaga singing to Alejandro. "I wonder what the Italian home remedy is for sexual frustration?"

A deep, male voice chuckles behind me, making me still, and then hang my head in resignation.

"Shit."

I glance back over my shoulder and sure enough, there he is, leaning against the doorjamb of the bathroom door, arms crossed over his *naked* chest and a mischievous grin on his delicious lips.

"Don't you know how to knock?"

"You didn't hear me over the music."

I stand and shut the music off, immediately sending the room into a shocking silence.

"What can I do for you?" *Can you please cover your ridiculously muscled chest?* Jesus, is that chest even legal?

"You didn't come down for dinner."

"I had work." I cross my arms over my chest, hoping to cover the fact that I'm not wearing a bra and tear my gaze from his torso. "And it was late by the time I was done."

"You know, I have people who do this." He gestures to the cleaning supplies on the floor.

"I clean when I'm stressed."

His face sobers. "What's stressing you out, *cara?* I'll take care of it."

I bark out a humorless laugh. "Right."

"Talk to me."

I bite my lip and then shake my head. "I'm fine."

"That's number two." His normally calm and easygoing voice is now hard, just like his eyes.

"Okay, you want to know what's wrong with me?" I push away from the sink and pace across the bathroom. "I had too many construction issues to deal with today, which put us behind by *hours* that had to be made up *today* in order to stay on deadline."

I pace back toward Dom and immediately regret it when I see his eyes narrow and his biceps bulge when he crosses his arms again.

"I lost the wedding with Tonya. Yes, she's a first class pain in the ass, but the commission was good."

I pace away again.

"I hurt Blake's feelings, and I *never* hurt his feelings. I sometimes forget that he has feelings. And I was insensitive and bitchy with him, and he didn't deserve it."

I turn back to Dom, all riled up and unable to stop the purging of words out of my mouth.

"And here *you* are, all sexy and funny and kind, and you make my body crazy! I'm so sexually frustrated I can't fucking see straight."

My chest is heaving with labored breaths as I stare at him, mortified that I said what I just did, and still pissed off.

Suddenly, he walks to me with measured, carefully controlled steps and lays his hand on my hip, urging me toward him.

"Do you think you're the only one, *cara?*" His eyes drop to my lips and then return to mine. "I've wanted you since the minute I saw you."

He's backed me up, like he did earlier in the sunroom, and suddenly my hips are pressed into the vanity.

"Why?" I whisper.

"I recognized you, and I'd never seen you before. My body yearns for you. I can't get enough of your laughter. And if I don't get my hands in your fucking hair *right now*, I'll go out of my fucking mind."

With my eyes pinned to his, I reach up and pull the knot out of my hair and let it fall around my shoulders. Dominic takes a long, deep breath as he pushes his hands gently into it at the base of my neck and tilts my head back.

"If you're going to say no, say it now, Alecia."

Seven

Dominic

Her eyes dilate as her chest heaves with her labored breathing, and I've never seen anything so fucking sexy in all of my life. Her body is on fire, pressed against mine. My hands are fisted in her long, soft hair, tugging her head back so I can look into her chocolate brown eyes.

She swallows hard and licks her lips, and my sanity is holding on by a fucking thread.

I tilt my head down, but don't kiss her. Not yet. My lips are hovering over hers, my nose brushes lightly over the tip of hers, and her eyes flutter.

"Yes or no, *cara?*"

"Dominic—"

"Answer me."

"Yes!" She surges up and takes my lips with hers in a frustrated kiss, plants one hand on the nape of my neck, keeping my lips over hers, and her other small hand goes on a long journey all over my bare torso, down my chest, across my stomach and around my side to my back, then around again, as though she just can't wait to touch me everywhere, all at once.

And fuck if I don't feel exactly the same way.

I boost her up onto the vanity, then brush her hair back over her shoulders and allow my hands to travel down her arms and up under the thin material of her white tank top.

She's not wearing a fucking bra.

I didn't think my cock could get any harder, and then my thumbs brush over her hard nipples and her hips surge against my pelvis, and that's it.

Game over.

She manages to reach into the waistband of my gym shorts and tug them down around the middle of my ass, just far enough to unleash my cock, and my eyes cross as she pumps my dick in two long, fluid motions.

"Jesus, Alecia." My voice is rough.

"Your skin is dark everywhere," she murmurs, her eyes watching the hand that's wrapped around my shaft. I'm not going to last if she keeps this up.

I take her hands in mine, kiss them both, then pin them behind her back, thrusting her breasts high, perfect for my lips.

"Wanna touch you," she gasps, then lets her head fall back on a long moan as I pull one perfect nipple into my mouth and suck, then release it with a loud *pop* before turning my attention to the other one.

"Love your tits, *cara*," I whisper. I glance up to find her eyes closed and her bottom lip clenched between her teeth. Her tank is pushed up above her breasts, under her armpits, and her hips are moving in a rhythmic circle.

I cup her sex, over her yoga shorts and grin when she gasps and gazes up at me with wide eyes.

"You like that?"

"Touch me," she whispers.

"Oh, I plan to do a whole lot more than that," I reply, releasing her hands. She immediately braces herself on my arms as I reach between her legs and rip her shorts and panties right off her, leaving them in shreds under her sweet ass.

"I would have taken them off for you," she says with a wry grin.

"No time," I reply, and take my cock in my hand, but instead of plunging right inside her, I drag the tip of my cock through her wet folds, up around her clit and back down again, and then I let it simply rest against her pussy and lean in to take her mouth again.

I thrust my hips against her, nudging her clit with every push, making her squirm and clench her legs around my hips, her hands on my back, pulling me closer against her.

But I'm not sinking inside her. Not yet.

"Dom," she says with a growl.

"Yes."

"Inside. Me. Now."

"Not yet."

"Oh, my God!" she cries as I fall to my knees, spread her wide, and feel my heart stutter.

Mother of God, she's stunning.

She covers her stomach with one hand and balances herself on the other, and I frown up at her in confusion.

"That's not my best side," she says, her cheeks reddening.

"Are you fucking kidding me?"

She's self-conscious?

I take her hand and press a wet kiss to her palm, then press it against my cheek as I stare up into her deep brown eyes, full of lust and excitement, and just a little fear.

"You're beautiful, *tesoro*. Don't hide from me."

I lift up and kiss her breasts, down her stomach to her navel and over the slight swell of her abdomen to her bare pussy, and just when I rest my lips against her clit, her hips pulse again and she buries her hands in my hair, keeping me pressed against her sex.

I take a deep breath, inhaling the musky scent of her, and kiss her long and deep, dragging my tongue through her folds and plucking her lips with mine, until she's about to fall off the bathroom vanity.

"Dominic," she moans. Her thighs are beginning to shake uncontrollably, and I know she's close.

I push one finger into her wet pussy and clamp my lips around her clit, and she comes spectacularly, crying out, and pulling my hair. It's the most amazing reaction I've ever witnessed.

Before she can recover completely, I stand and swoop her up into my arms and carry her to the bed, lay her on her back and cover her completely, my pelvis nestled between her legs, my pulsing cock cradled in her folds. I brush her hair off her cheeks as she stares up at me, trying to catch her breath.

"That was one."

"One what?" she asks breathlessly.

"One orgasm."

"You're counting?" She giggles, which makes her core flex against my cock, stealing my breath.

"Oh, yes, I'm counting. You won't have the brain cells to keep track."

"How many are we going for?" She pushes her fingers into my hair, brushing it off my forehead. Nothing's ever felt so good. I love the way she touches me.

"As many as possible."

"I'm good with one." She shrugs one shoulder, but I smile down at her.

"I'm not." I rest my lips against hers, brushing back and forth. I pull my hips back and the tip of my cock is just about to slip inside her when her eyes go wide.

"Stop!"

"What? What's wrong?"

"Condom!"

I lean my forehead against hers with a frustrated groan. "I wasn't exactly expecting this."

"I've had an IUD for a while. I can't get pregnant. Are you clean?"

"As a whistle."

A soft smile spreads over her gorgeous face as her hands glide down my back, grip onto my ass, under the elastic of my shorts, since I didn't take the time to remove them, and she pulls me inside her in one long, slow motion, making us both moan and shudder.

"So tight," I whisper, keeping as still as possible. My fingers brush down her cheeks, and I can't help but let my lips dance over hers lightly as her body stretches and adjusts to me. "So fucking small."

"I think you're just big," she replies with a laugh, hitching her legs up around my hips, opening herself wider, and making me swear under my breath. I can't help it, I have to move; I have to feel how it is to slip in and out of her hot, wet flesh.

"*Si sente così fottutamente incredibile.*" *Dio*, I can't hold back.

"English," she says with a breathless laugh.

"*Mi dispiace.*" I laugh and shake my head. "I'm sorry. I said, you're so fucking amazing."

"Oh, I like that," she says, and braces her hands on my chest.

"God, you make me forget my English. I've *never* forgotten my English."

I want to lift up and look between us, to watch my cock surge in and out of her, but I can't resist covering her and kissing her, holding her beautiful face in my hands as my hips pick up speed.

I feel her tense up, her pussy is milking my cock for all it's worth, and I know she's about to fall over the ledge into another orgasm.

"Go," I whisper against her lips. "Go."

"Oh, my God," she whimpers.

"*Si,*" I reply.

She shakes her head back and forth and stares up at me almost desperately as her pussy clamps down and the ripples start. Her back arches and I take one of her nipples into my mouth and roll the tip with my tongue as she cries out, bursting with pure energy.

"That's two," I say with a growl, pull out of her and flip her over onto her stomach. I shimmy out of my shorts impatiently and straddle her legs, spread her ass cheeks, and guide my cock back inside her, making her cry out, and I almost explode as she clamps around me.

Not yet.

I begin to fuck her in earnest, my hips hitting her ass hard. I brush her hair off her back, exposing one shoulder and lean over to bite her, where her neck and her shoulder meet, and her pussy spasms around me again.

Her neck is her sweet spot.

I grin and repeat the motion, careful not to leave marks. Her hips surge up, arching her back beautifully. I grasp one hip in my hand to hold her still as I fuck her hard, and feel my balls tighten and lift; the base of my spine tingles, and I know I'm about to lose it.

"Come again, Alecia," I order her with a firm voice. She gasps and clenches around me. "Again," I repeat as I push in as far as I can and hold firm. "Now!"

She cries out as the third orgasm takes her over, and I come with her, hard.

Wrecked.

Undone.

Dios, what has she done to me?

When I can breathe again, I pull out of her and return to the bathroom, wet a cloth and when I walk back to the bedroom, I smile when I see she hasn't moved an inch.

"Did you fall asleep?" I ask softly, and press the warm cloth between her legs, startling her.

"What are you doing?"

"Cleaning you up," I reply calmly. She sighs and lets me finish wiping her clean, and then I toss the cloth on the floor and rejoin her. "How do you feel?"

"Thoroughly fucked," she replies with a grin as I push her onto her side so I can slide next to her on my back and pull her against me, her head resting on my chest. I sink my fingers in her hair and watch the blonde strands sift through my fingers.

"Well, you were thoroughly fucked," I reply with a smile.

"It was rather unexpected," she says softly.

"You asked what the Italian home remedy is for sexual frustration. I thought it best to just go ahead and show you."

"Mm," she murmurs. I can feel her smile against my chest. "I was so pissed."

"So I saw." I kiss her head and take a deep breath of her citrusy shampoo. "You seem to be calmer now."

"Mm," she murmurs again.

"It's going to be a pleasure keeping you on your toes." I can't help but smile at the thought.

"Yeah, right," she replies, and nuzzles her nose against my chest, making my cock stir.

"Just wait and see, *tesoro*."

She takes a deep breath and drags her leg up mine, linking them together. Her arm is draped around my stomach and her ear is pressed to my heart.

I'm content to simply lie with her, brushing my fingers through her hair. I'm exhausted, but I don't want to sleep.

I'm finally in Alecia's bed, and I don't plan to miss a moment of it.

"I should go to sleep," she whispers against my skin. I grin and kiss her head.

"Go ahead."

She tenses, every muscle in her body waking up, and she lifts her head to frown at me.

"We're not sleeping together."

Blow to the gut.

"Excuse me?" I keep my voice even and lift an arrogant brow.

"We fucked, but that doesn't mean we're going to spend the night together."

She sits up and tries to hop out of bed, but I'm faster. I pull her back onto the bed and cover her body with mine, my face inches from hers.

"We didn't *just fuck*."

"Yes. We did." She tries to wiggle out from under me, but I'm much stronger. "Dominic, you're hurting me."

Back at you, sweetheart.

I immediately release her and shake my head. My feelings are hurt. This is new.

I glance back at her to see that she's wrapped the sheet around her, and she's gazing at me with uncertainty. Not fear, just as if she's not sure what I'll do next.

"I'll go." I pull my shorts on and turn back to her. "But I'll be joining you for breakfast."

"That's not—"

"It's necessary to me, Alecia," I reply and lean down to capture her swollen lips with mine. "I'll see you in the morning."

I turn and leave without looking back and stalk down the long hallway back to my own room.

She fucking kicked me out.

That's never happened before.

I flop onto my back on the bed and stare at the ceiling. I can still smell her, and it makes me wish she were still pressed up against me. I think back over the evening, wondering where things went wrong.

The sex was . . .

Amazing.

Fantastic.

The best I've ever fucking had.

And I know I wasn't alone in that. The way she responded to my touch was extraordinary.

But it was when we were cuddled up, ready to sleep, that she panicked.

My *piccolo tesoro* is uneasy with intimacy.

I feel my lips tip up in a smile, as I realize just how much of a pleasure it's going to be to keep her on her toes.

Just as she's keeping me on mine.

And fuck if that isn't sexy.

IT'S EARLY WHEN I let myself into Alecia's room. She's still in bed, under the sheets, curled into a ball on her side. The gentle rise and fall of her delicious curves are outlined with the white sheet. Her honey-blonde hair is fanned out behind her on the pillow, her cheeks are pink with sleep, and her rosy lips are parted and wet.

She's an angel.

I set the breakfast tray on the table beside the bed, tether my iPhone to her wireless speakers via Bluetooth and press play on the new *Alecia* playlist. It's full of soft, moody music like Sarah Bareilles and Adele. Unable to resist, I pluck the pink tulip from its vase and slip under the sheet next to her as Adele begins to sing *Chasing Pavements*. I'm still wearing my gym shorts. I'd rather be naked, but I'm not even sure she won't scream the house down when she realizes I'm in bed with her.

I inch close to her, drag the petals of the flower, then my fingertips, down her soft cheek and grin when she presses closer to my touch, as if even in sleep she's drawn to me.

"Alecia," I whisper before pressing my lips to her forehead.

"Mm." She frowns in her sleep.

She's adorable.

"Alecia," I repeat and kiss her nose. "Wake up."

"No." She opens one eye half-mast, snags the flower and snuggles it next to her cheek, sniffing it, then wiggles down further into the covers.

I chuckle and wrap my arms around her, drawing her against my chest. *Ah, that's better.*

"I brought you breakfast."

"Why are you in bed with me?"

I smile against her head and press a kiss to her hair as she wraps her arms around my waist and holds on sleepily.

"Because it's morning; I didn't sleep here as you asked, and I needed to see you."

"I can't resist your charm when I'm half asleep," she murmurs and kisses my chest sweetly. "If you brought me tea, I'll let you live."

"Tea and fruit and some other delicious things."

"Strawberries?" she asks.

"Do you enjoy strawberries, sweetheart?"

"Yes. I like it better when you use the Italian words."

I chuckle and pat her ass through the sheet. "I'll remember that."

"I thought you were mad at me," she admits with a small voice. I tip her head back so I can look into her deep brown gaze and shake my head.

"Confused, but not mad."

"Sleeping together pushes this into a category that I'm not sure I'm okay with."

"We're already there, Alecia." She begins to stiffen again, but I kiss her forehead and tuck her against me, not willing to allow her to pull away again. "But that doesn't mean that we won't go at the pace you're comfortable with. We have all the time in the world."

"What if sex is all I can ever give you?"

My heart hurts for her. Who taught her that love means pain? Why is she afraid to see where this leads?

"Then I'll be a very sexually satisfied man," I reply, rather than ask my questions. She sighs deeply and relaxes against me again, and I can't help but smile in satisfaction. "Alecia, as long as I can feel you come apart in my arms, and share moments like this one, and like the one the other night by my fireplace with you, I'm content."

"For now."

"Hey." I lean back so I can look her in the eye. "Right now is all that matters. I'm not asking to put a ring on your finger."

She bites her lip and looks so uncertain.

"I need to be honest, Dominic."

"Always," I agree.

"I don't think I believe in love. If you think that that's where you want this to go, you should know that I am not capable of that."

Bullshit.

Rather than argue, I sigh deeply and rub her upper arm soothingly. "Understood."

"Really?"

Fuck no.

"Really."

She sighs in relief and offers me a sweet smile. "Okay. I'm hungry."

"Me too."

"I'm hungry for fruit and tea," she clarifies with a laugh, and my stomach clenches. I love her laugh and her smile when she's happy and carefree like this. It happens so seldom.

I want to give her lots of smiles.

"Let's feed you then, *tesoro.*"

"What happened to *cara?*"

I've been slowly falling for you for a long time, and I'm afraid I fell the rest of the way in love with you last night, and you're so much more than my dar-ling. You're my treasure.

But that would send her screaming back to Tacoma. Instead, I simply laugh and shake my head as I pour her tea. "You're very authoritative when it comes to terms of endearment."

She shrugs and sips her tea. "I like the Italian."

"And you'll get it, *cara*. I'm right here."

She pops a slice of pineapple in her mouth and watches me speculatively. "What did you mean last night when you said I made you forget your English?"

"Just that," I reply, and spread strawberry jam on a toasted English muffin. "I didn't even realize I wasn't speaking English, I was so lost in you." This thought seems to make her happy. She smiles softly.

"How long have you spoken English?"

"Since I *could* speak. My mother raised me to be bilingual."

She takes in this information while she chews her fruit, then takes a bite of my muffin, licks jam off her lip, and then grins at me.

"So, it was good then?"

"*Good?*" I shake my head. "No."

"No?"

I shake my head again and set her tea on the tray, moving it out of my way so I can scoop her up and pull her into my lap. She wraps her arms around my shoulders. After I left last night, she must have pulled her tank and fresh panties on. Her hair is loose, falling in waves around her face, washed clean of makeup.

She's so beautiful she makes my heart stop.

"It was—" I slide my fingertip down her temple, then hook her hair behind her ear. "It was the most amazing," I kiss her lips, "arousing," kiss her cheek, "life affirming," kiss her jaw and down to her neck, "time of my life."

"You should know that if you kiss my neck, I'm not responsible for my actions."

I grin against the smooth skin of her neck and slide my hands under her tank.

"Challenge accepted, *tesoro*."

eight

Alecia

God, I love it when he's shirtless. I plunge my fingers into Dom's hair and hold on tight as his hands move under my tank, up my sides and around to gently cup my breasts, his thumbs barely brushing over my nipples, already puckered and primed for his attention.

"I love the way you touch me," I murmur against his lips. It's the honest truth. His hands do things to me that I didn't even know were possible.

And I'm no virgin.

"Your skin is so soft," he whispers, and nibbles his way back down my neck, sending shivers through me.

Sarah Bareilles begins to croon out *Gravity* through my speakers and I grin softly. "I love this song."

"It's appropriate," he replies before nipping my chin.

"How so?"

He pulls back, cups my ass in his hands, and grinds his hardness against me. "I can't stay away from you, Alecia. Knowing that you might throw me out of here this morning, I still couldn't stay away, any more than I can fight gravity."

And that terrifies me because the feeling is entirely mutual.

Before I can respond, he pushes my tank over my head, tosses it to the floor, and covers my breast with his lips; his hands are roaming my back, his fingertips digging into my flesh deliciously.

His passion is intoxicating. When he touches me, he *touches me*. There's no half-way about it, no wondering what he's thinking.

It's perfectly clear what he's thinking. He's thinking about me.

And fuck if I can think of anything at all but him.

I wrap my legs around his waist and grind my core against him, grinning when he releases a long, low growl. There's something decidedly thrilling about making a strong, controlled man like Dominic Salvatore come apart at the seams.

He moves quickly, placing me on the bed, grips my panties at my hips and slowly guides them down my legs, tosses them over his shoulder and gazes down at me like I'm a feast and he hasn't eaten in days.

"Do you have any idea," he murmurs and places light kisses on the inside of my thigh, "how beautiful you are? You're all soft, and warm, and still a bit sleepy, and I'm going to steep myself in you, Alecia."

I can only bite my lip and watch as he continues to kiss my skin, up one hip, to my belly and between my breasts. My hands roam over his muscled shoulders, arms, back. His skin is smooth and warm and so fucking *masculine*, I can't take my eyes off of him. I hook my toes in his shorts and push them down his hips, and he grins down at me roguishly, that sexy dimple in his cheek winking at me.

"You're not so bad yourself, you know." My breath catches as his fingertips brush up my side, then down my belly and between my legs, and breathing is out of the question altogether, as his fingers play my pussy like a freaking musical instrument. "Holy shit," I whisper. His lips are glued to my neck, wreaking all kinds of havoc, and he has the nerve to chuckle as I'm ready to come out of my skin.

"Do you need me to stop?" he asks.

"Don't you dare," I say, and grip onto him harder, afraid that he'll do just that. His fingers are sliding through my folds, spreading my wetness around, and if I wasn't so damned turned on right now, I might be just a little embarrassed at just how wet I am already.

My hips are moving of their own volition, circling, following his lead. And just as I'm about to fall apart, he stops.

Fucking *stops*.

"What the hell?" My eyes fly to his. I expect to find him smiling smugly, but he's intense and hot, and breathing just as hard as I am. "Why did you stop?"

"I don't want you to come yet."

"Why?"

He shakes his head and kisses my cheek gently. "I have a plan."

"There's a plan?" I cup his face in my hands and stare up at him as he hovers over me, catching his own breath. His cock is lying, heavy and full, against my belly. "Maybe you should reevaluate the plan."

"It's a good plan, *tesoro*." His lips nibble mine, almost lazily, and my body is still humming. He buries his hands in my hair and just kisses me for long minutes, softly at first, and then deeply, passionately, rubbing his chest against mine, moving his body over me in an ageless dance. I reach between us to take his cock in my hand, but I only get two good pumps in, and feel the drop of dew with my thumb, before he pulls away, laces his fingers with mine and pins my hand over my head.

"No touching is part of the plan?" I whisper.

"You have me on the edge."

"I've barely touched you." I search his bright blue eyes and feel my heart thud when he leans his forehead against mine and takes a deep breath.

"All you have to do is look at me and I feel like a teenager."

"Now you're just being charming."

He chuckles as he rears his hips back and slowly slides right inside me, all the way inside, and then all the laughter is gone from his face as he stares down at me. My body shimmies and moves under him, adjusting to him, and his jaw tenses.

"God, you're tight, *cara*."

I take a deep breath. "I'm going to come," I say, and close my eyes. God, I can't help it. He's plunged all the way in, he's pressing against my clit, and *holy shit*.

"Go ahead," he whispers, and begins to pulse his hips, nudging the root of his cock against my sweet spot, over and over, and I can't stop the eruption that starts at my core and shoots out of my every nerve, making me clench onto him and ride it out.

He swears ripely, but tenderly cups my face in one hand, releases my other hand, and grips onto my ass cheek, pulling me even more firmly against him.

"Open your eyes."

I comply and stare up into his icy blue gaze as he begins to move faster, his hips pumping, his cock plunging in and out of me, and his hand gripping onto my ass so hard, I'm sure I'll have bruises there later.

I can't wait to see them.

"Again," he growls.

"I can't." I shake my head, but he kisses me hard and grinds his pubis against my clit. Every muscle in his impressive body is tight, flexed in raw sexual need.

He's simply breathtaking.

"Again," he insists. "Oh God, Alecia."

The hoarse whisper of my name is all it takes to send me over the edge again. I cry out, holding onto him for all I'm worth, as my world crumbles out from under me. Dominic hardly makes a sound, aside from his harsh, labored breathing, as he succumbs to his own release.

Jesus. Neither of us can breathe. We're gasping, trembling.

I've never had an orgasm like that.

Make that like the last half-dozen or so he's given me in the past twelve hours.

A girl could become addicted to this.

"That's the plan," he says, with a cocky grin. I must have said that last part out loud.

"I need a shower." His eyes light with excitement, like a kid on Christmas morning, and I laugh and swat at his arm. "We have work, sex maniac."

"We could conserve water."

I shake my head, but can't help but grin as he leans down and kisses me like he always kisses me, with a lazy confidence, as though it's our first kiss all over again.

He's so fucking *good* at that.

"Are you okay?" He brushes his knuckles down my cheek and watches me closely.

"Yes," I reply, and realize that I mean it. I *am* okay. He studies me for another long minute, and then kisses my nose and rolls away, giving me space to sit up and stretch. "But you have to go away. No more distracting me. I have to get to work."

"That hurts." I spin and then relax when I see he's lying with his hands behind his head, a confident smile on his lips. "I thought I was more than a distraction."

"You're a sexy distraction," I qualify and, without covering my nakedness, stalk away and into the bathroom.

I start the shower and am just about to step into the hot spray when Dominic walks into the bathroom, wearing his shorts again, and scoops me up into a big hug. His hands glide over my back, down to my ass, and up again, but rather than join me in the shower, he plants a kiss on my head and murmurs, "Have a good morning. I'll see you later."

Dominic Salvatore gives the best hugs *ever.* I hold on for a moment, soaking in his warmth, his calm, his musky scent, before backing away and giving him a bright smile.

"You enjoy your morning too."

He tilts his head to the side and narrows his eyes. "Thank you."

He sees too much.

I nod and turn to get into the shower, but he takes my hand, making me look back at him over my shoulder. "Yes?"

"Finish your breakfast when you're done."

"Yes, sir." I pat his hard chest, then get into the shower and close the glass door. "See you later."

"Later."

He leaves and shuts the bathroom door behind him, and I immediately deflate like a balloon. What in the hell am I doing? Last night was . . . God. I don't even know how to categorize it. I've never felt that connected to anyone in my life.

Not even Blake.

Not even my ex-husband.

I wanted him to stay. I wanted to lie in his arms and feel him breathing all night long, so I did the only thing that made sense to me and sent him away. The hurt look in his eyes will forever be burned in my mind. I wanted to say *never mind*. Ask him to come back to bed.

But he *scares me!* He makes me feel things I have no business feeling. And he can deny it all he wants, but he'll eventually want to take this farther than just sex.

Hell, I might eventually want to take it farther than just sex.

And that would be a disaster, because I don't do love. I can't.

Like Jonathan used to say, I'm not capable of it.

I can't do this. I can't face Dominic today. I have to figure out how I'm going to tell him that this was a one-time deal.

Okay, a two-time deal.

I finish showering, my mind is made up, and dress quickly in a blue summer dress with black heels, twist my hair up, grab my computer and my handbag, and set out downstairs.

"Isaac!" I call out to the tall man as I approach the reception site.

"Hey, Alecia," he says with a smile. "Things are going to go more smoothly today. I promise."

"Great." I smile and gaze about the area, pleased with the progress already today. "It looks like things are pretty well under control today."

"They are." He takes in my handbag and tilts his head. "Do you need to leave?"

"I do." *I so do.* "But I'll have my cell on me, and if you need me for anything, I can be back here within the hour."

"We'll be fine," he assures me. "See you tomorrow?"

"You're coming every day?" I ask with surprise.

"Yes. This is my brother's wedding. There won't be any more mistakes. Between Mark and me, we have it under control."

"Sounds good." I nod, not really paying attention to him, just needing to *go*. "Thanks for everything, and don't hesitate to call if you need me."

He nods as I turn and walk briskly around the villa, almost running into Celeste as she's arriving for the day.

"Oh! Hi, Alecia."

"Hello, Celeste."

"You're leaving?" She raises a brow. "Is everything okay?"

"Yes," I lie. "I have some business to see to. Can you please pass the message on to Dominic? I won't be back until tomorrow."

Coward, my mind taunts me.

"Sure, I'll let him know. Have a good day." She waves and disappears inside, and I make a hasty retreat, immediately regretting leaving, but unable to turn around.

FOUR HOURS LATER, I'm pacing my living room. I've talked myself in and out of pursuing a physical relationship with Dominic six times.

Six. Times.

I'm sick of myself.

I scoop up my phone, and before I know it, it's pressed to my ear and ringing.

"So, you *do* remember that I exist," Blake's dry voice comes through the speaker and I want to cry. I bite my lip and stare out my window at the boats floating on the blue water of the sound and concentrate on breathing. "Hello?"

"I'm here."

"What's wrong?" he asks, immediately concerned, and that makes me want to cry too. "Damn it, Leash, talk to me."

"I'm an idiot."

"Sometimes," he agrees, and then chuckles, and I take a deep breath. "Why this time?"

"You're not helping."

"Start at the beginning. What's up?"

"I slept with him." I walk numbly to the glass and lean my forehead against it. The cold feels good on my warm skin. "And I liked it."

"I hope you liked it. If not, what in the hell is the point?"

"Not helping."

"Who, exactly, did you sleep with?"

"Dominic Salvatore." I swallow and close my eyes. "I slept with him last night, and again this morning, and then I ran out of there and came home. I'm an idiot."

I can hear Blake shuffling around and then his chair creaks as he leans back in it. "Why is sleeping with Dominic a bad thing? He's a good guy."

"That's just it. He *is* a good guy. And he's sexy and hot and the best sex I've ever had."

"Hey!"

"Oh, stop it." I roll my eyes and pace back toward the kitchen.

"So I'll ask again. What's the problem?"

"This isn't just a fuck buddy situation, Blake. I'm way too . . ." I wave my arm about, trying to come up with the right words.

"Beautiful? Amazing? Wonderful?"

"I was going to say incapable of having a real relationship." I bite my lip and then feel myself grin. "But thanks for the compliments."

"I don't know what the fuck Jonathan did to you, but I do know that he did a number on your view of relationships. Leash, of course you're capable of having a relationship. You and I have been in one for more than three years."

"That started as sex, and now we're just friends. And I love you, but not in that way."

"And you think you could love Dom in that way?"

Much to my distress, tears fill my eyes. "I like him."

"Do you think he likes you back, or is he just looking to get laid?"

You make me lose my English.

"He likes me."

"He'd be stupid not to." Blake chuckles ruefully. "Alecia, you are a sexy, beautiful, smart woman. Not all romantic relationships work, but some do."

"Not for me."

"Shut up for a minute. Jesus, you're fucking stubborn."

"Did you just tell me to shut up?"

"Yes, and you're not good at taking orders, obviously."

Come, Alecia. I'm good at taking orders from Dominic.

"Just take a deep breath, Leash. You're over-thinking this. I know you. You had a good time, and it scared you, and now you're doing the girl thing, over-analyzing it all."

"I *am* a girl."

"I'm aware," he says with a chuckle. "I love you, kiddo. You're the best friend I ever had. You're still the best *sex* I ever had."

"Blake—"

"You deserve to be happy. Just be happy, Leash."

"I want to be happy too," I choke out.

"So, just do that. Be happy. Fuck him senseless. Laugh with him. Let him teach you about wines and all that other fun shit, and don't worry about the rest of it."

"How did you get so smart?"

"I was in love with you for a long time, and you couldn't love me back." My heart stumbles to a stop as my eyes widen and my jaw drops. "I'm lucky just to have you in my life. I got over it, and now I think of you more like a sister, but don't shut Dom out the way you did me. Not if you think it could work out between you."

"Blake."

"I mean it. Go back out there."

"I'm going to go help Emily out tonight at the Haverland wedding." I'm still stuck like stupid on *I was in love with you for a long time.* "Blake, I didn't know."

"You weren't in a good place then, kiddo. You're good now. I'm okay."

"We're okay?"

"We will be if you go back to the vineyard tonight. Emily doesn't need your help. The Haverland wedding is tiny, and she has it handled."

"It's *my* business. I should be there."

"It's *your* business, and you've hired good people. You're being stubborn again."

"I love you too, you know."

"I know. Go to the vineyard."

"No."

"I'll give you a thousand bucks."

"I don't need it." I giggle and flop down on my couch, feeling more relaxed than I have since this morning when I was in Dom's arms. "You're bossy."

"Fine. Do what you want." He sighs dramatically. "What do I care if Salvatore gets laid?"

"He already got laid today. He's fine."

"I don't want to know this."

I chuckle again and then take a deep, cleansing breath. "So, I overreacted."

"Probably. What's up with women? Why can't y'all just fuck like rabbits and then get on with your day? Why do you have to sketch out a three-year plan and talk it to death? Just enjoy the sex, for Christ sakes."

"People should pay you for this advice," I say dryly. "Speaking of sex, are you seeing anyone?"

"I'm seeing a few someones," he replies with a smile in his voice. "I don't have sex hang-ups."

"You're gross. Tell me you're being careful."

"I buy condoms by the case."

"Ew."

"You asked, sweetheart."

nine

Dominic

"**G**ood morning, Mr. Salvatore."

I glance up from my computer as Celeste walks briskly into my office. "Good morning."

"I just saw Alecia," she begins, and opens her iPad to go over notes with me, as is our usual morning routine. "She was just leaving."

My heart stills. "Leaving?"

"She said she has some business that requires her attention, so she asked me to pass the message on to you."

"Fine." I nod, as the rest of me sighs in relief. Business. Yes, it's just like my Alecia to run off at a moment's notice if her business needs her. I love her work ethic, her passion for her job.

Yet, it's interesting that while she loves the planning, she's as cynical as they come when it comes to love.

I wonder if I can change her mind in that area.

I begin rattling off duties for Celeste to see to during the day. "Mick, the head of security, will be here tomorrow morning, and every day thereafter until the wedding."

"Yes, I have that on the schedule," Celeste replies with a nod. "Do you want me to have lunch brought in for your brothers today?"

"My brothers?" I ask with a raised brow.

"Yes, all of them are here."

I blink at Celeste in confusion. "All of them?"

"Whether related by blood or marriage, they're here. The backyard is a huge mass of testosterone. Can you bring them by more often?"

I laugh as I stand and shake my head at my assistant. "They're all completely in love with their women, you know."

"I don't have to touch them to appreciate them. I'm sure their women would understand."

"Would Clay understand?" I ask, referring to her husband of more than a dozen years.

"Clay doesn't have to know." She smiles and follows me out of my office. "So, lunch?"

"Yes, have sandwiches brought in from that café I like in Olympia. I'll be in the backyard."

"Lucky bastard," I hear her mutter, and can't help the smile that comes to my lips. I'm secure enough in my masculinity to admit that the Montgomery side of my family is a handsome one. I don't see any of them as my eyes scan the reception area, but I can hear raised voices coming from the ceremony site in the vines.

"Why do you smell like me?" Isaac asks Matt, the second eldest brother, with a scowl.

"I had to use your body wash when I caught a shower at the office before we came here," Matt replies calmly, with more than a little mirth in his trademark Montgomery blue eyes.

"Are you fucking kidding me?" Isaac yells, as the rest of the brothers laugh. "You can't use my body wash!"

"It's soap, dude," Caleb says with a shake of the head. Caleb is only a year older than me.

"I have to burn the fucking body wash now," Isaac mutters.

I stand back and take them all in. Not only are all four of my brothers here, both Luke and Mark Williams are here, along with Leo Nash and Nate McKenna as well.

The whole fucking family.

Mark is measuring boards and Isaac is manning a saw. I frown as I realize they're all in jeans, holding tools, hammering boards.

Even McKenna.

"Are we having a party that I wasn't aware of?" I ask as I approach.

"Oh, good, you're here." Will grins and shakes my hand, then claps my shoulder. "We're making the arbor."

"We are?" I glance toward Isaac. "Don't you have a crew for this?"

"We decided this would be more meaningful," Luke replies with a smile. "We're making the arbor, and Will is going to take it home after the wedding and put it in their garden."

"It's something from the brothers," Leo adds with a grimace. "I tried to talk them into just letting me write a song, but Will has his pansy ass set on something pretty for the garden."

"Fuck you, man, Meg loves the garden," Will replies, and then grabs Leo into a headlock and rubs his head with his knuckles. "You telling me that if Sam said she wanted pretty in the garden, you wouldn't give it to her?"

"I'd give her anything she asked for," Leo replies as he wrestles out of Will's hold. "And did just this morning."

"Watch it," Luke advises. "She may be your wife now, but she's my sister, and I can still kick your ass if need be."

Matt shakes his head and rolls his eyes. "Anyway," he says, and grins at me. "We were waiting for you. You have to hammer some nails for your soon-to-be sister-in-law too."

I roll my sleeves and take an offered hammer from Mark.

"How's the baby?" Caleb asks Nate, and we all crack up when the tall, tough former fighter breaks out in a goofy grin.

"Stella's awesome." Nate wipes his sweaty forehead on his black T-shirt and takes a long drink of water. "She's fucking beautiful."

"Well, look at her mother," Mark says off-handedly as he measures out more boards, earning a raised brow from Nate.

"Have *you* been looking at her mother?" Nate asks, and we all glance at each other, trying to hold our laughter in.

"Sure, I mean—" Mark suddenly stops and frowns and then looks at Nate. "Dude, not like *that*. It's Jules, for fuck sake."

"I'm well aware of who Stella's mother is," Nate replies with a chuckle. "And you're right. She's gorgeous, so it makes sense that I'll have my hands full with Stella."

"This family is good at producing beautiful babies," Isaac agrees.

"I find it a bit disturbing that there are no women around and we're talking about babies," Will says. "Shouldn't we be talking about sex and cars and football?"

"If you talk about sex," Leo begins, "you'll be talking about my sister, and that's not okay."

"How are things with Meredith?" I ask Mark, steering the conversation away from sex and babies.

"Great." He grins and passes a board to Isaac for cutting.

"And how are you feeling?" Caleb asks him. We all sober as we wait for his response. Mark was hit by a car while on the job more than a month ago, and while the injuries weren't serious, it was a scary time for the family.

"I'm good as new," he replies. "But I don't mind having Meredith around to coddle me now and then."

"And how are all your beautiful girls?" I ask. The guys all nod and grin, thinking of their women. I can't help but think of *my* woman and smile myself.

"My woman is gonna love this," Will says, as he gestures to the wood lying in a heap on the ground. "She has no idea. And it's going to mean more to her because you all made it for her." Will's face sobers as he looks at each of us. "No one's ever needed family more than my Megan."

"Well, she has it in spades now," Caleb replies and strips his sweaty shirt off, tossing it aside.

"Okay, boards are cut," Isaac announces and then begins giving us all instructions on the most efficient way to assemble it, and we break off into teams.

"You're quiet today," Caleb comments as he, Matt and myself work on the top of the arbor.

"I'm quiet every day," I reply. "Besides, you're one to talk."

Caleb shrugs and passes me a handful of nails.

"Who is she?" Matt asks quietly.

"Who is who?"

"The woman that put that shit-eating smile on your face earlier."

"That's an unfortunate turn of phrase," I reply.

"It's a woman," Caleb confirms. "He's evading."

"I'm not evading."

They both stop what they're doing and stare at me, then bust up laughing.

"I've just started seeing Alecia."

"Holy shit! You talked her into it?" Matt asks.

"Wore her down is more like it," Caleb replies, then bumps fists with Matt.

"She's an interesting woman," I reply, rather than take the bait to get angry. I may not have grown up with brothers, but I did grow up with cousins. I know baiting when I see it.

"Interesting how?" Nate asks from a few feet away. I glance around to find that everyone has gone quiet, listening to me.

These men are worse than a bunch of gossiping women.

I shake my head and hammer a nail.

"She's sexy as fuck, but she doesn't know it," I begin, then tap another nail in place. "She's feminine, but tough as nails."

"I wouldn't want to take her on," Luke adds. "I've seen others try, and she tramples them under one of her gorgeous heels without breaking a sweat."

I nod. "She's excellent at her job, but she doesn't believe in love."

"Hold up." Caleb stands and turns to me. "What the fuck does that mean? She plans weddings for a living."

I shake my head, just as confused as the rest of them. "And she loves it, but says she doesn't believe in happily ever after."

The guys frown, and I swear under my breath. "That doesn't mean you should fire her from planning family events. She does an excellent job—"

"No one's firing her from anything," Nate replies calmly, as the others shake their heads in agreement. "But it's a definite surprise."

"Just shows she's professional," Mark says.

"True," Leo says with a shrug and tugs his Metallica tank over his head. "I mean, I don't always love all the music out there, but I have a passion for mine. She's good at the organization of it, and she gets results."

"She's bossy," Will adds with a grin. "And she's sexy while she's doing it."

"I think we can all agree that we're all attracted to strong women, since that's what we all have," Luke agrees with a smirk.

"Meg's not bossy," Will says with a scowl.

"That's what she's let you believe," Caleb says and slaps Will's shoulder.

"Well, she's not bossy in the bedroom."

"I don't imagine any of us would let them take control in the bedroom," I say with a smile.

"Are you going to talk her into giving love a try, or are you just in it for a piece of ass?" Nate asks.

My eyes narrow on his and my hands flex into fists.

"He's been waiting too long for her for it to just be about the sex," Isaac says. Nate doesn't answer; he just continues to watch me with calm grey eyes.

"I'm not just fucking her."

"Okay then."

"What if I was?" I ask out of curiosity.

"Well, that's your business," Nate replies, and turns back to hammer more nails. "But I think that Alecia is worth more than that."

"She's worth everything," I mutter under my breath before taking a long drink of water.

"We're going to the Mariner's game the week after the wedding, right?" Mark asks.

"Yes, we have tickets," Matt replies. "And I might need your help with something that day."

"Don't do it like that, man," Caleb says with a roll of the eyes. "It's cheesy as fuck."

"Not the way I'm thinking of doing it," Matt replies with a scowl.

"Is he going to propose at a baseball game?" Will asks. "Dude, you should have done it at the fucking Super Bowl. We won, for Godsake."

"I wasn't ready," Matt replies.

"Don't do it in public," Luke says, and runs his hand over the plank of wood that has Meg and Will's names and the date of their wedding carved into it. "Make it more special than that."

"Oh! I know! Since Nic owns the cupcake place, bake her some cupcakes and put the ring in one of them and she'll find it when she eats it." Mark looks pleased with his idea, but Caleb clocks him in the back of the head.

"That's ridiculous," Leo says. "She'll choke on it."

"Trust me, I have an idea." Just as Matt begins to outline his brilliant idea for his proposal to Nic, my phone vibrates in my pocket.

Blake.

I walk away from the brothers and answer the phone.

"Hello."

"Hey, man, is this a bad time?"

"This is fine. What's up?"

Blake sighs heavily on the other end of the line and then curses ripely.

"No, I don't believe I'm interested in fucking you sideways," I reply with a smirk.

"I shouldn't be calling you."

Something in his voice has the hair on the back of my neck standing up.

"What's wrong?"

He swears again, and now I'm just pissed.

"Blake, what the fuck?"

"First, let me say this: everything Leash ever tells me is in confidence, and I don't make a habit of breaking that confidence."

"Understood." I turn to watch my brothers, not really seeing them, and narrow my eyes. "What's going on?"

"I just got off the phone with her. Have you spoken to her?"

"I saw her just this morning. She left for some work that she needed to take care of."

"That's bullshit," Blake says grimly. "She ran, man."

"What exactly do you mean, *she ran*?"

"She's not working, she's at her apartment over-thinking the fact that she slept with you. She's scared. She has her reasons, and they're her reasons to tell you, but intimacy scares the fuck out of her."

"I figured that out," I reply, and feel my blood heat. It has nothing to do with the heat of summer.

"Yeah, well, I thought you should know."

"Why?"

"Why what?"

"Why are you telling me this?" I turn my back on my brothers again and pace away.

"Because I think you'll be good for her, and because when I got off the phone with her a little while ago, she sounded regretful that she left, and I know she won't fix it on her own."

I push my hand through my hair and shake my head in exasperation. "I'm on my way to her place."

"I think she was going to go help out with a wedding tonight, but you might catch her if you leave now."

"Thanks, man."

I hang up and return, just as Matt scowls at Caleb and shouts, "Are you just going to stand around all fucking afternoon?"

"No," Caleb replies sarcastically, "I'm gonna fuckin' riverdance, asshole."

The guys laugh at Caleb's witty response as I slip my phone in my pocket.

"I have to go, guys."

"Everything okay?" Will asks.

"No, but it will be. If you need anything, Celeste is just inside."

"We're fine," Isaac says. "We'll have this done in an hour, tops."

"Is she okay?" Caleb asks.

"I don't know." I shove my hands through my hair again. "I'm going to go figure it out."

"Let us know if you need anything," Matt says.

"Good luck," Luke says with a grin, as the others wave. I run through the house, grab my keys and wallet, and set off to Alecia's apartment.

She fucking *ran*.

⚲

I TAKE THE stairs up to Alecia's floor, rather than wait for the elevator. Just as I burst through the stairwell doors, Alecia is stepping out of her apartment and her eyes go wide when she sees me stalking toward her.

"What are you doing here?"

"That's my question," I reply, and stop a few feet away from her.

"I live here," she replies and props her hands on her hips, pulling her pink blouse tight over her full breasts, and making my cock take notice. "But I'm about to go to work—"

"No, you're not."

Her jaw drops at the hard tone in my voice.

"Yes, I believe I am."

"You're going to invite me in your place so we can work out all the reasons why you ran from the villa today."

Her eyes narrow on my face. "I didn't *run* anywhere."

"Like hell." I step forward and cage her in against her door, my hands on either side of her face, and lean in, but don't touch her. Not yet. She takes a deep breath and lays a hand on my chest to push me away, but instead swallows hard and stares at my mouth.

"I couldn't stay there," she whispers before catching herself. She grips my shirt in her fist and scowls up at me with bright, angry brown eyes. "And it's none of your business if I decided to come home for the day."

"It's my business, *tesoro*, to make sure you're okay, and you clearly weren't if you felt that you couldn't stay in my home after I'd just spent the better part of last night and this morning inside you." Unable to resist touching her for one more moment, I drag my knuckles down her cheek, and feel the flare of satisfaction when her eyes close and she leans into my touch. "Invite me in, please."

"I told Emily I'd help her tonight."

"You can un-tell her."

"You're not going to leave, are you?"

"No, *cara*, I'm not leaving."

She opens the door at her back and motions for me to follow her into her apartment, closes and locks the door and pulls her phone out of her bra.

"Emily, I'm sorry, something's come up, and I won't be able to help you after all." She smiles as she watches me lean my hips back against her kitchen counter. "I know you didn't really need me in the first place. But you know where to find me if you do need anything. Good luck." She clicks off and sets the phone and her handbag on the table by the front door. "Happy?"

"No." I sigh and cross my arms over my chest. "No, I don't think *happy* is the right word to describe how I feel."

"How do you feel?"

"Frustrated. Concerned. Baffled. To start."

She nods slowly and walks past me to the kitchen, pours us each a glass of Merlot, then passes one to me.

"This isn't one of mine," I comment wryly and take a sip.

"No, but it's nice." She walks out of the kitchen toward the living room and I can smell her citrusy shampoo as she passes by.

"Hmm." The wine is nice, and I have a feeling she needs it to bolster her courage.

"Have a seat," she says, motioning to the couch, and I have to take a breath to rein in my temper. This morning, she was writhing beneath me and now she's speaking to me like I'm a business associate.

So, I sit right next to her and brace my arm on the back of the couch behind her head and pull the pins out of her hair, letting it spill into my fingers.

"That took me a while to put up," she says.

"I like it down."

"I've noticed."

"Talk to me, *cara*."

"What do you want me to say?"

"Fuck this." I take her glass and set them both on the coffee table, then cradle her face in my hands and kiss the hell out of her. She gasps and grips my shirt in her fists at my sides and holds on tight as I take the kiss from hot and hard to soft and lazy and back again, before pulling away and staring into her eyes. They've gone soft and glassy, making me feel satisfied. "That's better."

"You're good at that," she whispers with a sigh.

"As are you. I don't want you to pull away from me, *tesoro*. Not now. Not after last night."

She tries to look down, but I catch her chin with my thumb and finger and keep her gaze locked on mine. "If you get scared, or nervous, or have doubts, you run *to* me, not *from* me, do you understand?"

"This is so far outside my comfort zone, I don't know what to do."

"I think that's the most honest thing you've ever said to me," I murmur and kiss her forehead. "I'm not letting you slip through my fingers, Alecia. I'm not going anywhere, today or any other day. But I can't understand if you don't talk to me."

She shakes her head and closes her eyes, but not before I see the pain there, and my own heart cracks for her.

"Being naked with you is easy compared to talking to you about my past."

"I love it when you're naked with me," I murmur with a smile. She opens her eyes and grins back at me. "But I need you to talk to me. Let's start with what we were talking about the other night. I believe you said something about not believing in happily ever after." She squirms and finally pushes me away, and then stands.

And just when I think she's going to throw me out of her apartment, she surprises me with, "Let's take a bath."

Ten

S he doesn't stop to see if I'm following her as she walks purpose-fully into the bathroom, wine in hand, and turns on the taps of the garden tub.

"Nice bathroom," I comment calmly as I lean a shoulder against the doorjamb, watching her as she bustles about, keeping her hands busy pinning her hair back on her head and setting out towels.

"It sold me on the place," she replies with a grin. "I haven't used the tub yet. No time."

She kicks out of her sexy black heels and begins stripping off her clothes as the tub fills and the room heats up, and I can only stand here and watch her. She's not trying to tease me, she's not trying to be enticing.

And yet I want to rush to her, strip her bare and fuck her against the bathroom vanity more than I've ever wanted anything.

Except to hear what she has to say. She won't make eye contact, and I let her take her time to get comfortable. She pours something into the water that makes the room smell like jasmine. Turning her back from me, and this will be the last fucking time she ever does that, she strips bare and sinks down into the water.

"Are you just going to stand there and look at me?" she asks testily.

"Was that an invitation?"

She exhales deeply and closes her eyes, then offers me a shy smile. "I'm sorry. Yes, please join me."

I push away from the doorway and unbutton my shirt, slip it off my shoulders and hang it on the hook behind the door. I don't take my eyes off of her as I undress, and can't help the smile that comes as her eyes follow my hands, gliding down my body. She licks her bottom lip as her eyes widen and her breathing picks up. I walk toward her, but rather than sit behind her, I sink into the water opposite her, pick her foot up and begin to dig my thumb into the sole, earning a low moan from her sweet lips.

"Oh, God, that's good."

I'm not sure what to do for her, and this is a first for me. So I simply sit and wait, letting the hot water work its magic, relaxing us both, and finally, after long minutes of me rubbing her feet and calves, she leans her head back on the edge of the tub, closes her eyes, and begins to talk.

"I'm not a particularly lovable person, Dominic."

And pisses me off from the first words out of her gorgeous mouth.

"My mother never made it a secret that she didn't want children."

"Are you an only child?" I ask quietly, casually.

"Yes. My parents didn't plan to have kids, and I was a mistake."

You're not a motherfucking mistake.

"From the time I was small, it was clear that I was an interruption. They loved each other, very much, and intended to always be a couple." She pauses and bites her lip, a small frown between her eyebrows, as though she's choosing her words carefully. "It wasn't that they didn't love me, in their way, they just weren't interested in me."

I rub my hands up her calves, massaging the muscles in her slender legs and concentrate on keeping my breathing even and face calm.

"From the time I was old enough to eat by myself, my mom would fix me a plate and set me up in front of the television to eat, so she and dad could eat together in the kitchen. That was *their time*. It still is." She shrugs her shoulders, making her nipples surface above the water line and pucker from the cold air. Her cheeks are flushed pink from the warmth of the water. She's pink everywhere.

Gorgeous.

"They kept me busy in school," she continues. Her voice is perfectly calm. There's no anger, no sadness. Just composure. "I also play the piano. I had lessons twice a week from the time I was four until I graduated from high school. Then, when I wasn't involved with piano, they had me in soccer, basketball, and softball."

She cringes and then laughs. "I fucking hate to run."

"You hate to run?" I ask with a smile.

"I do. I hate it. And they always signed me up for things that involved running. I asked if I could do cheerleading or *anything* else, but those sports were on a regular rotation, so I was always doing something after school." She sighs. "That's probably why I don't like to exercise much now and my ass is too big."

"Your ass is not too big," I reply calmly, but inside I want to beat the shit out of her parents. Who the fuck treats their child like they're an imposition? "Besides, you run around plenty for your job. In heels, no less." I drag my thumb along her arch, earning a groan from her.

"I'm used to the heels," she replies and smiles at me, then leans her head back again and continues her story. "So, I was in school all day, practicing *something* each afternoon, then doing school work until bedtime each day."

"Surely your parents attended your games. Your recitals?"

"No, those were their date nights," she replies quietly. "I don't recall them ever going to an event."

My hands still on her foot, and tighten just a bit as pure rage seers through me. Alecia's head comes up and she frowns at me. "What's wrong?"

I shake my head and resume rubbing her foot. "Nothing. Go on."

Her eyes narrow on mine for a moment, then she shrugs and leans her head back again. "You've got good hands."

"You've got good feet," I reply, waiting her out.

"So, when I was a senior in high school, I met Jonathan. He was . . . attentive."

"Attentive?" I ask.

"He paid attention to me. I was always kind of shy. I didn't make a lot of friends, mostly because I was always too busy to spend time with them after school. But Jonathan paid attention. He was also a senior. He used to say he liked the looks of me." She giggles.

"Why wouldn't he like the looks of you?"

"It was the turn of phrase that made me laugh. He could be charming. And he was interested in me."

And you soaked that up like a sponge in the ocean, fiorellino.

"My parents happily sent me off to college. They didn't care which one, as long as I went away."

How in the fucking hell can she be so calm? My heart is aching for her, and she's as cool as can be. I continue to rub her, sure to be quiet, so I don't spook her. I have a feeling at this point she's just relaxed and talking on autopilot.

"So, Jonathan and I went to the same college, and eloped to Vegas our junior year." She chuckles and shakes her head. "I thought he was the sexiest, funniest person in the world. I was a stupid, young girl."

"How long did it last?" I ask quietly.

"Longer than it ever should have," she replies with a sigh. "Jonathan made it clear from early in the relationship that I was a huge disappointment."

I can't take it anymore. I grip her foot tightly and pull her toward me, turn her around, and settle her between my legs, wrap my arms around her and plant my lips on her head.

"Go on."

"Are you okay?" she asks with surprise.

"I am now." *No, I'm not fucking okay.* I have to take another deep breath, inhaling in the sweet scent of her, feel her against me, warm and strong and whole, to calm myself. "How did he make you feel like you were a disappointment?" My voice is deceptively calm.

"I *was* a disappointment, Dom."

"Why?"

She shrugs and laces her fingers through mine, then hugs our hands to her chest.

"I didn't like the same things that he did." She falls silent for a minute, and then swears ripely, surprising the hell out of me. "He liked to go to sex clubs, shows, places where clothing was optional. I didn't feel comfortable going to those places."

"Okay." I'm clearly missing something.

"No, not okay." She kisses my fingers. "He wanted me to wear skimpy clothes that I wasn't comfortable in. I know I'm not horrible on the eyes, but I do have curves, and I don't feel that it's appropriate to walk around half naked in front of people I don't know. Hell, I don't particularly like walking around half naked in front of people I *do* know." She chuckles, but I don't find it fucking funny. "It would make him angry. He wouldn't yell at me, though. No, he would just ignore me."

"Ignore you?" I can't help the tightness in my voice.

"Yeah." She sighs. "He knew that ignoring me was the best way to hurt me. I'd been ignored most of my life."

"So, he ignored you as a punishment."

"He did. And as time passed, it got worse. He would sleep on the couch, which he knew made me crazy. Wouldn't speak to me for days, sometimes weeks at a time. When I started the business, and completed my first wedding, I asked him to take me out for a fun dinner to celebrate."

I hug her closer to me.

"And he said, 'Why? It's just a fucking job.'" She chuckles and shakes her head, then glances over her shoulder at me.

"He was an asshole," I mutter.

"Yeah. But—"

"But?"

"Well, I'm not going to say I deserved it, because that's ridiculous, but he was right. It was just a job."

"It was something you worked hard on, and you wanted to celebrate it. It wasn't *just a job* for you. And if he'd loved you the way he should have loved his wife, he would have seen that."

"Hmm," is her only response. "So, back to the love thing."

"The *love thing?*" I ask with a laugh.

"It's just not in me," she replies and shrugs a shoulder, but then plants another kiss on my hand. "So, I'm comfortable with pursuing a physical relationship, if you're still interested in that, but don't expect much more from me, because you'll just be disappointed."

Her voice is perfectly matter of fact and reasonable and I want to just . . . shake her.

What?

She leans her blonde head back and gazes up at me. "Dom?"

"Ah, *tesoro*," I murmur and glide my wet knuckles down her cheek softly. "Let's table this discussion for now, okay?" I grip her hips in my hands and lift her to her feet, then pull myself up behind her, help her step out of the tub and reach for a towel. I wrap it around her shoulders, and gripping each end in my hands, I pull her against me, making her grin shyly.

"No more talking?" she whispers, her eyes pinned to my lips.

"Maybe less talking." I lower my lips and gently brush them over hers, barely touching her skin, before nibbling the corner of her mouth and then gliding my tongue along her bottom lip to the other side, where I can nibble some more.

She shivers, so I let my hands roam over the towel, drying her off. When we're both dry, I lift her in my arms, snag her bottle of lotion from the sink and carry her into her bedroom.

It's dark now. With Alecia cradled in my arms, I pull the linens back on her bed, switch on the sidelight and gently lower her onto the bed, laying her on her back.

She's watching me through dreamy eyes, relaxed from the warm bath.

"You are sure handsome to look at," she murmurs, and lifts my hand to her lips.

"You have such a sweet heart," I whisper, as I lean in and kiss her forehead. "Close your eyes."

"It's too early to go to sleep," she replies.

"I'm not trying to put you to sleep." I rub lotion between my hands, warming it, then begin to massage it into Alecia's soft, smooth skin. I run my hands over her arm, her shoulder and her hand and grin when she sighs deeply and closes her eyes.

"You're good with your hands," she says.

"They enjoy touching you," I reply, as I move to the other side, then add more lotion and glide my hands over her upper chest, between her breasts and down her sides. "You have the smoothest skin I've ever seen."

"The skin is the largest organ in your body. You should take care of it," she says primly, making me chuckle.

"Brains as well as a beautiful face." I work my way down her legs and give her feet another good rub, earning a long sigh of contentment from her. "Don't the shoes you wear kill your feet?"

"No," she replies immediately, then bites her lip and squints one eye open to gaze at me warily. "Okay, can you keep a secret?"

"Anything you ever say will stay between the two of us, *cara*."

"They fucking kill me," she says, and closes her eyes again, but the corners of her lips tip up in a smile. "But I love them too much to ever wear anything else."

"You look fucking amazing in them," I reply, as I urge her to turn over onto her belly. She cradles her head in her arms and sighs deeply as my hands glide up and down her slender back, kneading and stretching her muscles. "You have great legs."

"That comes from walking in four-inch heels every day. Sweet Jesus, that feels good." I move over the spot on her right shoulder again, and if I'm not mistaken, she purrs. "Don't ever stop touching me," she whispers with a blissful sigh, and my heart catches.

"That's the plan." I lean in and kiss her neck, right in the spot behind her ear that drives her mad. She sighs again, and her hips tip up, brushing her ass over my already hard cock. Her lips are still curved at the corners, and a blush creeps up her cheeks as she rotates her hips once again, feeling the heavy weight of my dick against her ass.

I grin and kiss her neck again, then drag my lips down to her shoulder and over between her shoulder blades. Her hand grasps the pillow, but I whisper in her ear, "Relax, babe," and she lets go, then frowns up at me.

"I prefer the Italian."

I raise a brow. "Is that so?"

"You know it is." She purses her lips in a pout and closes her eyes again as my fingertips trail lightly down her back and up her sides, making her squirm.

"That tickles."

"You'll learn, *babe*," I begin, and continue to make her skin tingle, "that you won't top me in bed." I nip her shoulder as she takes in a quick gasp of air and bites her lip. "I know what you prefer, and I plan to continue learning. Your body is expressive." I straddle her legs and sit back on my haunches, grasp her ass cheeks in my hands and squeeze gently and she shivers and lets loose with a low moan that shoots energy straight through my cock, making it slap the crack of her ass. "See, you like that."

"I do," she agrees with a whisper.

"And you like this." I cover her body again, nip at her neck and slip a hand between her closed legs, pushing on her clit with my fingertips, spreading her juices through her lips.

"Oh, God, I so love that."

I grasp her hand in mine, and she quickly links our fingers and tucks my hand under her face. I grip my cock and guide it down her crack and inside her, and we both groan at how amazing she feels wrapped tightly around me, tighter still because of her thighs pressed together between my own.

"Fuck, you feel good, Alecia."

"How is it possible that you grew since this morning?" she asks in awe.

"It's the angle," I reply with a chuckle, and then feel my eyes roll up into the back of my head when she clenches around me. "God, do you have any idea what you do to me?"

"I have a fairly good idea," she replies smartly and rolls her hips. "It's inside me as we speak."

"The fact that you can speak means I'm not doing my job," I reply and with my free hand I brush her hair off her face, then drag it down her back, her side, and hold onto her hip firmly, keeping her from moving, and begin to thrust my hips in earnest, loving her long and slow, just slower than I know she wants me to. She growls and turns her face, resting her forehead against my hand.

"Harder," she moans.

"Not yet," I reply and keep up the long, slow pace. "I'm going to eventually make you understand how amazing you are, *tesoro*," I whisper into her ear. She frowns in surprise, but is pinned beneath me. She can't do anything but feel and hear me all around her, and I take full advantage of her vulnerability. "You are *not* a quick fuck for me. If that were the case, I wouldn't have followed you here today." I adjust my grip on her ass, spreading her cheeks further apart so I can plunge in even deeper, but not faster. "You are sexy, yes, and God knows I want you so bad I'm blind with it, but that's not all you are, Alecia."

"Dominic."

"I didn't say you could talk." I nip at her earlobe. "It's your turn to listen."

She bites her lip as I seat myself as far as I can and pulse my hips, hitting her G-spot and her clit at the same time. I can feel her about to lose it.

"Yes, this is scary," I whisper. "It's not exactly in my comfort zone either, but the thought of not having you terrifies me. If you thought you'd scare me off earlier, you were wrong. I'm not going anywhere."

"I wasn't trying to scare you off," she says as her pussy pulses around me. "I was being honest."

"And I appreciate your honestly, *cara*." I pull back, dragging my cock almost all the way out of her, and then switch up the intensity again, taking my time to sink back into her. She's panting, and her lips are wet and parted. "You are precious. You are worthy of so much more than you know. Knowing that others made you feel insignificant pisses me off, but it's their loss."

I press my lips to her ear. "It's their loss."

"Dominic," she whispers as her body begins to writhe and tremble under me.

"Yes, *tesoro*," I reply and finally give her what her body is craving, moving faster, a bit harder, inside her. "Come for me."

"Oh, God," she breathes and her body shudders, tenses and comes apart at the seams beneath me, crying out my name.

My name.

"That's right," I say raggedly. I pull out of her and urge her onto her back, settle between her legs, and sink inside her still-trembling pussy as her arms and legs envelope me tenderly. She sinks her fingers in my hair and watches me with wide, glassy brown eyes as she hitches her knees up around my hips, opening herself up to me completely. "This is *me* with you, Alecia. Not your ex, or any other idiot who let you get away from him. It's just you and me." I nibble her lips and make slow, sweet love to her, drunk on her. I push one hand under her ass, bringing her flush against me.

"You and me, understand?"

"You and me," she agrees, before pulling my lower lip between her teeth, and I can't hold myself back any longer. I bury my face in her neck as the orgasm shoots its way through me. I rock my pelvis against hers and come inside her as she cries out and clenches around me once again, coming along for the ride.

After I catch my breath, I brace myself on my elbows, taking my weight off of her and grin down at her softly. "I think we need another shower."

"I think you're right." She chuckles and her pussy squeezes me, instantly making me hard again.

"Later," I murmur with a smile and hitch her leg up over my shoulder. "It seems I'm not finished with you."

eleven

Alecia

"It's just you and me." Dom's words echo in my mind as I slowly slip from a dreamless sleep to lazy wakefulness. His arm is draped gently around my waist, his chest pressed against my back. Even in sleep, he's holding me against him.

You and me.

I grin and take a deep breath, then shimmy around so I'm facing him. His face is relaxed in sleep, his lips closed, his eyelashes brushing his cheeks.

What's up with men having better eyelashes than women?

I nudge the tip of his nose with mine, then place a gentle kiss on his lips and scoot out from under his arm and pad sleepily into the bathroom.

I desperately need that shower we never got around to last night.

Not that I'm complaining.

My body is humming, extra sensitive from all of Dominic's attention as I step into the spray of water and grin to myself as I begin soaping up my body.

I'm still scared out of my mind. I'm not going to lie to myself and try to think that I'm suddenly a hearts and flowers kind of girl. I'm still not so sure that shit exists, but what Dom said last night made complete sense. What I feel with him is unique to him. To *us*. It has nothing at all to do with either of our pasts.

He has nothing to do with Jonathan, or my parents.

It's just him and me.

And damn if it's not the safest feeling I've ever had.

I finish shaving my legs, grinning when I see his fingerprints in my thigh muscles.

Yep, damn sexy.

Is it weird that I think it's hot that Dominic left fingerprint bruises on my skin?

I shrug, turn the tap off, quickly dry my skin and wrap up in a large, fluffy, blue towel, then lean across the vanity and swipe the fog from the mirror before moisturizing my face.

If he touches me the way he did last night, he can leave bruises anywhere he wants.

I smirk and brush out my hair, then twist it up onto the back of my head, securing it with pins. Just as I lower my arms, Dom appears behind me in the mirror. He doesn't say anything, but his eyes are pinned to mine as he gently squeezes my shoulders and kisses my neck, in that spot that he knows makes me weak in the knees. His hands glide down my arms, to my hands, which he guides to the counter top.

"Leave your hands right here," he whispers against my ear.

I bite my lip and close my eyes, but he leans past me, his long arm reaching around me and wipes the fog that has reformed on the mirror away.

"Keep your eyes open, *cara.*"

I find his gaze in the mirror once more. His lips twitch with humor, his dimple winks at me, and the next thing I know, my towel is gone and tossed on the floor. My eyebrows climb as his eyes rake over me, from my face, down my chest, to my stomach in the mirror, then he pulls back and his eyes take the same tour of my body from behind.

And just like that, I'm on fucking fire.

"Dom—"

"I didn't say you could talk," he murmurs lazily, but his eyes are direct and firm as they meet mine in the glass.

I love it when he gets bossy.

He pulls the tip of his finger down the nape of my neck, and continues down my spine, sending gooseflesh over my skin. When he reaches the small of my back, he grips my hips in both hands and urges me back, bent over, sticking my ass in the air. His hands slide back to cup my ass gently, reverently, and I can already feel the moisture forming between my thighs.

Jesus, I want him like crazy, and I just had him a few hours ago.

"I thought about taking you like this last night," he says softly, his fingertips gliding up and down my sides. It would normally tickle the hell out of me, but all it does is make my nipples pucker in anticipation. "But I decided this wasn't what you needed then."

He leans over me and plants his lips in the crook of my neck, then finds my gaze with his again as he grips my hands and moves them from the countertop to the mirror.

"Lean on the glass," he instructs me firmly. He cups both of my breasts and tweaks my firm nipples with his thumbs. "I like you in this position. With your ass pushed out, spread open for me."

My jaw drops as I watch his tanned hands move over my white skin.

"I want you to keep your hands on the mirror, *cara*. And I don't want you to watch me."

I frown at him, not understanding.

"You're to keep your eyes open, but I want you to watch *you*." He kisses my spine, right between my shoulder blades as his thumbs continue to torture my nipples. "I want you to see what I do to you."

I know what he does to me. He makes me completely crazy. He makes me feel like my body is turning inside out.

He makes me lose myself.

I open my mouth, but before I can speak he says, "Don't argue with me, unless you want this to stop."

Forget bossy. Try tyrannical.

And with those last words of instruction, he kisses his way down my back and squats behind me. It feels bizarre to watch my own face as I'm getting turned on.

"How do you feel?" he asks before he plants a kiss on my left ass cheek, as if he's reading my mind.

"Shy," I reply immediately.

"Good girl," he says and drags his hand up the inside of my right thigh and skims his fingertips through my folds and against my clit, then retreats immediately. I gasp, my lips part, and I can see the pulse in my neck pick up speed.

"Look at the way you blush," he whispers. The very tips of his fingers, his short fingernails, scrape up and down my ass slowly, softly, making me catch my breath. "I love it when your cheeks get red with arousal."

I've never noticed it before. I didn't know I did that. A blush spreads from my cheeks, down my neck to my chest, and my hands form into fists, still leaning against the mirror. I can see his shoulders on either side of my hips, and I bite my lip at the thought of his face being eye-level with my pussy.

"You blush down here, too, you know." He plants another wet kiss on the opposite cheek, just as his hand takes another trip up the inside of my left thigh and into my dripping wet folds.

I moan and drop my head, my eyes closing, and he's suddenly . . . *gone.*

"If you stop, so do I, *cara.*"

My head whips back up. He's shifted to my left side, watching me in the mirror.

"I mean it."

I bite my lip again and nod, and he moves behind me once again, grips my hips in his hands, and without further ado, leans in and swipes his tongue, from my clit to my anus, in one long, firm, wet motion.

I'm panting now, my pulse scattered, the blood rushing in my ears. He presses his thumb to my clit and pulls my lips into his mouth, gently pulsing, then his tongue sinks inside me. He rubs his nose against my puckered anus, but then he switches it up again, drags his lips down to my clit, flicking it softly, just before he sinks two fingers deep inside me and makes a *come here* motion, hitting my goddamn sweet spot.

"Dom!" I shout, my hips bucking. God, my eyes are glassy, the pupils dilated. My skin is glistening with a light sheen of sweat, and my lower lip is swollen from my own teeth.

He's going to fucking kill me.

"That's right, baby," he says loudly, before gripping onto my clit with his lips once more, sucking firmly, turning me inside out. I watch in wonder as I tumble over the edge, crying out, pounding my fist against the mirror as I go blind, seeing only stars as I come hard.

I can't fucking breathe.

Before I know what's happening, Dom stands and turns me in his arms, boosts me onto the vanity and pushes inside me, smoothly burying himself in my dripping wetness. He covers my mouth with his, leans his own hands against the mirror and begins to drill in and out of me violently, as if he's a man possessed.

I'm clinging to him, my legs wrapped around his waist and my hands gripping his upper arms as his mouth plunders mine. I can taste myself on him, and it only makes me want him more.

With one hand, I reach between us and press my fingertips on my clit, then sink them lower and press against the base of his cock as he moves in and out of me. He growls and tears his mouth from mine so he can watch my hand, then turns those feral blue eyes on mine.

"Che è così fottutamente sexy," he groans. "God, you're so fucking sexy."

I can feel my body tightening as another orgasm gathers in the core of me, then explodes through me. I lean in and bite Dom's shoulder as I buck and shudder against him.

"Fuck yes," he growls, one hand planted on my ass as he pulls me even more firmly against him, grinding his pubis against my clit, and comes long and hard, emptying himself inside me.

We stay right here for long moments, me clinging onto him so I don't fall back, Dom gripping my ass almost painfully, while leaning on the mirror with his other hand, chasing our breath. Finally, he tips his forehead against mine and shakes his head.

"Do you see how damn sexy you are?"

"I see—" I begin, but he stops me with one firm look.

"No smart ass responses."

"Yes. I see it."

"Thank Christ."

He kisses my forehead tenderly and backs away, helping me off the vanity.

"I want to spend the day with you," he says.

"Well, we'll be out at the vineyard, so—"

"No, away from the vineyard."

I turn to stare at him. "Dom, I spent the day away from the vineyard yesterday. I have work to do."

"It's Sunday, *cara.*" He throws me a cocky grin. "No one else is working today."

I chew my lip as I think of all of the things I should be doing today, but he cocks a brow at me, and I cave. I want to spend the day with him.

"What do you have in mind?"

He flips the water on in the shower before tugging me against him and plants a kiss on my nose, then my lips. "I want to take you somewhere special."

I TOSS CRACKERS and grapes into the basket I'm putting together for our day out and shake my ass in time with Matt Nathanson, singing "Faster." I add cheese, salami, and strawberries, then shimmy over to my wine rack and choose a bottle of Dom's red, two glasses, and then bounce around the kitchen, singing along with Matt.

Suddenly, Dominic's strong hand takes mine, and he gracefully spins me into his arms, dancing us both about the kitchen.

"I love watching you move," he whispers against my temple as he holds me close.

I chuckle and move my hips suggestively, playfully, just as he pushes me away from him again, then pulls me back in, my back against his front, my ass pressed against his crotch.

I wrap my arm up around his neck and tilt my head back so he can kiss my nose, and then, Patrick Swayze-style, he twirls me one more time, then dips me low as the song comes to an end.

"Very nice, Mr. Salvatore." His lips twitch, and that dimple winks at me as he pulls me back to my feet and lays a quick, hard kiss on my lips.

"Are you ready to go?" he asks. My eyes wander down his casual white button-up and sexy jeans, then back up to his face to find a half smile on those amazing lips and his eyes shining with . . . *lust*. "Keep looking at me like that, *cara,* and we won't get far today."

I simply bite my lip and keep looking, enjoying the way he looks back at me. Finally, he shakes his head and laughs.

"We're going. Out. Now." He gathers the basket, then takes my hand in his spare one and plants a wet kiss on my knuckles. "Come on."

"I DIDN'T KNOW this was here," I comment, as Dominic and I walk side-by-side up a long pier that overlooks the sound. It's a bit overcast today, keeping us cool, but the scenery is no less stunning. "It's only a few miles from my condo."

He nods and gazes out at the water, then frowns at the chain-link fence with locks of all different shapes and sizes hanging from it.

"Locks of love," I murmur with a grin. "I guess they're trying to copy the place in Paris?"

"I don't get it," he says, before glancing down at me with a raised brow. "Is it supposed to be romantic?"

"It's supposed to be symbolic," I reply with a shrug. "You know, obviously if we place a lock here with our initials with all of the rest, our love is true." I smirk and shake my head. "It's like Valentine's Day."

He blinks in surprise. "Okay, you have to explain that to me."

We lean against the railing and watch sailboats float past. The water is deep blue and choppy. We shed our shoes at the base of the pier, along with the basket and wine. Dom takes my hand in his and lifts it to his lips, planting a firm kiss right on the back of my hand as I lean my cheek against his shoulder and take a deep breath of the salty air.

"It's a gimmick," I say simply.

"You're so not a romantic, *tesoro.*" He chuckles and kisses my hand again, and I'm not sure why, but that doesn't sit well with me.

"I am," I insist, and turn to lean my back on the railing so I can face him. "I am when it comes to what matters."

"What matters?" His voice is quiet, but insistent, and his deep blue eyes are pinned to mine.

"Romance isn't about proving to someone you love them with flowers and greeting cards and chocolate. Or even a lock on a fence. It's a daily reminder. It's saying, *I choose you. Today and every day.*" I shrug, and look down, embarrassed now. Why in the bloody hell did I say that?

But Dom tilts my head up and smiles down at me in that gentle way he does. "I hear you."

I turn back to the water and take a long, deep breath. "God, I love it here."

"Why?" he asks suddenly.

"Why?" I repeat and frown at him.

"Why do you love it here?"

I glance back out at the water and then to the tall, dark man next to me. "Are we not looking at the same scenery?"

"Don't be difficult. What is it about this place, this water, that you love?"

I sigh and turn my gaze to the water, the islands, the birds, the boats.

"It centers me. I knew when I bought my condo that I had to be on the water, and I scrimped and saved until I could afford my place. There was nowhere else I wanted to be." I take Dom's hand and lead him down the pier toward the grass. "I love everything about the waterfront. The smell, the way the wind hits my face and filters through my hair. There's nothing like watching a parasailer, or catching a glimpse of a sea lion in the water."

Dom lifts the basket and the wine and I take my shoes and the wine glasses and follow him out into the wide grassy area, where we drop everything and sit facing each other.

"This is my home." I shrug one shoulder and pluck a blade of grass out of the dirt.

"I get it," he replies with a nod. "It's where you fit."

"Exactly."

"That's how the vineyard is for me," he says, and squints as he gazes out at the water. "And Italy."

"I would love to see Italy. Tell me about it."

He grins, and then before I can react, he's pulled me in his arms, and onto my back in the grass, covering me with his solid body.

"Close your eyes."

"There are children nearby," I reply dryly, making him laugh.

"Close your eyes," he repeats. I wrinkle my nose at him and then do as I'm told, relaxing in the grass.

"I'm not even going to think about the bugs that could be crawling around in my hair right now," I comment lightly.

"I'll protect you," he replies and suddenly, his fingertips are grazing along my cheekbone, and I melt. "Italy is unlike anywhere else. Tuscany, specifically, is the most beautiful place I've ever been."

His fingers journey up my temple, along my forehead, and over my eyebrows, making me sigh in contentment. Dear sweet Jesus, the man is good with his hands.

"The villages are busy, bustling with people, but they're the friendliest people you'll ever meet." His fingertip drifts down my nose. "And the colors are just spectacular. The hills are vibrantly green. The sky boldly blue, but when the sun is hanging just right, everything is gold." The last few words are whispered as he traces my lips with the pad of his thumb. "Watching the sunlight bounce off the dew on my grapevines is as close to heaven as I'll ever be. It smells . . . *clean*. New. Every day is new."

Now he sinks his other hand in my hair, brushes tiny tendrils off my forehead and cheeks, sending sparks of awareness through me, yet I'm the most comfortable I've ever been.

His voice is soothing. His hands are calming. I can't believe how gentle his touch is when I know how rough he can be.

I can't get enough of him.

He leans in close and whispers in my ear, "I can't wait to show it to you. Italy is going to love you."

Before I can respond, he covers my lips with his, in a long, slow, sweet kiss, in that way he does that feels like it's the first time he's kissed me all over again. His fingertips continue to tickle my forehead, while his other hand drifts down my side, barely brushing over my breast, down to my hip, where he holds me as his lips brush back and forth over my own. He nibbles his way to the corner of my mouth, then licks along my bottom lip, tugs it with his teeth, and settles in to kiss me long and slow once more.

When he finally pulls back, I can't open my eyes. My lids are heavy with desire and need, and his fingertips on my skin are making me nuts.

He kisses my cheek, then my nose, and whispers, "Open your eyes, *cara.*"

They flutter open and I'm staring up into the brightest blue eyes I've ever seen, surrounded by dark lashes, olive skin, and raven hair.

"How do you always kiss me like it's the first time?" I ask breathlessly.

His eyes flicker down to my lips, then back to my eyes. Instead of answering, he offers me that heart-stopping smile, and moves in to kiss me all over again.

I grip onto his strong back and go along for the ride, enjoying his lips on mine, his body covering me, his manly scent flowing around me.

I'm in way over my head. And I don't want to be saved.

twelve

This week has flown by. The second Dominic and I returned to the vineyard, it was full speed ahead with Montgomery wedding plans.

"We're heading out, Alecia, unless there's something else you need," Mark says, as he waves goodbye to his crew.

"I don't need anything," I assure him with a grin. My heels click on the hardwood dance floor as I approach him. "This is beautiful."

His blue eyes take in the massive tent, floor, and stage and he gives me a satisfied nod. "We did good."

"You did excellent," I agree.

"We'll hang the lights and set out tables tomorrow, and that's about it."

I can already picture the white twinkling lights strung throughout the tent in my head, the tables set up and decorated with beautiful flowers, smiling people dancing and laughing.

I can't wait.

"Rehearsal dinner tomorrow night," I remind him, as he turns to leave.

"Like I could forget that." He shakes his head and laughs. "I hope you're ready for the party about to ensue tomorrow night."

I cock my brow and tilt my head in question.

"The girls will drink and celebrate, let loose. Our family won't feel comfortable letting loose at the reception, but given that tomorrow night is private, well . . ." He shrugs and offers me a roguish grin. "Game on."

"Thanks for the warning." I wave him off and walk toward the house, let myself in through the side door and run right into Dominic as he comes out of his office. "Hey there, handsome."

A soft smile spreads over his face, and before he can respond, I rise up on my tip-toes, wrap my arms around his neck and press my lips to his in a quick, chaste kiss, then pull away and drag my hands firmly down his arms to his hands and clench them tightly in mine.

"Hi yourself," he responds.

"How's your day?"

"It's gone well. I'm assuming yours has as well?"

I nod and kiss his palm, just before he cups my cheek and rubs his thumb over the apple of my cheek. "I have a few more things to see to."

"I'll see you soon, then."

I smile and squeeze his hands once more before walking away toward the kitchen. Unable to resist, I toss a glance over my shoulder to find him watching me walk away, one hand resting on his chest over his heart, his deep blue eyes smiling at me.

Dear sweet Jesus, my man is hot. And the way my heart skips at the look on his face is just almost disgusting.

And I don't even care.

I wiggle my fingers in a wave and saunter happily into the kitchen where Blake is whistling while he works, looking handsome in his chef jacket, with the sleeves rolled up to his elbows, showing off his flexing forearms.

"Something smells good," I comment lightly, and lean over the stove, reaching for the lid of a pot.

"Hands off, sister."

"I'm hungry."

"I'll feed you, but get your nose out of my pots."

I stick my tongue out at him and cross to the fridge. "Did the food come in for tomorrow's dinner?"

"Yes, boss."

"Are the artichokes fresh?" I poke at the large, beautiful vegetables.

"Get your hands off my shit."

I close the fridge and turn to find Blake glaring at me while he chops something briskly.

"You're going to cut your fingers off if you don't watch what you're doing."

"Why are you in here pestering the fuck out of me?"

"Because I love you?" I bat my eyelashes at him and then laugh when he cocks a brow and smirks. "Because I'm checking to see if you have things under control."

"When have I *not* had things under control?"

"It's my job to check."

"So, you checked. Are you done micro-managing the rest of the crew for the day?"

"Yep." I reach around him and pluck a piece of red pepper off his cutting board and pop it in my mouth. "You were my last stop."

"Good," Dom says, as he saunters into the kitchen with two bottles of wine in his hands. "Is dinner almost ready?" he asks Blake.

"Yep."

"Wait. Are we having a party?" I ask.

"We're having dinner," Blake replies with a grin. "I know how you get when you work. You forget to eat, and then you get hungry and you annoy the piss out of everyone around you."

"That's not true," I insist.

"Which part?" Dominic asks, as he pulls three wine glasses out of a cupboard.

"If you guys are going to gang up on me, I'll go home."

"No you won't," Blake replies, as Dom just narrows his eyes at me and shakes his head slowly from side to side. "I made your favorite. And if you leave, you can't have any."

"Homemade mac n' cheese?" I ask hopefully, making Dom smile widely.

"And . . ." Blake says in a sing-song voice.

"And turkey breast?" I clap my hands in excitement.

"And . . ."

"If you say collard greens, I'll kiss you."

"No," Dom interjects lazily, as he pulls the cork out of the first bottle, "you won't."

"I'll give them to you for free," Blake says with a laugh. "And it's just about ready."

"Woot!" I offer Blake a fist bump and help the guys carry everything outside to the table near the fire pit. We all settle in, Dom right next to me and Blake across from us, loading our plates, sipping our wine, and I can't help but wonder if this is going to be . . . weird. I've slept with both of these men, and they're both very special to me.

"So it looks like it's pretty much done back there," Blake says, as he takes a bite of the mac n' cheese, gesturing to the tent.

"Yep, just a few odds and ends to finish tomorrow," I reply, and load a bite of turkey, greens, and mac n' cheese all on my fork, then groan loudly when they all hit my tongue. "So good," I say, my mouth full of food.

"You're such a lady," Blake smirks.

"I don't have to be a lady when you feed me this," I say, and take a sip of wine, eyeing Dom over my glass. "He doesn't feed me this very often," I inform my sexy Italian.

"You always tell me the pasta will make you gain fifty pounds," Blake reminds me.

"It will."

"Women," Blake says with a shake of his head.

Dominic leans in and whispers in my ear, "Your body is perfect." He kisses my cheek and returns to his meal.

Blake doesn't miss a thing. He grins widely. "This is nice."

"Emily will be here tomorrow morning," I say, trying to change the subject. "She and I will start handling the nitty gritty things."

"Nitty gritty?" Dom asks with a smile.

"The little things," I reply. "Greeting the florist for tomorrow's flowers, and meeting with her about Saturday's flowers. Placing calls. Picking up favors, double-checking the guest list and forwarding it on to security." I sip my wine and continue to tick items off in my head, then blink and look around. "Sorry."

"I already spoke with Emily," Blake says nonchalantly, and won't look me in the eye as he cuts his turkey.

"When?" I ask.

"Last night," he replies.

Last night?

"There wasn't an event last night," I say, and chew on my own turkey.

"No, there wasn't," Blake replies. I glance up at Dominic to find him watching me closely. I can't tell what he's thinking, but he quirks a brow at me and I shrug.

"But you saw her last night?" I ask in confusion.

"I did."

"Did you enjoy yourselves?" Dominic asks and sips his wine as I stare at Blake in shock.

Blake and Emily?

"Very much," Blake says with a grin.

"You're seeing Emily." It isn't a question.

"Problem?" Blake asks defiantly.

I set my fork down and clear my throat. "It's Emily."

"We've established that, Leash." Blake's mouth is set in a firm line.

"I know you," I murmur quietly.

"As do I," Dominic interrupts, still the epitome of calm. "And because I do, I know Emily will be well taken care of." He takes my hand in his and kisses my fingers, and then says in a low voice, "Don't say something you'll regret."

I look back and forth between these men and swallow hard.

"Jealous?" Blake asks and winks at me, trying to be funny.

"I love you both," I reply honestly. "You're two of my dearest friends, and I don't have many of those, Blake. So if this falls apart, and I have to choose—"

"God, you're dramatic," Blake says with a roll of the eyes.

"I'm being honest," I insist.

"I'm dating her, yes."

"Are you fucking her?"

"Alecia," Dom says, with a shake of his head.

"Yes, I am, Leash," Blake replies frankly.

"This has disaster written all over it," I mutter, and take a long drink of my wine.

"She's different," Blake says, and stares down into his wine. "I don't have the urge to run away from her."

"There are things you don't know, Blake." I shake my head and think back on the long conversations that Emily and I have had about her abusive past.

"I know," he replies and pins me in his sober gaze, the one I don't see often. "And I'm sticking for as long as she'll have me."

I stare at my friend, Dom's hand still in mine, holding on to me tightly.

"Be nice to her," I say quietly. "She deserves to have someone be nice to her."

"I've been very nice to her," he replies with a cocky wink.

"God, you're a pig." I scowl at him, but soften when he lets out a belly laugh.

"You've never warned me off a woman before," he says.

"I've always found out about them long after they left your bed," I remind him, and then turn to Dominic. "If I'd known them beforehand, I would have told them to run screaming in the other direction."

"Oh, they scream all right."

"Yuck," I grumble, and then chuckle as I drink more wine. "Have you always been so disgusting?"

"Pretty much," he replies, as he clears his plate. "Don't worry, Leash."

"Worry is my middle name," I remind him.

He sighs and finishes his wine. "I'm going to head out." He reaches for his dishes, but Dominic waves him off.

"I'll handle this," he says.

"You cooked," I say with a grin.

"I usually cook and clean when you're around," he says as he stands.

"That's bullshit. I like to clean."

Blake laughs. "I'll see you tomorrow."

"Drive safe," Dom says with a wave, as Blake lets himself out. He sips his wine thoughtfully as I finish my dinner and sigh in contentment.

"I wish he'd tell me how he makes this mac n' cheese," I grumble, as I gather dishes. Dom stands and helps me, and soon we are bustling about the kitchen silently, each of us lost in our thoughts as we clean.

I stack the last plate into the washer and close the door and look up to find Dom leaning his hips against the counter top, his arms crossed over his chest, watching me quietly.

"What's wrong?" I ask.

He shakes his head and frowns. "Nothing is wrong."

"What's on your mind?"

"You really are just friends. With Blake."

I tilt my head. "Don't tell me you were feeling threatened by Blake."

"I wouldn't call it threatened," he replies and rubs his fingers over his lips. "I've never spent any significant time with both of you before. I can see that you care about each other, but not on an intimate level."

I nod slowly. "Like I said, he's one of my dearest friends. We had a physical relationship a long time ago." His nostrils flare at that, his eyes narrow, just a bit, but he listens calmly. "It was obvious that we're much better as friends. He means a lot to me. He's the one person in my life that I know will never leave me."

Dom's eyes narrow as he watches me. "I'm not going to leave you, Alecia."

I swallow and shrug a shoulder, not sure what to say.

"Okay." He nods, as if that settles something and crosses to me.

"Okay?"

"Okay," he repeats and pulls me in for a hug, kisses my forehead, and breathes me in all in one smooth move. "You smell amazing."

I grin and enjoy the feel of his arms looped around me, pulling me tightly against him.

"You're a bit tense," he continues.

"It was a long day."

"Come." He pours a glass of wine, then takes my hand and leads me through the house and up the stairs to his master bathroom. He magically produces a single pink tulip and hands it to me with a soft smile. I rub the petals against my nose and breathe the sweet scent in as he turns and runs me a bath, lights candles, and then turns his attention back to me.

With sure fingers, he unzips my dress and pushes it off my shoulders, letting it pool around my ankles.

"You're beautiful, *cara*." His eyes roam up and down my torso. "This bra is pretty." His fingertips skim my skin over the light pink cups of my demi bra, making my nipples pucker before he unclasps it between my breasts and it joins the dress on the floor. With his eyes on mine, he hooks his thumbs into my panties and guides them over my hips and down my legs.

"Step out of those killer heels, please." He takes my hand in his and leads me to the bathtub, watching as I sink into the steamy water and settle back with my head leaning on the ledge of his vast bathtub. "Here's your wine," he says with a grin as he sits on the ledge.

"It's pretty in here."

"With you here, yes it is."

"You're a charmer."

"I'm just calling it like I see it," he replies with a half-smile, showing off that sexy dimple.

"I like your dimple."

"I hope that's not all you like."

I shrug. "Probably not."

He chuckles and drags his fingertip down my cheek.

"Actually, there's more to you than the flirty, charming Italian that I've known you to be."

His blue eyes find mine, and he watches me calmly as I take a sip of wine.

"You're not going to ask me what I see?" I ask boldly.

"What do you see, *tesoro*?"

I take his dry hand in my wet ones and plant a kiss to his palm. "I see a professional, intelligent, kind—"

"Just don't call me *nice*."

"Sexy, sweet man."

"You're the sweet one, Alecia."

"This bath is nice."

"I'll take your word for it."

"You're not joining me?"

"No." He sweeps my hair off my forehead with one fingertip. "I want you to relax. Take a deep breath." He leans in and kisses my head, then stands and leaves the room.

Damn, he's sweet.

I set the wine glass on the ledge of the tub and sink as far into the water as I can without sinking my mouth and nose under the water, take a deep breath, and the next thing I know, strong arms are lifting me out of the tub.

"No falling asleep and drowning, sweetheart."

"I'm getting you wet," I murmur against his chest and burrow closer to him, my arms around him, my nose pressed to his neck. "But don't put me down."

He chuckles and kisses my forehead. "I have to set you down for a second to dry you off."

He dries me off quickly, and before I can get cold, I'm back in his arms, being carried into the bedroom, where he gently lays me in the bed and pulls the covers up over my nude body.

I watch him with heavy-lidded eyes as he quickly sheds his clothes and joins me, pulls me against him, into him, his arms folding around me and hugging me tightly, as if he's afraid I'll roll away from him.

Not a chance in hell of that.

I never knew that falling asleep in someone's arms could be so comforting.

Because it never has been before.

I sigh deeply and press a kiss to Dominic's neck. "This is delightful."

"Mm," he replies and kisses my hair. "Sleep, sweet girl."

"We're not going to have sex?" I ask with surprise, and pull back far enough to look him in the eye. His fingertips dance down that sweet spot on my neck, sending shivers down my arms, just as his other hand takes mine and he laces my fingers through his, then brings them up to his lips.

"I want to sleep with you," he whispers roughly. "I don't mean have sex with you, although I always want to be inside you. I want to sleep with you, in my bed, with your head on my chest and my arms wrapped around you. With my nose buried in your hair so I can breathe you in all night long." He takes a deep breath and kisses my fingers again. "I want to sleep with you, here in this chilly room, so we have to cuddle closer. No talking, just being here, with you. I just want to *be* with you, Alecia."

I swallow hard, my eyes pinned to his lips as he speaks, and feel my heart trip and my stomach tighten at his words.

"I can live with that," I whisper hoarsely.

"Good. Sleep, *cara.*" He kisses my fingers again, rests our hands on his chest and guides my head down onto him, where I just seem to fit perfectly, despite our immense height difference.

I take a deep breath and feel myself relax against him. I feel him grin against my head as his fingertips tickle my neck again.

"Keep doing that and I won't sleep," I whisper.

"You'll sleep," he replies confidently.

I don't speak again. I simply lie with him. *Be* with him, and after long minutes I feel him slip into sleep, but I lie awake for a while, listening to him breathe, listening to his heartbeat against my cheek.

Listening to the silence around us.

Is this what it feels like to be in love? This contentment, this attraction? This trust?

I can't resist planting a kiss on his chest, and I feel his arms tighten around me in his sleep.

I'm quite sure that if this is what love is, I've tripped over and fallen right in.

thirteen

"**S**eriously, this is like hot man overload," Emily whispers to me as we sit in the white chairs before the arbor Dominic's brothers made for Will and Meg's wedding. The whole family is here for the rehearsal. All of the Montgomery siblings and their spouses, all of the parents, even the kids. It's a huge family party, and they're having a great time ribbing each other.

"And here," the pastor says patiently, as two of the brothers, Matt and Caleb, snicker at something Isaac whispered to them in the front row. "Is where you recite your vows to each other. Will, you first."

Will, with a perfectly sober and serious expression on his impossibly handsome face, takes Meg's hands in his and stares down at her intently.

"Megan, I promise to never make you work out with me. I know how you value your laziness." His lips twitch as his brothers snicker. "I vow to send cupcakes to your work regularly." He grins wickedly, and I know we're about to get an earful of something fun. "I vow to remember where all your sweet spots are on that fantastic body of yours, and pay the appropriate amount of attention to them on a regular basis."

"You're the reason we have to put instructions on shampoo bottles in this country," Samantha calls out, earning a fist bump from Brynna.

"I'm not going to say the *real* vows today," Will says, his eyes still pinned on his bride. "Those are for Saturday."

"Your turn, Meg."

"I'm not saying mine either," she says with a grin. "I want to get to the kissing part."

"That's my girl," Will agrees and leans in to kiss her, but she slaps her hand over Will's lips and leans away, looking at the pastor.

"Wait! How are we supposed to kiss?"

"No tongue!" Leo yells out, making us all laugh.

"Mmph hump smeethart," Will says against Meg's hand.

"What?" she asks, pulling her hand away with a smile.

"I've never needed instructions on how to kiss, sweetheart." Will slips his hands around Meg's waist and pulls her flush against him, bending at the knees to match his lips up with hers, and suddenly they're in a passionate embrace, kissing with great enthusiasm.

"Stop it right now!" Jules cries and covers her sleeping infant daughter's eyes where she's perched on Nate's shoulder. "There are children here!"

Will dips Meg dramatically, never taking his mouth from hers. Dominic turns in his seat and smiles at me, shakes his head, and then shrugs as if to say, "What can you do?"

"Okay, we get it, you love her," Steven says as he stands. "Let the poor woman breathe, son."

"Sweet Lord, if a man kissed me like that, I'd die," Emily whispers in awe, making me laugh.

"I hear Blake has been kissing you just fine," I murmur, and watch her face flush.

"I was going to tell you." We watch quietly, not looking at each other, as the Montgomery family stands and chats, the girls fussing with babies and kids, the guys admiring their handiwork on the arbor.

"As long as you're happy, I'm happy," I tell her honestly.

"I'm happy."

I nod once and drop the subject, standing to get back to work.

"Okay, guys, good job." I clap my hands as I walk to the happy couple. "Dinner is being served in the tent. We might as well break it in, right?"

"Alecia, this is spectacular," Meg says with a wide grin. "It's so pretty."

"If you like it now, just wait for Saturday."

"You heard the woman!" Will announces almost urgently. "Food!"

"Will hasn't eaten in about an hour," Isaac says with a roll of the eyes. "He thinks he's starving."

"Be nice to my boy," Gail, their mother, admonishes Isaac as she lifts Luke and Natalie's daughter, Olivia, into her arms and kisses her cheek, then follows the others toward the tent, where the servers have set up a vast buffet spread. A DJ is playing soft music, and the twinkle lights have been turned on, giving the space a dreamy glow.

Emily marches ahead, talking into her earpiece, alerting the kitchen staff that we're moving into the tent and ready for drinks.

I bring up the rear, but before I can get far, Dominic joins me and brushes his fingertips down my neck, in that way he does that sends shivers down my spine.

"How are you?"

"I'm great. Meg and Will are happy, that's all that matters." I grin up at him as he takes my hand in his, kisses my knuckles, and walks with me into the tent.

He and I hang back, taking in the scene before us. The tables have been set up for Saturday, and five of the round tables have been covered and dressed prettily for tonight's dinner. The flowers Meg chose as her wedding flowers, tiger lilies, roses and calla lilies, serve as centerpieces. The lights hanging above are pretty and cast a glow about the room.

The parents are seated at one table together, laughing and talking, some holding babies. Steven has his arm wrapped loosely around his wife's shoulders, and he's watching her with loving eyes as she tells the table at large a story.

The others are scattered about the other tables. Meg and Will invited their entire family, including Meredith's best friend Jax and his fiancé, Logan.

It's a smaller party, but full of love and fun.

Will is already seated with a heaping plate in front of him, eating and joking with his brother Caleb at the next table.

"Dude, you totally slipped Bryn the tongue when you got married!" he says.

"Hell yes I did, and I'd do it again."

"You're all disgusting," Jules grumbles, but smiles at the server who delivers her a drink, almost making him stumble over himself. "Oh, thank you. You're my newest friend."

"Don't flirt with the waiter, baby," Nate says with a chuckle. "You'll make him trip."

"He's fine," she says and waves Nate off. "Alecia! Come sit by me."

"Oh, I have to work."

"No." Meg shakes her head and points to the empty chair next to Jules. "You worked already. It's beautiful. Now I want you to be my guest."

I frown, but Emily speaks into my earpiece, "I got this, boss. Easy peasy. Enjoy yourself."

"Excellent idea," Dom agrees, and plants his hand on the small of my back, guiding me to the table with Jules, Nate, Luke, and Natalie. He pulls the chair out for me, and when I sit, he leans in and whispers in my ear, "I'll go get you something to eat."

I frown up at him, but he's already marching away toward the buffet.

"This is weird," I announce, and gaze around the table. "I'm supposed to be working."

"You're our friend," Natalie says with a smile and kisses her infant son's cheek. "We want you to celebrate with us. You'll be busy enough at the wedding."

I nod and gaze around the room, taking in the way Matt's hand rests on his girlfriend, Nic's neck. It's a gentle touch, yet almost . . . commanding. The beautiful woman is smiling at Stacy, Isaac's wife, as Stacy and Brynna discuss which of Nic's cupcakes they enjoy the most. Isaac, Caleb, and Matt are watching their girls with contented smiles.

It sounds like the tiramisu is winning the cupcake contest.

"I'll take one of those lemon drops martinis, Linus," I say to my young server, who is still blushing from Jules' attention.

"Daddy!" Olivia calls from Gail's arms across the room, holding her hands out and grinning at Luke. "Kiss you, Daddy!"

"I think that means she wants you," Nat says, as Luke stands and crosses to his daughter, lifting her easily into his arms and burying his face in her neck, blowing raspberries.

Seriously, that might make my ovaries explode.

That might make *any* woman's ovaries explode.

Luke Williams, former movie star, is maybe the hottest thing on this planet.

Not that I'll ever admit that out loud.

"We need to discuss Stella's first birthday party," Jules says to me.

"She's not even six months old," Nate says, as he brushes his hand down his wife's hair. "Let her be little, Julianne."

"She'll need a great party," Jules insists, but leans into her man's touch.

"She'll have one," I assure her. "But he's right. Let her be little for a while." I gaze at the pretty baby with the pink bow on her head, her little pink dress and big blue eyes staring back at me.

"Would you like to hold her?" Nate asks, as Luke returns with Livie.

"Oh, I don't think—"

"Here." Jules passes the baby to me, and suddenly I'm sitting here, at this party that I planned, that I'm supposed to be working at, with a gorgeous baby in my arms and my man setting a heaping plate of food before me.

"Who do you have here?" Dominic asks as he sits next to me. He kisses Stella on the cheek, then pays the same attention to me. "Hello, *bella*," he croons to the baby, *"il mio dolce bambino."*

"I love it when you call her your sweet baby," Jules says with a smile. "It sounds pretty."

"She's pretty," I murmur and instinctively cradle Stella against my chest, kiss her head and bury my nose in her wispy blonde curls, inhaling her baby smell. "Babies always smell so good."

"Not always," Jules says with a laugh.

"Well, I don't have to change their diapers," I reply with a smile.

"You look good with her," Natalie says, and sips her drink.

"Let me take her, *tesoro*, so you can eat," Dom says, and smoothly takes the baby from my arms.

"What did that mean?" Nat asks.

"What did what mean?" Dominic asks and smiles at Stella. "Goodness, you're getting big, *bella*."

"You called Alecia *tesoro*," Jules says. "We've never heard that one. You always call us *bella* or *cara*."

Dom rubs his nose against Stella's and then laughs with the baby, barely paying attention to his sisters. "*Tesoro* means my treasure," he says, and glances over at me with warm eyes. "I'm calling her my treasure."

I feel my eyes go round as I swallow the bite of food I'd just taken and gape at him.

His treasure?

His treasure.

Well, if that doesn't spark butterflies, I don't know what does.

And then it occurs to me, he's been calling me his treasure since the first time we made love.

"Charming Italian," I whisper, earning a laugh from Jules.

"Oh, he's definitely that," she agrees.

"I think it's very sweet," Nat says with a smile. I can feel Dom watching me as I focus on my food. "Why does this make you shy?" she asks me.

I shrug a shoulder, frown and drink the rest of my martini, then gesture to Linus for another.

"We know you're seeing each other," Jules assures me happily, and I want the floor to open up and swallow me whole, but I smile brightly, not wanting anyone to think I'm uncomfortable. I had no idea we were making our relationship public. "And, can I just say, it's about time."

"Excuse me," I murmur and stand.

"Are you okay?" Dominic asks.

"Of course." I smile again and nod. "I just need to check on a few things."

I make it out of the tent and around the store building, where the hills roll, full of grape vines as far as the eye can see and take a long, deep breath.

His family knows we're seeing each other.

Isn't it too soon for that?

"Here she is," Natalie says as she and Jules come around the corner and stand on either side of me, flanking me, staring out at Dominic's land.

"It's gorgeous here," I say.

"Do you often have the undeniable urge to leave a party and stare at the scenery?" Jules asks, as she drops her arm around my shoulders.

"Maybe," I reply primly.

"We didn't mean to scare you off," Natalie says.

"I just needed some fresh air," I lie.

"We scared you," Jules says. "Is it because we know you're doing the nasty with our brother?"

"Well, I'm scared now," I reply and shake my head ruefully. "I had no idea that you guys chatted with your brothers about who they have sex with."

"Ew." Jules scrunches up her nose and shivers. "We don't do that. But we can tell that you're doing the sex stuff."

"*Sex stuff?*" I snort. "Is that the scientific term for it?"

"He's been interested in you for a long while," Natalie says softly, watching the horizon, as she slips her hand in mine. "There were times I'd see him watching you with so much want in his eyes, it was almost painful."

"So, he wanted in my pants."

"You're a smart girl," Jules says. "You know that's not all it is."

I don't say anything in return. What is there to say? It's not just sex, for either of us.

He calls me his *treasure*, for Godsake.

"If that's all it is for you—" Natalie begins, but I immediately interrupt.

"It's not," I say firmly.

"Good." Jules kisses my cheek just as the DJ switches the song to "Blurred Lines." "Now, let's go get our drink on and dance, friends. We have a wedding to celebrate."

"I LOVE YOUR mom," I tell Jules, as she and I sway on the dance floor, not unlike junior high students at a school dance. We've had countless lemon drops, and if we let go of each other, I'm not so sure we'll stay upright.

Okay, we most definitely won't stay upright.

"I love her too!" Jules yells right in my ear.

"No, you don't understand." I take her face in my hands and hold her still so I can talk to her. "When she was leaving to take the babies home, she hugged me and *thanked* me for this dinner. She's the sweetest person ever born. Ever."

"I know." Jules leans her forehead on mine and now she's even more blurry than she was before. "She rocks. I love my mommy."

"Batting for the other team now, Jules?" Mark asks from a nearby table. "It would be hotter if you two would take off your clothes."

"The men in this family are all perverts," Jules tells me seriously. "You need to be aware of this now."

"Come sit down, Julianne." Suddenly, Nate is standing next to us, pulling us in to either side of him; his strong arms wrap around our shoulders, and he leads us to a table where most of the others are sitting and talking.

Everyone except Meredith's best friend Jax and Brynna, who are currently dancing like crazy on the dance floor.

"Wait. Where are Will and Meg?" I ask, as I continue to survey the table.

"They disappeared a few minutes ago," Isaac informs me.

"Orgasms," Stacy sighs. "She's getting some right now, I'll bet."

"Lucky bitch," Sam grumbles from her perch on Leo's lap. "Are you gonna give me some orgasms tonight, rock star?"

Leo grins and whispers something in his wife's ear that has her cheeks going pink and she bites her lip. "Hell to the yes," she says happily.

"You know what orgasms are?" Nic says suddenly.

"Seriously, why do these women talk about nothing but sex when they've had liquor?" Caleb asks, as Dom takes my hand and pulls me into his lap. He nuzzles my temple and I easily curl up against him, happily fuzzy from too much alcohol.

"I know what orgasms are," I hear myself say, and then clap my hand over my own mouth. I can feel Dominic laugh beneath me.

Damn, he's strong.

"You're strong," I say, attempting to whisper, but I don't think it comes out that way, based on the way the boys all snicker at my comment.

"Orgasms," Nic continues, "are nature's way of saying, 'Yeah, life sucks ass, but here, have some candy.'"

"Does your life suck, little one?" Matt asks Nic, planting a kiss on her hair.

"Not even a little, but you gotta admit, that shit's funny."

"Orgasms are *so* like candy!" Jules exclaims.

Brynna and Jax return to the table, sweaty and panting. Brynna collapses in Caleb's lap and kisses his cheek as Jax sits next to his man, Logan, who has been content to sit and listen quietly, a soft smile on his handsome face.

"There are some seriously hot men at this table." I'm mortified to hear the words actually come out of my mouth. "I was supposed to say that for my own brain, but my mouth didn't get the memo. Sorry."

"You're right," Brynna replies with a smug smile. "We could open a store. Hot Men R Us."

"You're trying to sell us off?" Isaac asks.

"I bet we could get a lot of money for you," Natalie says, and smiles up at her husband. "Especially this one."

"Plus, Dominic has the sexy Italian speak going for him. Chicks dig that," I add, and wiggle in my man's lap. He presses his lips against my ear.

"Keep moving like that, and I'll need to find a private spot to fuck you silly," he whispers.

And just like that, my girl parts are wide awake and completely sober.

My brain isn't sober, but that's okay.

"I'm so fucking drunk," Stacy mutters, and rubs her nose on her husband's shoulder vigorously. "And my nose always itches when I get drunk."

"Then you're not drunk enough," Jules says with one eye closed.

"Why is your eye closed?" I ask her.

"It stopped working."

"I think you're drunk too," I reply with a laugh, wiggling slightly in Dom's lap and feeling him growl in my ear.

"You know what rhymes with drunk?" Sam asks. "Sex!"

"Nuh uh," Meredith replies with a frown. "But fuck does!"

"Drunk and fuck do not rhyme," Mark says with a surprised laugh.

"It's closer than sex," she says defensively.

"Everything rhymes with sex when you get to have it with an apa," Jules says.

"Julianne," Nate warns her.

"It's true!"

"What's that like, anyway? I've always wanted to know."

"You can't have sex with my husband." Jules frowns for a second, then a smile spreads over her gorgeous face. "Well, maybe you can."

"No," Nate replies quietly, "she can't. No offense, Alecia."

"None taken." I grin at the crazy-hot man. "You're hot as fuck, though."

"He really is," Jules agrees happily. "And the apa . . . wow."

"Will you get one?" I ask Dominic, just as he takes a sip of wine, and he immediately chokes.

"Fuck no."

"Maybe I'll have to find someone with one," I say thoughtfully. "Just to give it a try."

"That's it." Dominic stands with me in his arms and doesn't even set me down as he begins to stalk out of the tent.

"Where are we going?" I look over his shoulder and see the others laughing and watching us leave. I wave happily and they all wave back.

They're so friendly.

"I'm going to teach you a lesson, *tesoro*."

"A lesson?" I giggle and bury my nose in his neck, breathing him in. "I'm kind of dizzy."

We pass by the barn. I can hear voices, heavy breathing and Meg giggling.

"I think we found Meg and Will," I whisper into Dom's ear, as he hurries past.

"*Merde*, I didn't need to ever hear that," Dominic grumbles, making me giggle more. He strides around the store building, where I stood a few hours ago with Jules and Natalie, sets me on my feet, and pins me against the wall.

"I dare you," he begins with fire in his bright blue eyes, "to say again that you're going to go find another man to fuck."

"Um, it was a joke, babe."

His eyes narrow and his nostrils flare, and I know I'm in big trouble.

"Are you jealous?" I ask incredulously.

"Not usually," he says. "I'm not the jealous type, but what's mine is mine, Alecia. And you're *mine*. What I have with you, I don't want with anyone else. You're all I fucking think about."

He's gathering my skirt in his hands until it's bunched around my waist, and he slips his finger inside the elastic of the crotch of my panties and brushes the lips of my pussy, making me gasp.

"Dom!"

"That's right." He bites my lower lip, then soothes it with his tongue and pushes his finger farther into my panties. "*Me*. I'm the only one who can touch you here, or anywhere. This is mine."

With those words, his finger slips inside me deeply and he presses against that spot that he knows so intimately, sending me up onto my tiptoes.

"Holy fuck," I whisper.

He wraps his free arm around my waist, pulling me flush against him as he finger-fucks me, dragging his palm against my clit in the process, making me fucking crazy.

"I'm going to come," I whimper, but he pulls his hand away.

"Not yet," he growls.

"Hey!"

But before I can say anything more, he spins me around, bends me over, and shoves my panties aside, while I hear the zipper lower on his slacks and he's suddenly slamming inside me. I have to brace my hands on the building for leverage as he fucks me hard and fast. His breath is harsh, his hands almost bruising on my hips.

I bite my lip, but I can't be quiet as he fucks me unlike he ever has before. It's primal. Rough.

Fucking amazing.

He leans over me and groans, presses his lips to my ear and whispers.

"You. Are. Mine. This is mine. Don't ever forget that, *tesoro*."

I push back on him and grin when I make him groan, but suddenly his fingers are pressing on my clit as he fucks me hard, and that's all I can take. I come brutally, biting my own arm so as not to cry out, spasming around him.

"That's right," he says and pushes in me twice more before he stills and surrenders to his own climax, resting his forehead on my back.

Finally, he slips out of me and turns me to face him. He cups my face tenderly in his hands and kisses me gently, but when he pulls back, his eyes are no less fierce.

"Mine."

fourteen

Dominic

She's fucking magnificent.

"I want six men at the parking lot," Alecia says as she paces back and forth across my back patio. She's holding every one of the twenty four men's rapt attention. Her voice is sharp and no-nonsense. Her back straight. Her eyes hard.

I've never seen anything like her in my life.

"I was planning on four," Derek, my head of security, replies. Derek is a former Army ranger, six-foot-five and built like a fucking brick house.

Alecia doesn't even bat an eye.

"I need six."

"No one knows where the wedding is being held," Jason, the head of Alecia's security, points out logically. "The guests are parking ten miles away and we're bussing them in."

"I'm aware," Alecia replies. "Look, guys, I'm going to be a hard ass on this one. Will Montgomery won the Super Bowl last year, and it's not just him that the paparazzi are interested in. You're all aware that we have rock stars coming, movie stars, producers, and other football players. Security can't be breached. If even *one* paparazzi follows a bus here, or figures out the location and spreads unauthorized photos, I'll have all of your dicks on a platter."

"Montgomery was smart about this," Derek reminds her. "The guests were simply given an address to park their cars. Even they don't know where they're going."

"I'm aware. I set it up," she replies.

I lean my shoulder against the wall, cross my arms over my chest, and watch my woman take control over two dozen strong men.

I want to kiss the fuck out of her.

"If we put two more guys on the parking lot, that's two less that will be here."

"You'll have eighteen men here," she replies with a shake of the head. "Are you being a pain in the ass because I'm a woman, or are you just always this stubborn?"

Derek stands, his jaw ticking and watches Alecia for a long minute. She's staring him down, and it's the most amazing bout of chicken I've ever seen in my life.

"Fine," he says at last. "You'll get your six."

"Yes, I will. Follow the guest list. I don't care if someone claims to be a long lost grandma and turns on the big crocodile tears. If they're not on the list, they don't get in. Period. If you have questions, talk to me. I'll have my earpiece in all day."

"You know, I like a bossy woman."

This comes from a younger kid, as tall and built as Derek, but clearly too young to know to keep his mouth shut. Alecia stops in her tracks, narrows her eyes and pins him in her glare.

"Do you?"

"Yes, ma'am," he replies with a cocky smirk.

Oh, you young idiot.

"What's your name?" she asks him.

"Stokes," he replies.

"Stokes." She crosses to him, props her hand on her hip and smiles sweetly at him. "Do you have mommy issues, Stokes?"

The other men smirk, but Stokes' eyes go hard as his face sobers.

"No, I just think it's fucking sexy when a woman has a backbone."

Alecia tilts her head to the side and then nods. "Good. Because I have one. Don't fuck this up, Stokes." She backs away and nods to Derek and Jason. "That's all. Let me know if there are any issues."

"There won't be," Jason replies, and turns to continue briefing his men as Alecia walks away.

"She should be in the military," Stokes says with new respect in his voice.

She's too good for the military.

"Good job, Lieutenant," I whisper as I fall into step beside her.

"I will cut off someone's junk if I find out they only put four men out there," she grumbles.

"You're awfully angry at the male genitals today, *cara.*"

She smirks and then lets out a short laugh.

"I'm around a lot of men today."

"Everything is going to run like clockwork."

"Don't say that. You'll jinx it. I should go see Blake."

"Blake paid me five thousand dollars to keep you out of the kitchen today."

She frowns and blinks up at me.

"He did not."

"He did." Okay, he didn't, but she'll just make them both crazy if she stomps in there and harasses him today. "Everything is set. The food already smells amazing. The tables are set, and the florist is working her magic on the arbor and the tent."

"The cupcakes—"

"Get here in a few hours and Nic will set them up. She's awesome." I take her shoulders in my hands and kiss her forehead gently. "But I get it. This is what you do. So go get 'em, tiger."

She grins up at me before gripping my shirt in her fist and pulling me down for a quick kiss. "Thanks. I'll catch up with you later."

"Alecia." She stops about twenty feet away from me and turns back with a raised brow. "This fierce side of you? It's sexy as fuck."

She doesn't answer; she simply smiles before turning and walking away, with just a little more sway in her magnificent hips.

God, I fucking love her.

I HAVEN'T SPOKEN with Alecia since that moment this morning. The family began to arrive, and chaos has descended on the vineyard.

And I love it.

The guys are in my playroom, shooting pool and yelling insults at each other, which is pretty much par for the course with my brothers.

The girls are out back in the tent, helping Nic set up the cupcakes.

Or, getting in her way, and she's too nice to tell them to get lost.

Meg is getting ready up in the bridal suite, and to escape said chaos, I decide to head up there to say hello.

Alecia opens the door to my knock and steps back, letting me inside. Natalie has her camera pressed to her face and is quickly snapping photos.

And Meg is standing before the mirror, dressed in her gorgeous gown. It's lacy, but not frilly. It's sleeveless, and the neckline plunges deep between her breasts. The skirt hangs straight, with no train.

It's elegant, chic, and completely perfect for our Meg.

"You are stunning," I tell her, as I lean in and kiss her cheek, careful not to muss her up.

"Thank you."

"I didn't think you were the photographer," I say to Natalie.

"Just for this part," Nat assures me.

"I didn't want a stranger taking photos of me getting dressed." Meg wrinkles her nose and turns back to the mirror. "It's pretty, isn't it?"

"It's perfect," I assure her. "I've never seen a more beautiful bride."

"Don't make me cry!" Meg whines. "It took forever to get my makeup like this."

There's another knock on the door, and then Leo walks in and stops in his tracks, his eyes wide as he takes Meg in from head to toe. And then a slow smile spreads over his mouth as he tucks his hands in both of his pockets and rocks on his heels.

"Ah, Meg-pie," he whispers.

"Does the dress suck?" she asks, making both Nat and Alecia roll their eyes.

Leo crosses to her, gently folds her into his arms and rocks her back and forth slowly.

"You are so beautiful, Meg-pie."

"You're going to wrinkle me," she says against his chest.

"No, I'm not." There are tears in his eyes as he presses his cheek to her hair. "I love you so damn much. You know that, right? There isn't anything I wouldn't do for you, Meg."

"I know."

"You're my sister in every way that matters. You're my constant. Before Sam, it was you and music, and I need you to know that I haven't forgotten that, Meg."

"Leo," she whispers, and I nod at Alecia as Natalie quickly snaps pictures.

Alecia and I slip out the door, leaving Meg and Leo to have their special moment. She leans her back against the wall and closes her eyes tightly.

"Hey, are you okay?" I cup her smooth cheek in my palm and watch as she turns tear-filled eyes up to mine.

"I don't know what it feels like to be loved like that," she whispers, breaking my heart.

"Holy crap," Natalie says as she sneaks out of the room and closes the door behind her. "That was the sweetest moment I've ever witnessed. I'm so glad I captured it."

"Those photos are going to rock," Alecia agrees, and wipes the tears from her eyes. My gut hurts from seeing the pain in her beautiful brown eyes.

"Alecia."

She shakes her head and offers me a shy smile. "I'm fine. It was just a really emotional moment. Can you please go check on the boys?" Her eyes are begging me to drop it, so I do, but I lean in and kiss her cheek.

"We'll talk later," I murmur, and kiss Nat's forehead as I walk back down the hall.

She's going to know what it feels like to be loved like that if it's the last thing I do.

I CLASP ALECIA'S hand tightly as Leo walks a nervous Meg down the aisle. I talked Alecia into sitting next to me during the ceremony as my date last night while I was buried inside her and she couldn't even remember her name.

Playing dirty? Damn right.

It worked.

The sun is setting behind us, casting everything in gold, making Meg's auburn hair shine. She's on Leo's arm, walking to "Baby, I Love Your Way" being played by Leo's band, Nash.

The guitarist, Jake, is singing the lyrics in his rough voice, perfect for the song, and for Meg.

She's smiling brilliantly, her eyes pinned to my youngest brother, whose eyes have gone glassy.

Of all of my brothers, I've come to learn that Will is the one that isn't afraid to show his emotions. Whether he's happy, sad, hungry, angry, it doesn't matter. He doesn't hold back.

I couldn't respect him more.

"Who gives this woman to this man?" The pastor asks when the music ends.

"I do," Leo responds, kisses Meg, then joins his own wife next to me.

"Unca Will!" Olivia exclaims and points to Will excitedly.

"Yes, baby," Nat whispers in her daughter's ear as Will turns and winks at the toddler.

"Dearly beloved."

The pastor speaks of love. Commitment. The sanctity of marriage. The promise.

And I can hear him, but all I can focus on is this woman at my side, with her hand in mine, and all of the promises I want to make to her. Telling her this now would send her running into the hills, but Alecia is it for me. I love her. I can't imagine my life without her.

If that's not commitment, I don't know what is.

"And now, the vows. Megan, I'll ask you to recite your vows first, please."

The pastor steps back and all our eyes are pinned to Meg as she takes a deep breath and stares up into Will's eyes. She grins.

"I wrote it all down, but I just realized that I don't need to read a piece of paper to tell you how I feel about you." She swallows hard and her face sobers. "I take you, Will, to be my husband. I vow to always be honest, to be fair, to be spontaneous, and to always hold you in the highest regard. I promise to dream with you, to support you, and to always be your biggest fan. I will be your faithful partner, your unyielding encouragement, and your forever love." She blinks and one tear falls down her cheek, but Will catches it with his thumb and rubs the apple of her cheek tenderly. "I promise you this today, and every day, for the rest of my life."

"Will, your vows, please," the pastor says kindly, as Will brushes a tear of his own away.

"Megan," he begins and has to pause to swallow hard. "I hope you understand today how very much I love you. I wonder if you'll ever truly understand how much of me belongs to you. You are the delight of my life. Loving you is an adventure that I wouldn't miss for the world. I'm honored, my love, to take you as my wife today. I vow to spend the rest of my life giving back to you what you give to me every day. To be your constant companion, your most trusted confidant, and your truest friend. I vow to never keep score. I vow to accept you, to honor you, as you are, for the rest of my life. I will be faithful to you, forsaking all others. I will choose you, always."

"Wow," Jules whispers, and wipes the tears from her face.

Meg and Will exchange their rings, their faces bright with smiles and tears, and finally, the pastor says, "You may now kiss your bride."

Will sweeps Meg right off her feet and into his arms, kissing her soundly, and making us all laugh.

"Atta boy, Montgomery!" his teammate yells, as we all stand and applaud.

"It's my honor to present Mr. and Mrs. Will Montgomery!"

IT'S TIME TO take my woman upstairs.

The crowd is thinning considerably. At just after two in the morning, Will and Meg are still dancing in the middle of the floor. Most of Will's teammates are still here, talking, mingling, and hitting on a few of the nurses that work with Meg at the hospital. All of the food and cupcakes were long ago inhaled. I lost count hours ago of how many bottles of wine we went through tonight.

I know it's in the hundreds.

I'm so damn proud of Alecia for not only pulling off the event, but for making it spectacular.

My eyes find her, smiling and talking with Blake and Emily, at the empty cupcake table.

"Emily," I say as I approach, "can you finish up here?"

"I can't leave—"

"Yep," Emily says, interrupting Alecia with a broad smile. "Blake will help me."

"There are still guests here. I have to stay."

"No, you don't." Blake pulls her in for a hug. "You kicked ass today, Leash. Go celebrate."

"Are you sure?" Alecia asks Emily.

"Absolutely."

Alecia turns to me, and for the first time today I can see the exhaustion settling in. If I have my way, she'll sleep for three days straight.

"Let me say goodnight to Will and Meg."

I nod and watch her walk to my brother and new sister-in-law. They both hug her tightly, and wave at me as she returns to me, tucks her hand in mine and says, "I'm ready."

She doesn't speak as we walk into the house and up the stairs. The silence is comfortable.

Welcome.

I reach around her to open the door to my master suite and gesture for her to go in before me and smile when she lets out a gasp of surprise.

"What is this?" She turns those wide brown eyes to me in wonder.

"A celebration, *tesoro*." I close and lock the door behind me and lead her further into the room. Candles flicker around the room, the only light in the space. Pink tulip petals have been formed into a heart on the bed, and right in the center of them are . . .

"Shoes!" she exclaims and hurries to the bed. "Oh, my God."

"What is it?" I press my chest to her back, my hands gripping her shoulders, and kiss the top of her head.

"There are blue boxes in those pretty pink shoes."

I grin. "Indeed."

"And the pink shoes are strappy."

"Right again."

She crosses her arms and grips my hands with hers, holding on tight. "We're celebrating Will and Meg with designer shoes and blue Tiffany boxes?"

"No." I turn her to face me and cup her face in my hands. "We're not celebrating the wedding, *cara*. We're celebrating *you*."

She frowns in confusion.

"You were amazing, not just today, but during this whole process. You should be so proud of yourself, sweetheart." I kiss her soft forehead, her nose, and then gently lay my lips on hers, kissing her lightly before pulling back. "Don't you want to open the boxes?"

"Desperately." She chuckles, and turns back to the bed.

"Wait. Let's get comfy. I'll rub your feet while you open the boxes."

"Wow. This is a lot of pampering, Dominic."

"You haven't seen anything yet." I wink at her and help her get comfortable, leaning against the pillows. I pull her shoes off her small feet, sit on the bed, and begin kneading the arches.

"Oh, God." Her eyes close and she leans her head back against the headboard. "You're seriously good with your hands."

"If you fall asleep, you won't see what's in those boxes."

She bites her lip and raises her head and looks at me.

"You didn't have to do this."

"Yes, I did. Open them."

First, she examines the shoes, her eyes bright with feminine lust for such things, which makes me laugh.

"I kind of like looking at them like this," she confesses. "I mean, the blue looks so pretty in these pink shoes."

I raise a brow and wait for her to finish admiring the shoes, and finally she can't resist any longer. She tugs one box out of a shoe.

"Oh my," she breathes when she opens the box. "There's a lot of pink happening around here tonight."

She's quiet for a long minute, her lip gripped in her teeth as she simply stares at the white and pink diamond necklace nestled in the blue box. Her brown gaze shoots up to mine as she reaches for the other box.

"Lots of pink," she says again, when she sees the matching bracelet.

"They match the pink shoes," I whisper, and continue to knead the muscles in her calves. "Your calves are tight."

"I was walking in heels for roughly fourteen hours today."

Finally, without another word, she simply climbs over to me, into my lap, and wraps herself around me, clinging on tightly.

"I don't know what to say," she whispers.

"You don't have to say anything."

"They're so beautiful. Thank you so much."

"They're going to look amazing against your skin, *cara*. That's why I chose pink. You wear pink so well."

She buries her face in my neck and kisses me gently. Now is the time to tell her how much I love her.

But instead, I stay quiet, plucking pins from her hair until it's falling around her shoulders and plunge my fingers in it, pulling it to my nose.

"You smell amazing."

"*You* smell amazing," she replies, her nose still pressed to my skin.

"You were remarkable to watch today. You were so in control, so focused."

"That's my job."

"You're excellent at it."

She smiles against my neck.

"Are you going to let me lay you down and help you get more comfortable?"

"I'll let you lay me down and make love to me," she says with a small voice.

You don't ever have to ask me twice.

I tip her onto her back and hover over her, helping her shimmy out of her beautiful blue dress and matching underwear, until she's spread out under me, the pink tulip petals around her, her golden blonde hair fanned around her head, looking like nothing short of an angel.

"You take my breath away," I whisper.

She grins as she works on the buttons of my shirt, shoving it over my shoulders and tossing it aside, then making quick work of my pants. When I'm naked at last, I settle over her, bracing myself on my elbows, my heavy cock nestled in her slick, hot folds.

I brush imaginary tendrils of hair off her forehead and cheeks with my fingertips, sweep my nose over hers, anything to touch her.

I'll never get enough of feeling her skin with mine.

"Dominic," she whispers, then gasps as I move my hips, just a bit, sliding through her wetness.

"Yes, my treasure."

Her eyes flare at the term of endearment.

"Are you more comfortable hearing it in Italian, *tesoro?*"

"I guess I'm surprised to hear it at all," she replies truthfully.

"You are my treasure." I kiss her cheek, then drag my lips down to that sensitive spot by her ear. "You are the best part of my life."

Her hands glide up and down my back, then her fingertips follow the same path, making me even harder. I rear back and sink slowly inside her waiting heat, watching her gorgeous eyes as I press in as far as I can, then rest there, watching her.

"So proud of you, Alecia."

"Thank you." Tears fill her eyes and she closes them.

"Don't close your eyes," I whisper and brush a tear aside. "You don't ever have to hide from me."

"I'm not." She shakes her head lightly, then looks back up at me, with her heart wide open for the first time.

It's magnificent.

"Do you know how much you scare me?" she asks, her voice barely a whisper.

I begin to move, filling her, then pulling out, in long, smooth, sure strokes. Her breath hitches, her fingers dig into my back, and she clenches around my cock in the most delicious of ways.

"You are everything," I say into her ear, as I make gentle love to her. "And yes, *tesoro*, it scares me too, but not having you scares me even more."

"Me too."

I grip her hand in mine, lacing our fingers, and press it down into the bed as I begin to ride her harder, but not faster. I press the base of my cock against her clit and grind down, and that's all it takes for her to fall over the edge, coming hard, taking me with her.

I love you.

fifteen

Alecia

I've been waking up to his handsome face for more than two weeks now, and it never fails to take my breath away.

Or make me squirm in pure, unadulterated lust.

I mean, look at him. He's all dark skin and hair against my white sheets, gathered at his waist, giving me a prime view of his defined abs, sculpted arms, and magical hands with long fingers.

He's shown me what my body was made for. In the week since the wedding, he's spent every night here in my bed with me, leaving each morning to go back to the vineyard, but he always returns every evening for dinner, wine, conversation, and the best sex of my life.

I can't resist dragging my fingertips down his rough cheek, enjoying the way the scruff feels on my skin.

With his eyes still closed, he grins, flashing that dimple, and captures my hand in his, bringing it to his lips.

"Good morning," he whispers against my palm.

"'Morning," I reply and lean in to kiss his shoulder. "We need to get up soon. Baseball game today, remember?"

"I remember." He pulls me into his arms, into what I consider my spot, cozied up against his side, my head on his chest and arm wrapped around his ribs, where I simply fit just right. "But we should do this for a little while first."

"Do what?" I nuzzle my nose into his neck and take a deep breath, enjoying him.

"Just be," he says, and kisses my head.

"This is nice," I whisper.

"Mm."

"I'm not gonna be available every night next week," I say regretfully.

"Oh?"

"It's summer, so I have events every night next week. Except Wednesday."

"I have an event at the vineyard on Wednesday," he says with a sigh. "We'll survive five days apart, *cara*."

His hand travels down my back to my ass and back up again, into my hair, then down once more, lulling me into sleep.

"*Tesoro*," he whispers in my ear as he rolls me onto my back. His fingertip brushes down my temple and cheek. "Wake up."

"Hmmm."

"We slept another hour."

"We did?" I ask groggily and stretch, still not opening my eyes.

"We need to get ready to go."

"Okay." I don't move. I simply lay here and enjoy his hands on me, in this space right between sleep and wakefulness.

"This isn't waking up," he says dryly.

"I'm awake."

"I wish we could just stay here all day, *cara*, but it's kind of a big day for Matt and Nic. We have to go."

"I want to go," I reply and crack open an eye to find Dom hovering above me, that dimple winking at me, his blue eyes happy and pinned on mine. "Hello, handsome."

"*Ciao, bellissima*," he replies and flashes that charming grin at me.

"Dear God, I love your Italian. It's sexy as hell."

"It is?" His voice is heavy with sarcasm.

"You know it is."

He brushes his fingertips down my chest to my stomach. "*Hai la pelle più morbida*."

"What was that?"

"You have the softest skin," he whispers and plants a kiss on my shoulder.

"We don't have time for this," I warn him with a grin. Jesus, his lips are incredible.

Instead of answering me, he grins wolfishly and suddenly stands, pulling me with him. He tosses me over his shoulder and stalks into the bathroom, starts the shower and when the water is warm enough, sets me down in the large stand up shower.

"I could have walked," I inform him.

"But then I wouldn't have carried you," he replies, and reaches for my shower gel.

"Are we conserving water?"

"Smart girl." He lathers up his hands along with a wash cloth and begins to drag both over my skin, cleaning me up.

"That feels nice," I murmur, watching him.

His lips twitch as his hands glide south, over my belly, over my smooth pubis and into the most sensitive part of me.

"Dom!" I gasp and grip onto his arms, holding on tight.

"Yes?"

"Holy shit, you're good at that," I groan as his free hand glides down my ass, and now he's reaching me from both sides, rubbing my clit from the front and plunging fingers inside me from the back, and it's the most incredible sensation. He plants his lips on my neck, then bites me there, licks his way up to my ear and says in a firm, direct tone, "Come."

Jesus, who could refuse him? I come hard, shuddering against him. If he weren't holding me up, I'd fall into a boneless mass on the tile floor. With my forehead leaning on his chest, I struggle to find my breath, and my legs.

"Damn, babe," I say with a laugh. "That was fun."

"Yes, it was. Now, no more distractions. We have to go."

"But, what about you?"

He winks and slaps my ass playfully. "I'll collect later. Trust me."

◯

"HEYYYYY, BATTA, BATTA, batta!"

"Um, Bryn, this is batting practice. You can't heckle the players during practice." Matt shakes his head at his sister-in-law playfully.

"I can too. It's the freaking *White Sox*, Matt."

"Hey! I love the White Sox," Nic says with a frown. We're all here, all of the siblings with their spouses, and Nic is the only one wearing a White Sox shirt. The rest of us are in our Mariners gear.

"I didn't know you were so into baseball," Stacy says to Nic with a grin.

"I like it more than football," Nic admits, and then laughs. "And I can only say that because Will and Meg are still on their honeymoon."

"I'm so telling," Jules says.

"No, you're not," Nate says, and kisses his wife square on the lips.

These men seriously never stop touching their women. It's awesome.

As if to prove my point, Dom wraps his arm around my shoulders and leans in to kiss my temple. They're an affectionate lot, that's for sure.

"How did we get these seats?" Meredith asks, looking out at the field from our front row seats. We're right between first base and home plate, and we have a prime view. "I can practically smell the sweat."

"Ew," Sam says, wrinkling her nose. "No one said anything about sweat."

"You're married to a rock star, Sam." Stacy shakes her head at Sam. "You should be used to sweat by now."

"I'm married to a rock star," Sam repeats proudly. "My husband is a rock star."

"It's still new," Nat murmurs.

"I still get a kick out of calling you my wife," Luke says to her. "And it's not so new anymore."

"It's getting really girly around here," Mark says with a scowl.

"We have connections," Jules says to Meredith. "It doesn't suck."

"Not in the least," Meredith agrees.

"It looks like the Sox are almost done with practice," Matt says and pulls Nic to her feet. "Come on, we'll go get a ball signed."

"Rhys O'Shaughnessy is playing," Nic says, and claps her hands excitedly. "He's my favorite."

Matt leads her away, and everyone springs into action, pulling out their phones to capture photos.

"I'm getting Will and Meg on FaceTime right now," Jules says, and then grins when their faces appear on her screen. "Hi guys! He just took her down to the field."

"Jules, turn the camera. I want to see my brother get engaged, not your face."

Jules sticks her tongue out at her brother, then turns the camera around so Will and Meg can watch.

"He got her favorite player in on this?" I ask excitedly.

"He did," Dom confirms, gripping onto my hand, as if he's as nervous as his older brother.

"Rhys is running over with a ball!" Natalie says.

Nic is all smiles as the tall, handsome player hands her a ball, kisses her cheek, and shakes Matt's hand.

"I wish we could hear what they're saying," Jules grumbles.

"He wanted it this way," Caleb says softly.

Rhys points to the ball in Nic's hand, and she looks down at it, then her jaw drops as Matt lowers himself to one knee and takes her hand in his.

"Is it just me, or is this cheesy as fuck?" Mark asks.

"Shut up, it's not cheesy. It's brilliant." Brynna smacks Mark's arm, shutting him up.

We can't hear what's happening, but suddenly, Nic is nodding furiously, and Matt puts a ring on her finger, then stands and lifts her off her feet, hugging her tight, whispering in her ear.

Rhys and his teammates applaud and begin to circle around them to congratulate the happy couple.

"Fuck that! I want to hug them now too!" Jules, careful not to lower her phone, jumps up and leads us all down onto the field. Stacy, Brynna and Meredith jump the wall, garnering the attention of security, but Dom holds up a hand.

"That's their brother. They're just anxious to congratulate him."

"No more jumping down," the tall security man says sternly, then his jaw drops when he sees Leo. "Is that Leo Nash?"

I immediately walk to the man and speak quickly, in my no-nonsense voice. "This is a family outing. Not a photo op. I hope you'll remain discreet, please."

"Of course." He nods and walks away, minding his own business.

When I turn to rejoin the others, Nic and Matt are surrounded by family and players, but Dom is waiting for me with a sober face.

"What's wrong?"

He shakes his head. "Not a damn thing."

He takes my hand and leads me to the others.

"He wrote *Will You Marry Me* on a baseball!" Nic exclaims and shows everyone.

"Aww, and had your favorite player give it to you," Stacy says dreamily.

"I'm your favorite player?" Rhys asks, as if he didn't already know.

"Maybe," Nic says, and then laughs. "Yeah, you definitely are."

"Is it my undeniable good looks?" he asks.

"No, it's your batting record. Seriously, you have the most hits this year in all of the MLB, and watching you hit is like watching a dance. You're damn good."

Rhys cocks his head to the side and watches Nic more seriously. "Thank you."

"I'm sorry to break this up, guys," the security guard says, "but I need you to take your seats. We'll be starting soon."

"Okay, that was cool," Mark concedes as we go to find our seats.

"I want nachos," Brynna announces. "And a hot dog."

"Pizza!" Stacy agrees.

"We're going out for dinner after this," Nate reminds the girls.

"We're at a baseball game," I say, as if it makes perfect sense.

Because it does.

"We need Cracker Jacks too," Sam says. "And cotton candy."

"And a dentist," Luke says with a cringe.

"Beer." I add.

"The beer here is warm," Dominic says.

"I don't care. I'm at a game. I need beer and peanuts."

"Wait!" Meredith stands, looking about. "Where are Matt and Nic?"

We all turn and search the area, and suddenly Caleb points back down to the field. Matt and Nic are coming out of the White Sox dugout, headed for the field.

"Ladies and gentlemen," the announcer begins. "Throwing out the first pitch today is a young woman who just got engaged on our field! Give a big Seattle welcome to Nic Dalton!"

"Oh, my God, I have to get Will back!" Jules is furiously tapping the screen of her phone as we all jump up, cheering loudly.

"Atta girl!" Brynna calls down to the field. Dom and his brothers are whistling loudly.

"This is so fun!" I clap my hands, jumping on the balls of my feet.

Nic walks out to the pitcher's mound, ball in hand, but instead of standing in front of the mound, she stands on top of it and gives the catcher an arrogant look. Her lips twitch, but then she winds up and throws the ball perfectly, right into the catcher's mitt, as if she's a pro who's been throwing baseballs for years.

"Holy shit, Will, you're not the only one in the family with a hell of a right arm," Isaac says excitedly.

"That's so fucking awesome!" Will exclaims through the phone.

Matt and Nic wave at the crowd, then join us in the stands.

"You are so damn cool," Luke says to Nic as he pulls her in for a hug.

"I know," Nic replies, and laughs as she's passed from brother to brother.

"Okay, you all have your own girls," Matt says finally. "Hands off mine."

"Now, back to food," Brynna says, and flags down a guy carrying a box full of peanuts.

"It's going to cost us a thousand dollars to eat all this junk," Nate says.

"You can afford it, ace," Jules replies happily, and cranes her neck looking for another vendor. "Where's the pizza guy?"

"Were those rookies hitting on you when we were down hugging Nic and Matt?" Meredith asks Natalie.

"Yeah." Nat shrugs and shakes her head. "They didn't know any better."

"They do now," Luke replies mildly.

"What did you say?" Stacy asks.

"He didn't say anything," Nat replies and lays her head on her husband's shoulder. "He glared at them like a caveman and the one guy recognized him and they shut up."

"I'm a caveman?" Luke asks in surprise.

"You're all a bunch of cavemen," Meredith replies.

"Am I a caveman, *cara*?" Dom murmurs in my ear.

I snort and stare up at him, then lean in to talk into his ear. "I believe it was you who fucked me against the building on your property because I joked about fucking someone with an apa."

I pull back and see his eyes narrow. "And just hearing you say that makes me want to do it again."

"See? Caveman."

"I'M SO FUCKING full," Brynna says as we walk down the sidewalk outside of the stadium toward a nearby pub.

"That's because you ate everything except for the seat you were sitting in, legs," Caleb says with a laugh and takes her hand in his.

"I didn't eat any of Jules' pizza," she replies with a pout.

"I would have cut your hand off if you'd tried to steal my pizza," Jules says.

It's a beautiful summer night. Not quite dark out yet, warm with a light breeze. Perfect Seattle weather.

"I love nights like this," I breathe, as the others joke and chat around us. Dominic is walking beside me, slowing his strides to match mine. He kisses my hand, then tucks it in the crook of his elbow, content to let me lean on him as we walk. "Seattle is beautiful in the summer."

"Seattle is always beautiful," he replies softly. "Even when it rains."

"It's certainly always green," I reply with a nod. "Not so different from San Francisco."

"Why didn't I know that you're from San Francisco?" he says with a frown.

"I don't know." I shrug and laugh when Sam jumps on Leo's back, making him give her a ride. "It's not a secret. I guess it never came up."

"When did you move to Seattle?"

"Right after I left Jonathan." I lean my head on Dom's shoulder. "There was really nothing for me there anymore. And I've always enjoyed Seattle."

"It's lucky for me that you loved it here."

"Back at you," I reply sincerely. "What are the odds that we'd both be from opposite sides of the world and end up in the same city?"

"It's not odds, *tesoro*, it's fate."

I snort and shake my head, but when I glance back up at him I see he's completely serious.

"You don't believe in fate?" he asks.

"Not really. I guess I've never really thought about it."

He nods thoughtfully. "I would think that if ever there was a couple fated to be together, it would be you and me. Like you said, we're from opposite sides of the globe, neither of us started here, and yet, here we are."

"You two are slow pokes!" Sam calls back to us as Leo walks backwards. "If you trip and fall and drop me, rock star, we are going to have issues."

"I'm not going to drop you, sunshine."

"I want a ride too," Stacy says demandingly to her husband.

"I'll give you a ride, all right," Isaac replies with a cocky grin.

"Stop it!" Jules cries, just as Luke stops dead in the center of the sidewalk, pulls his wife into his arms and drops a kiss on her that would make the gods weep. "For the love of Christmas, we're in public!"

"I don't give a fuck," Luke replies calmly, still staring in Nat's eyes.

"God, you're gross," Jules grumbles. "I need cheesecake."

"We'll get you some," Nate replies with a laugh. "Just ignore the PDA. Or join it." He buries his face in her neck and bites her flesh, making her moan.

"Oh, that doesn't suck."

"You're all a very affectionate group of people," I observe, as we walk into the pub and score a big table near the back.

"Does that bother you?" Meredith asks.

"No, it's just unusual."

We settle in, glance at menus, order drinks and just when I think my comment has been forgotten, Luke continues. "If it does bother you, Alecia, just say so."

"Hey! I say so all the time and you do it anyway," Jules complains.

"I'm fine," I reply with a laugh. "It's not that it bothers me. I'm just not used to it."

"Were your parents affectionate?" Nic asks.

"They were with each other," I say slowly.

"But not with you," Nic replies.

I shrug and shake my head, as if it's no big deal.

"My mother hasn't touched me in six years," Nic says as the waitress sets a glass of water before her.

"What?" I frown at the beautiful woman, surprised.

"We don't get along well. Never have really. So all of this affection was new to me too." Matt kisses her temple gently.

"You'll get used to it," Jules adds. "I drink a lot, to dull the grossness."

Natalie laughs and throws a napkin at her best friend.

"I want hot wings," Brynna announces.

"I thought you were full?" Caleb says.

"I'm in the mood to suck the fuck out of a bone," she replies, and my eyebrows climb into my hairline.

"Excuse me?" I ask.

"Oh, just wait," Sam says with a grin. "You haven't seen anything until you've seen Brynna suck the fuck out of a bone."

sixteen

Alecia

"But I hate to run," I whine, as I pull into my parking space and cut the engine.

"Don't be a pussy," Blake replies into my ear. "I need a run and I want to talk to you, so I'm picking you up."

"You're using me as an excuse because I have the best running trails in my neighborhood."

"That hurts, Leash," he says. "It's true, but it hurts."

"You're a smart ass." I giggle and walk to my building.

"I'm a smart ass who's almost to your place."

"What? I'm just getting home."

"Well, hurry up and change. I just got off the freeway. See you in a few!"

"Damn it, Blake!"

But it's no use. He's already hung up. I hurry upstairs, let myself in, and immediately begin shedding clothes. My shoes come off first, tossed just inside the door, then I unzip and shed my skirt, leaving it in a wad by the kitchen.

My blouse and bra are flung next, one ending up on the couch, and I have no idea where the other went.

I'll pick them up later.

I hurry into a sports bra, tank and yoga shorts, and Blake bursts through my front door, just as I'm lacing up my shoes.

"You've gotten messy, Leash."

"Eff you. You didn't give me any time."

"Are you going to pick your clothes up?"

"I will later." I sigh and wave him off. "I have to take them in to be dry cleaned anyway. Are you really going to make me run?"

"Yes, ma'am." He winks at me and wraps his arm around my neck, kisses my head with a loud smack, and pushes me away.

"Why do I have to go? Can't you go running without me and just come back here when you're done?"

"God, stop whining," he says and rolls his eyes. "It'll be good for you."

We leave my condo, ride down the elevator and walk out to the sidewalk, then break out into a slow jog.

"This is as fast as you're going to go?" Blake asks me with a smirk.

"If you don't like it, go by yourself." I sniff and already hate the way it feels to run. I've always hated it. "How's Emily?"

"Why do we have to talk about this?"

"So it takes my mind off the fact that I don't want to be running."

"So, let's talk about *your* love life"

"Hell no, you're the one making me run. So start talking."

He sighs and stares out at the water, watching a boat drift by. "We're good."

"Well, that was informational."

Blake laughs ruefully. "One of the things I love about you is that you don't take my shit."

"You don't need me to take your shit. You have enough people in your life who do that for you."

"True enough." He picks up the pace, just a bit, and I growl at him, making him laugh again. "You're kind of a weenie, Leash."

"Emily."

"She's great." He sighs again, not because he's out of breath, but because he doesn't want to talk about this with me.

I don't care.

"She's funny. Smart. Has a banging body."

I shake my head and look up toward the heavens. "Seriously."

"She seriously has a banging body."

"Does it always go back to sex with men?"

"Pretty much, yeah." He seems to give this some thought and then shrugs. "So I enjoy sex. Sue me."

"I enjoy it too, but that isn't in the top three things that I talk about when I discuss who I'm dating."

"Okay, what are *your* top three things?"

"He's smart, sweet and funny."

"What's number four?"

"He's amazing in bed."

He laughs long and loud, then high fives me. "You're funny."

"I know."

"I really enjoy Emily," he says, serious now. "She's fun to be around, and she also doesn't take my shit. If I cook something she doesn't like, she's honest about it. She's sweet."

"She is sweet," I agree. "I'm glad it's going well."

"You are?" he asks, surprised.

"Of course. I want you to both be happy."

"When we were at Dom's, you didn't seem so convinced."

"I admit, I always imagined you'd be happy with someone other than each other," I admit with a shrug. I'm breathing harder now, and that pisses me off. "But you're adults."

"How are things with Dom?"

I grin before I can stop myself, and Blake being Blake, he catches it.

"That good, eh?"

"I like him."

"Thank you, captain obvious."

I laugh and elbow his arm.

"He's nice to me."

"He'd better be, or I'll kick his ass, friend or not."

"That's sweet."

"Out of morbid curiosity, what do you like about him?"

I frown and ponder the question, running in step with him, our feet pounding the pavement. We pass an older man walking his dog, and a young mother with a baby in a stroller.

"I respect him," I begin. "When I first met him, I thought he was just a player. Some charming Italian who melts panties off women with just a few pretty words, and works his way from bed to bed."

"Wow, you got all of that from meeting him at family gatherings?"

I shrug and keep talking. "But he's not that person. He loves his family fiercely. He's proud of his business. He's so damn good to me."

"I'm glad."

I glance over to find Blake watching me with serious eyes.

"You deserve to be happy too, you know."

I nod and then laugh. "And as ridiculous as this sounds, I think I'm in love with him."

"Oh, I could have told you that."

"What? How?"

"You should see the look on your face when you talk about him," he says with a grin. "You're such a girl."

I shake my head as we turn back toward the condo.

"I don't think I've ever been in love before, B."

"You've been married," he says.

"I'm learning that doesn't mean much," I reply honestly. "I mean, I think I *thought* I loved Jonathan when I married him; I hope I did, but it was nothing at all compared to this. And it's going to sound silly, but I miss him."

"Why is that silly?"

"I just saw him Monday morning. I've been too busy this week to see him, and I miss him."

"Why are you running with me on your one free night this week rather than spending it with Dom?"

"Because he has an event at the vineyard, so he's not free tonight."

"Have you told him you love him?"

"Are you nuts?" I shriek. "No way."

"Why not?"

"Because I've only been seeing him for a few weeks. It's too soon."

"Women." He rolls his eyes and speeds up more as my building comes into view, but I let him go ahead of me, and stay at my pace. When I approach my building, he's panting, stretching his legs by the front door. I immediately begin to stretch with him.

"You should go see Dom tonight, Alecia."

"He's busy."

"Not too busy for you to show up and tell him you love him."

"I can tell him this weekend."

"Why wait? You miss him. You love him. Go see him. Seriously, life's too short for this bullshit."

I let us into my condo, frowning at my friend. "When did you become a dating expert?"

"Look." He takes my shoulders in his hands and forces me to look him in the eye. This is very un-Blake. "What if you don't get the chance to tell him? You'll always regret it."

"Have you told Em you're in love with her?"

"Hell yes, I have."

I'm struck dumb. I stare up at him, and then fling my arms around his neck, hugging him tightly. "I'm so happy for you."

"Go be happy for *you*. He'll love seeing you."

"Are you trying to kick me out of my own condo?"

"Hell yes, I want to use your shower. The spray in there is fantastic."

I laugh and walk into my bedroom closet, blindly change my clothes, and then scowl when I realize I'm sweaty.

"I should take a shower."

"Yeah, no man wants to hear his woman say I love you while she smells like a gym rat."

I stick my tongue out at him and march back into my bedroom, stripping out of my clothes on my way to the shower.

What the hell am I going to do, just show up in his office and blurt out, "I love you! Surprise!"

That's lame.

Maybe I should take him dinner or something. Except, he said he has to work tonight, so that won't work.

Why am I overthinking this so much? Just go tell the man you love him!

But what if I do, and he just stares at me in confusion. Or worse yet, says *thank you.*

Dear God, I would die of horror.

Maybe this isn't such a good idea. I should wait. It's still early in our relationship. There's no need to rush this.

You're my treasure.

Would a man say that to someone he doesn't love?

I don't think so.

I turn off the tap, and just as I reach for a towel, there's a commotion in the living room, and I hear a very angry Dominic yell, "What the ever loving fuck is going on?"

seventeen

Dominic

I miss her.

It's been less than three days since I last held her, tasted her, and I miss her as if she's a part of me.

Because she is.

I'm tempted to say fuck it and just go to her tonight. Let Celeste handle the event. That's what I pay her for, isn't it?

I reach for my cell to text Alecia when my office line rings.

"Salvatore," I answer briskly.

"*Ciao*," my cousin Gianna says in my ear, but I can hear an edge in her voice, with just that one word.

"What's wrong, *bella?*"

"I need you here, Dom."

"You do this every three months like clockwork, Gianna. I can't just pack up and come to Italy. I have a business here. A life."

"Marco has been robbing us blind."

I sit forward in my chair, frowning, sure I've heard her wrong.

"*Mi scusi?*"

"You heard me." She sighs the sigh of one who is bone-tired. "The vineyard is broke, Dominic."

"How?"

"A little at a time. I think he's been gambling again." I close my eyes and everything in me stills.

That little motherfucker.

"Where is Marco, Gianna?"

"I can't find him."

"Son of a bitch!" I pinch the bridge of my nose, already making plans to fly to Italy today.

"Dom, you're the one that knows figures. You're the only one who can fix this. I need you here."

"I'm on my way."

"*Grazie*," she begins, but I cut her off.

"And when I get there, we are going to have a long talk about why it took you so fucking long to call me."

"Just get here."

She hangs up, and I'm tempted to hurl my phone across the room, but instead I yell for Celeste.

"What's wrong?" she asks, as she comes into my office.

"I have to leave for Italy this evening."

"Is everything okay?"

"No." I swear and pace behind my desk. "I'll need you to stay this evening for the event. I want someone here to supervise."

"I can do that."

"Good. I'm going up to pack."

"Do you want me to book the airline?"

"No, I'll do it. You'll be able to reach me in Italy if you need anything."

"How long will you be gone?"

"I don't know." I sigh, already sick to my stomach at the mess that awaits me there. "It could be a few weeks. A month at the most."

"Don't worry about anything. Everything will be fine here."

"Thanks, Celeste."

I quickly gather my laptop, iPad, cords and pack my briefcase, pocket my phone and jog upstairs, taking two stairs at a time.

I dial the airline as I unzip a suitcase and begin filling it with clothes and essentials.

I'm an excellent multi-tasker.

"I need to be on a plane to Italy tonight, from SeaTac, first class."

I can hear the agent get to work, her nails clicking on her keyboard as she works on finding me a flight, and I remember that Alecia tried to call while I was talking with Gianna.

Alecia.

Fuck, I have to tell her I'm leaving.

"I have a flight available at eight this evening," the agent says.

I check my watch. That gives me an hour to finish up here before I have to leave for the airport.

And I need to talk to Alecia, preferably in person.

Or, I could just take her with me. She has a team of people who can manage her business without her for a few weeks.

I grin as the idea forms in my head.

"That works, but I'll need two seats, please."

"I have that," she responds. I give her the passenger information, pay with my credit card, and finish packing, suddenly excited at the spontaneous trip back home. I've been eager to show Alecia where I come from, to see her face light up when she sees my grandparent's land, or when I take her shopping in Rome.

With renewed energy, I check in once more with Celeste, then head out, driving toward Seattle.

I can't wait to see her, but first I place a call to Steven.

"Hello."

"Hey, it's Dom. I wanted to let you know that I'm heading to Italy rather unexpectedly."

"Is everything okay?"

The concern in Steven's voice always makes me pause. The way he's accepted me, so readily, always disarms me.

"No, but it will be. There are issues at the vineyard, and I'm needed."

"Of course. Be safe, son, and let me know when you get there, and if there's anything at all that you need."

"Thank you." I nod and smile to myself. "I'm taking Alecia with me."

"Is that so?" I can hear the smile in his voice as well. "So, not completely a work trip, then?"

"No, I want to show it to her."

"Good for you. Be safe."

I end the call and immediately call Matt, giving him the same information.

"You're taking her to Italy? Is she excited?"

"She doesn't know. It's a surprise."

"Now, that's one hell of a surprise."

"I know." I laugh. "Chicks dig shit like this."

"You sound more American every day, brother. Have fun. Call if you need anything."

I end the call just as I leave the freeway, headed to Alecia's condo. My Montgomery family is a special one, there's no doubt about it.

I walk quickly into Alecia's building, checking my watch. We have just enough time for her to pack a bag and to drive to the airport. I hope I don't have to get her naked to convince her to go with me.

Not because I don't want to get her naked, and sink inside her for the better part of the night, but because there's simply no time.

I check my watch again. Okay, maybe I'll just get her half naked.

I'm smiling at the prospect of taking her hard and fast in the kitchen when I approach her door, and open it without knocking, surprised that it's unlocked.

I glace down and frown when I see the shoes I gave her the night of Will's wedding tossed just inside the front door. Then scowl more then I see her skirt wadded on the floor by the kitchen, and her top and bra flung in the living room.

Sitting on the couch, with one ankle propped on the opposite knee, his arms stretched on the back of the sofa, sweaty and wearing only gym shorts is Blake.

His shirt has been thrown on the arm of the couch. He's sweaty, his hair a mess, and he looks . . . *satisfied*.

And I'm going to fucking kill him.

"Hey, man. Alecia is going to be surprised to see you."

"What in the ever loving fuck is going on?" I yell and advance on

Blake. He immediately stands, frowning as if he's confused, which only makes me want to punch him more.

What? She didn't see me for three days and decided to call Blake to scratch her itch?

I'm so fucking stupid.

"Dom?" Alecia says from her doorway. She's wet, fresh from the shower, wearing only a towel, and the world falls out from under me.

"Are you fucking kidding me?"

"Hey, man, it's not what you think—" Blake begins, but I advance, pressing my face close to his.

"What I *think* is that I thought I could trust you. You fucking lied to me."

"No, Dominic," Alecia says, as she lays her hand on my arm. I look down at her hand and then into her face, and she immediately pulls away.

I glare at both of them and pace away, pushing my hands through my hair.

"What, exactly, are you accusing me of?" Alecia asks angrily. Her brown eyes are on fire, her cheeks flushed, as she props her hands on her hips and glares at me.

"You're about to lose your towel," I say, trying to keep my voice calm.

"I don't care. Just say it."

"That's right." I shake my head and laugh humorlessly, pacing her living room. "Why should you care if you lose your towel? We've all seen the goods, right?"

"Hey," Blake begins, but I turn on him, hands fisted at my side, and suddenly Alecia is between us, hands on both of our chests.

"We didn't—"

"This isn't my first rodeo, Alecia. I've walked into this before, only last time it was my fiancé and my cousin."

"What?" Her face pales as she stares up at me. "And you think I would do that?" Her face reddens with anger. I simply shrug as Blake swears under his breath and paces away.

"You know what?" Alecia stomps to the door and opens it wide. "I think you should go."

"Say you didn't fuck him," I reply and advance on her.

"Jesus, Dom—" Blake begins, but Alecia interrupts him.

"I shouldn't *have* to! I want you out of my condo. Now."

"This isn't the end of this," I say, staring down into her angry eyes. I'm just as pissed off. I want her to say *no. Of course I didn't sleep with him.*

And if she hadn't, that shouldn't be so fucking hard to say.

"I'm not talking to you right now." She shakes her head adamantly. "We will finish this later."

When I step out into the hallway, she slams the door behind me. I hurry to my car and drive blindly north, through Tacoma, to the airport, getting angrier with each mile. She fucking played me.

I want to turn back and confront her again. Kick Blake's ass. But there's no time. I'm needed in Italy *now.* My family needs me.

I need Alecia.

Or I thought I did.

She just practically admitted to fucking Blake by not denying it.

Read the writing on the wall, man.

My cell rings, showing Gianna's name.

"What."

"Gee, that's a nice way to answer the phone."

"What do you want, Gianna? I'm on my way to the airport now."

"I want to say thank you again. I'm excited to see you, and I wish it were under different circumstances."

I sigh and rub my hand over my face.

"I'll be there by tomorrow night."

"Also, I just spoke with Liliana, and I might have mentioned that you're coming."

I shake my head and swear under my breath at the mention of my former fiancé.

"Gianna."

"She would love to see you."

"I'm not interested, Gianna."

"It's been a long time, Dom. I'm not suggesting you marry her. Just talk to her. She's missed you too."

She fucked Marco, is all I can think, but I'm too fucking pissed to argue.

"Fine." An idea begins to form. "Actually, Gianna, I will speak with Liliana. Invite her for dinner on Friday."

"I was hoping you'd say that! I already invited her."

"Good. I'll see you when I get there."

I hang up and tap my lips with my fingers, thinking about the two women that I've ever been stupid enough to give my heart to. One betrayed me with my own cousin, not even bothering to try to be discreet. I'm quite sure she intended for me to find them the night before our wedding.

It worked.

And thank Christ I discovered the truth before I married her.

But when I think of Alecia, it's a physical ache in my chest. How could she do this? Why?

eighteen

Alecia

"I can't fucking believe him!" I shriek and stomp into my bedroom to throw on clothes—any clothes, I don't even bother to see what I'm throwing on—and march out to the living room where Blake has pulled his shirt on and is staring out the window. "I can't believe I was going to tell him I *love* him!"

"You do love him," Blake says calmly, and turns to look at me. "And he obviously loves you."

"*Loves me?* He loves me and he accuses me of screwing around with my best friend?"

"Look around, Leash." His arm sweeps around the room. "Your clothes are everywhere. I was half naked, and you came out of the shower. If it had been me walking in on this, I would have killed him. I'm lucky my jaw isn't broken right now."

"He should trust me!" I yell in response. "I would never do that to him!"

"I agree, but did you know about the ex-fiance?"

"No." I shake my head and pace to the kitchen to open some wine. "And that's another thing that pisses me off. He was freaking *engaged*? How has he never mentioned that little tidbit before?"

And why in the hell does the thought of another woman wearing his ring make me homicidal?

"Sounds like it's not exactly a good memory for him," he replies dryly. "Besides, did you ever ask him if he'd been engaged before?"

"Why would I ask him that?" I turn and stare at Blake like he's grown an extra head, but all he does is shrug.

"You didn't help things, you know."

"Are you saying this is *my* fault?" I demand.

"Part of it, yes. He jumped to conclusions, but you refused to deny it, Alecia. Seriously, you were both pretty fucked up."

I sigh and hang my head as some of the mad leaves me. "What he accused us of is horrible."

"Definitely," he agrees. "But you didn't say, *Dominic, I would never fuck Blake. He's too good for me and the sex was too amazing and I can't ever do that again.*"

I roll my eyes, but he just grins.

"No, instead you said, and this is the Cliff's Notes version, but as a man, this is what he heard, *fuck you. I don't have to justify anything to you. Get the eff out.*"

"Shit."

"I have dinner with Emily tonight, so I'm going to go. I suggest you go to the vineyard and apologize, Leash."

I wrinkle my nose, but I know he's right.

"I hate the taste of crow."

"Take a salt shaker."

I TRY TO call Dom's cell phone, but there's no answer. In fact, it goes straight to voice mail.

He's so angry he shut off his phone?

Shit.

I pull into Dom's driveway and walk inside without knocking.

"Dom!" I poke my head into the playroom, the dining room, the kitchen.

No luck.

"Dom!"

I'm walking briskly down the hallway to his office when Celeste sticks her head out, surprise written on her pretty face.

"Alecia."

"Hey, is Dom in his office?"

"No, I'm sorry."

"Oh." I turn toward the back of the house. "Is he out in the barn?"

"No, he's on his way to Italy."

I blink and turn back to her, sure I've misheard her.

"Excuse me?"

"He's on a plane, Alecia. He got called home."

This is his home.

"When?"

"Not long ago."

He's on his way to Italy, and he didn't tell me?

"When will he be back?"

"He didn't know. It could be a few weeks. Maybe a month."

"He's going to Italy for a month." I sound like an idiot, repeating everything she's saying, but I can't help it.

Italy is going to love you.

"It could be less."

I nod and then shake my head, trying to clear it. He left for Italy without telling me.

"Are you okay, dear?"

"Oh, I'm fine."

"Do you want me to give him a message?"

"No." I shake my head and offer her a bright smile. "No message. Thanks."

I turn and walk as quickly as I can out of Dominic's house, to my car, throw it in drive and speed away, barely feeling the tears running down my cheeks. I try to call his cell phone again, but it goes straight to voice mail.

He's on a motherfucking plane.

I dial Blake's number.

"If you're calling me, it didn't go well."

"He's going to *Italy*," I reply, and hate the sound of tears in my voice.

"Seriously?" Blake asks.

"I can't make this crap up. The going gets tough and he runs off to freaking Italy. He didn't even stay and fight for me, Blake. What in the hell is up with that?"

Blake is trying to talk, but I'm on a roll, angry and frustrated and so fucking *hurt* I don't know what to do with myself.

"I mean, am I that big of an idiot? Am I so unlovable that people can just leave me without so much as looking back?"

"Alecia, stop. Take a breath."

I do as he says and wipe angrily at the tears on my cheeks.

"He was supposed to take me to Italy with him, and instead, as soon as he thinks the very worst of me, he hops on a plane."

I can't fucking believe it.

"Alecia, I don't think this has as much to do with Dominic as it does with you and your own issues."

"I don't have issues," I reply stubbornly.

"Oh, sweetheart, you have more issues than any of the *Real Housewife* chicks."

"I'm going to tell Emily you watch that crap."

"Seriously, Alecia. You don't know that Dom has abandoned you."

"People don't stay in my life, Blake," I reply softly. "They just don't."

I end the call and stare blindly at the freeway as I drive home. There are no more tears, just stunned silence. I park and walk up to my condo, let myself in, and stare in disbelief at the shoes Dom gave me where I left them when I hurriedly toed them off to get ready for my run with Blake. I pace around the space, stare out the window at the ferry floating by, and then pace some more.

People don't stay in my life.

And why don't they? I never speak to my parents. My ex-husband walked away from our relationship with barely a look back.

I'm tired of being disposable.

You're my treasure.

God, he was a damn talented charmer, I'll give him that.

With my mind made up, I fish my phone out of my bag and dial

Emily's number.

"Hey, boss."

"Hey," I reply, putting a smile in my voice, and quite proud that my voice doesn't shake. "I've had something come up. Would you mind taking over for me for the next week or so?"

"Sure," she replies, and I can hear the questions in her voice. "Is everything okay?"

"Of course," I lie. *I just have to go have it out with my parents, which is long overdue.* "I just have some personal things to see to."

"Okay. Don't worry about anything."

I swallow the lump in my throat and take a deep, silent breath.

"You're the best. Thanks."

"No worries."

nineteen

Gianna is fussing at the stove over our grandmother's red sauce, humming under her breath, then pulls fresh bread out of the oven. I missed this kitchen. It makes me think of *Nonna* and laughter and home.

Our grandfather updated this kitchen years ago, installing an industrial stove, oven and refrigerator, and *Nonna* made good use of it, always in the kitchen, always feeding someone.

If we'd been smart, we would have bottled and sold her red sauce while she was alive, rather than wine. It most likely would have sold better.

But she would have had none of it.

I sip my wine, a pretty little Merlot that came from this land, and page through my cousin's financials on her laptop one more time.

"So, he was making withdrawals of more than ten thousand Euros at a time, and you didn't notice? Come on, Gianna, I'm not stupid."

"He always had reasons," she says, flailing her arms about as she paces the kitchen. I check the time, conscious that Liliana will be here soon, and I want this wrapped up before she arrives. "His car was broken. He had medical bills."

"Marco has never been sick a day in his life."

"Why would I question him?" she demands, her deep brown eyes on fire. "Why? He's my brother, yes?"

"You would question him because he's done this before."

"But never like this!"

I sigh and push my fingers through my hair. I'm still exhausted from jet lag, from being angry at Alecia. From worrying about this vineyard.

"I'm going to go to the bank next week, Gianna. I'll get you figured out. I'm still digging through your records, which are a mess by the way, and trying to figure out exactly how much he owes you."

"He's not going to pay it back, Dominic."

"Oh yes," I reply, my voice full of steel. "He will. And when I find him, I'm going to kick his ass."

"That's not why I asked you here."

"Well, it's happening anyway. You wanted my help, and you're getting it."

She stops by the table, twisting the kitchen towel in her hands and finally wraps her arms around my shoulders and hugs me tightly. "Thank you for coming right away, Dom. Thank you for helping."

"You should have called me months ago."

"I thought it would stop. I thought maybe I could help him."

"He doesn't want help, Gianna. That's something you need to remember."

She smiles up at me sadly. "He's my brother."

The doorbell rings and Gianna pulls away. "I'll go get the door."

I close the laptop and stow away the paperwork before Gianna leads Liliana into the kitchen, both chatting excitedly.

"You're here!" Liliana exclaims and launches herself into my arms, plants her lips on my cheek and clings to me.

It very nearly turns my stomach.

"I'm here," I reply and pull her off of me and motion for her to sit at the table. "How are you, Liliana?"

"Oh, I'm great." She smiles, and I can't help but take her in, from head to toe. She's in stylish, brightly colored clothes that fit her long, lithe body like a glove. She's always been thin, almost too thin.

But her breasts are full and almost spill from her blouse.

She's had them done.

Her lips are bright red, her skin pale and perfect. Her raven black hair spills around her shoulders in loose curls, and her blue eyes are bright as she watches me, her lips tipping up in a flirtatious smile.

"I've missed you, Dominic."

I cock a brow. "Have you?"

"Very much." She leans over and grips my hand in hers, but I slowly lean back, out of her reach.

I don't want her touching me.

Gianna serves dinner, and the two of them chat happily, gossiping about mutual friends, giving me a chance to watch Liliana.

Was I ever really attracted to her? Of course I was, but the reasons why are a mystery to me. She obviously works very hard to make herself beautiful, and yet ironically, she's incredibly unattractive.

Being a cheating bitch will do that, I suppose.

"Oh, Dom, do you remember that weekend trip we took to Rome? That last one when we got engaged?"

I physically flinch before I can stop myself. Of course I remember the weekend trip to Rome.

"What of it?"

"Well, I was just there a few weeks ago, and that little bed and breakfast that we stayed in is for sale. Of course, I so longed to buy it, purely for sentimental value." She bats her eyes at me. "You should buy it."

"Why in the hell would I do that?"

"Because it's our special place, of course."

Gianna frowns at Liliana, and then watches me warily. I set my fork down, lean on my elbows, and watch Liliana over the rim of my wine glass.

"What's your game, Lil?"

"Game?" Her eyes go wide, innocently, and four years ago, I would have bought it hook, line and sinker. "There's no game. That place is special to me. I would hate for someone to buy it and turn it into something horrible."

"Gianna," I begin and stand, gesturing for Liliana to take my hand, which she does without hesitation. "I'm going to take Liliana outside to talk privately."

"Of course," Gianna replies, and begins clearing the table. I try to pull my hand from Liliana's, but she holds firm, smiling flirtatiously up at me, the way she used to do when she couldn't wait to get me home and rock my world, as I lead her outside and around the side of the house on the wrap-around covered porch.

"Thank goodness we're alone at last," she purrs and glides her hands up my chest, leaning into me, tipping her head back in invitation. "I'm so happy that you're home, *mi amore*."

I back away from her touch and cross my hands over my chest. "I'm not your love, Liliana. I'm not anything to you."

"That's not true."

I tilt my head to the side, watching her closely. "You fucked my cousin. The night before we were to get married."

Her lip quivers and tears spring to her eyes, but I don't for one minute believe they're genuine.

Liliana is a master manipulator.

"It was only cold feet."

"Or a cold heart," I reply calmly.

"I wish you would just forgive me, Dominic. It was a moment of weakness. It meant nothing at all."

I nod, considering her words. "Yes, Marco told me that you'd been fucking him for about three months. So, was that just a three month long moment of weakness then?"

Her eyes narrow and lips firm. "Did you come here to reconcile or not?"

"Not." I drag my finger over my lips, considering her. "I came here because my cousin needed me."

"Then why did you invite me to dinner?" She props her hands on her slender hips and glares at me.

"For a few reasons." I rest my hip on the banister casually. "One, I'd like to know how much money you've talked Marco into giving you over the past six months."

She starts to speak, but I hold a hand up, stopping her.

"I also wanted you to finally admit that you'd been fucking him since before I proposed to you. And I wanted to simply ask you why."

"Why what? Why does Marco give me money? Why was I fucking him?"

"All of it."

She tosses her head back and laughs. Not the sexy, lovely laugh I once knew her to have, but a vindictive, malicious laugh that only makes her look more ugly.

"Oh, come on, Dominic. You're an adult. We had a good time together. The sex was spectacular, we made each other laugh."

"The sex was mediocre," I correct her and smirk. Sex with Alecia was spectacular.

"It was never about *you*," she spits out. "As soon as I set foot on this vineyard when I came out here to take care of your mama, God rest her soul, I knew that I wanted it."

"You wanted the *vineyard*?" I ask incredulously. "For what? You're a nurse."

I rack my brain, thinking back to those months when Liliana came here to care for my mama when she was dying, how compassionate she was.

She'd been my rock during that time, and it was why I'd fallen in love with her.

"I'm a damn good nurse, but do you honestly think that's what I want to do forever? Watch people die?"

"What do you want?"

"I want money!" She shakes her head at me like I'm stupid. "You always talked of moving to America, starting over, and that wasn't what I wanted. I love it here. *Right here.* And I knew Marco would never leave."

"So, you seduced him."

"And I still do," she replies with a smug smile. "And he does pretty much whatever I tell him to."

"Including steal money from his sister," I growl.

"Hey, I've been asking Gianna to talk you into moving back home for a long time, Dominic. You were the one I wanted, but I wanted you *here.* And I wanted a claim on this vineyard."

"Have you forgotten that you'd signed a pre-nup, Lil?" I smirk, when her face pales and she glares at me. "And aside from that, Marco and I are not controlling owners in this vineyard. He and I only each own twenty-five percent. Gianna owns fifty percent. This is *her* vineyard."

"Well, then it's a good thing I've kept the mindless twit as a friend all these years, isn't it?"

"You're no friend of mine."

We both turn, shocked to find Gianna standing at the end of the porch, a bottle of wine in her hands, quivering with rage.

"Gianna, *bella*, you misunderstood me."

"No, I didn't." Gianna shakes her head and sets the wine on the railing. "All this time, I thought you were in love with Dominic." She turns her sweet eyes to Liliana and sighs. "I felt sorry for you."

"Well, that's something we have in common," Liliana replies coldly.

"You're going to need to get the fuck off my property now," Gianna says, surprising us all with her language. Liliana turns to me in a huff.

"Are you going to let her talk to me like that?"

"Absolutely. Get the fuck out."

"Dom," she begins, and softens her face into a soft, self-deprecating smile. "When your mama was dying, she told me that she hoped that you'd find a nice woman like me. She *wanted* us to be together."

"My mother didn't know what you are, Liliana. I do. Get off of Gianna's property before I have you arrested for trespassing."

Liliana glares at both of us, then stomps inside for her purse and slams out the front door. Gianna and I watch each other quietly as we hear her car start and the tires squeal as she tears out of the driveway.

"Are you okay, *bella?*" I ask her.

She frowns and nods, but then her face crumbles and she shakes her head no. I cross to her and gather her close, rocking her back and forth as she cries.

"I thought she was my friend."

"I know. I'm so sorry."

"I thought she loved you, and I felt sorry for her, and that's why I always ask you to come home."

"I knew that too."

"God, she's a bitch."

I chuckle and kiss her head, then lead her to the porch swing and help her dry her cheeks.

"You knew all of it," she says quietly. "You knew that she was helping Marco steal from me, and all the rest of it."

"I did."

"Why didn't you tell me?"

I tilt my head and watch her quietly, and finally she sniffs and nods.

"You tried. Right after it all happened, you tried, and I told you that you were imagining things and wouldn't believe you."

"She was your friend."

"You're my family," she replies.

I shrug and then nod, just as my phone rings in my pocket.

"Hello, Celeste."

"Hi, Dominic. I'm placing the food order for the family reunion being held here next weekend, and I wanted to make sure that you don't have anything to add to it."

"No, the last email I sent you is it. Check with Blake, though. He might have tweaked the menu a bit."

"Yes, sir. Oh, and did Alecia catch up with you the other day before you got to the airport?"

I frown, ignoring Gianna's look of surprise at Alecia's name.

"What are you talking about?"

"Oh, she was looking for you. She didn't leave a message, but it sounded important."

Of course it was important. I'd caught her with Blake.

"Thanks, Celeste."

"You're welcome. I'll see you in a few weeks."

She clicks off and I shove my phone in my pocket.

"Who's Alecia?"

"No one." *Everything.*

"What is it the American's say? Oh yes, bullshit. Who is she?"

I take a deep breath, and before I know what I'm doing, I've spilled everything to her. How I met her, how we came together, how much she means to me, all the way through to the day I was coming to Italy and I found out she'd been sleeping with her best friend.

"But she was trying to find you when you were on your way here. Celeste just said so."

"Of course she was," I scoff. "She got caught and she was trying to beg for my forgiveness, which she won't get."

"So, you haven't spoken to her."

"No."

Gianna sighs and murmurs something about pig headed men. "Perhaps you should talk to her before jumping to conclusions."

"I know what I saw, Gianna."

"You saw her best friend sitting on the couch."

"Half naked, sweaty, and their clothes thrown all over the fucking living room. It wasn't exactly innocent."

"Well, I'll concede that." She bites her lip. "I'm sorry. I'm clearly not the best judge of character, and I've never met your Alecia."

"She's not mine," I reply quickly.

"Isn't she?" Gianna grins and cups my face in her hands. "You love so strongly, Dominic. You always have. It's one of the things that both opens you up to great heartache and brings you such joy. Liliana dimmed that light in you for a while, but I can see that it's back. There's anger there, and I'm not saying it shouldn't be, but perhaps you should try to reach out to her."

"She hasn't tried to contact me either, Gianna."

"You're halfway across the world. It's been two days. Cell phones aren't always reliable." She leans in and kisses my cheeks then stands. "*Ti amo.*"

"I love you too." I kiss her hand before she walks away, lifts the forgotten wine bottle off the railing, and returns inside.

I know what I saw. There was no way to mistake it. Her clothes were everywhere; Blake was half dressed.

And she refused to fucking say that she hadn't just been with him. She wouldn't deny it.

If she came looking for me, it was because I found out about it.

Right?

I shake my head and scrub my scalp in agitation, and then decide *fuck it* and pull my phone out of my pocket and quickly dial her number.

It goes straight to voice mail.

I frown and try one more time, but it again goes to voice mail. It's either dead or she shut it off. I take a deep breath, and finally bring Jules up in my contacts and dial her number.

"Hello."

"Hey, Jules, I'm trying to reach Alecia and I can't get through on her cell. Have you spoken with her?"

"Dominic?"

"Who else would this be?"

"Your number came up as *unknown*. You're lucky I answered."

"Have you spoken to her?" I ask again.

"No, I haven't spoken to her since the baseball game. Is everything okay?"

I swear under my breath and rub my fingers over my lips. "No, it's not okay. But I'll figure it out."

"I'm sure she's fine, Dom."

"Thanks, *bella*."

She's probably right. I'm sure she's fine. But now worry has settled in. I need to get Gianna back on her feet and have words, and come to blows, with Marco, so I can go home and figure out what the fuck is going on.

twenty

Alecia

I didn't know I could hate a city as much as I hate San Francisco. And it's really not the city's fault. It's a beautiful city with lovely buildings and interesting people. Excellent food. There's always something going on here, whether it be an art exhibit or a festival.

And the views of the Golden Gate Bridge and the Pacific Ocean are stunning.

But there are nothing but bad memories for me here.

I drive my rental car through the neighborhood I grew up in. I know the streets like the back of my hand. I walked home countless times, alone, when one of my parents forgot to pick me up from school, or simply didn't come get me because it was inconvenient.

I could find their house blindfolded.

I pull up to the curb, cut the engine, and simply gaze about the tidy, middle class neighborhood. It's a beautiful, sunny summer day. The trees are heavy with green leaves, the sidewalks tidy and busy with kids on bikes or running around with friends. Two of the neighbors are mowing their lawns.

I step out of the car and stare at Mom and Dad's house. They must have had it recently painted. Instead of the solid, dependable dark grey from my childhood, it's now a rust color, and the green shrubs on either side of the small porch look even brighter against the house.

I take a deep breath and walk slowly up the sidewalk, climb the stairs of the porch, and ring the doorbell. My eyes can't help but travel to the corner of the porch where I used to sit for hours on end, watching the other kids in the neighborhood, wishing I didn't have to go to another piano lesson or basketball practice or day camp.

The door opens and my mother, her blonde hair curly and a bit unruly around her thin face, dressed in a simple white T-shirt and blue jeans rolled up to mid-calf, opens the door with a surprised smile.

"Alecia! Oh my goodness, what are you doing? Come in, darling." She steps back, letting me in and kisses both of my cheeks. "Alan! Alecia is here!"

"Hi, Mom."

"Well, this is a delightful surprise. Are you visiting from Sedona?"

"Seattle," I correct her and clench my hands into fists. "I live in Seattle."

"That's right, dear. Come on back to the kitchen. Your father and I were just about to have some lunch."

The furniture is the same. Brown leather couches and a tube TV at least fifteen years old sit in the living room. The same worn dining room set in the kitchen.

Even the mug my dad is drinking out of in the kitchen is one I gave him for Christmas when I was nine.

"Alecia," he says kindly, and kisses my cheek. "How nice of you to visit. It's been, what, at least six months?"

"Three years," I reply, and blink back tears. Why does this always surprise me?

Mom frowns and begins gathering lunchmeat, cheese, and bread to make sandwiches.

"No, it can't be that long," she says and shakes her head. "I'm quite sure we spoke to you at Christmas."

"No, you didn't," I reply firmly. This is what I'm here for, right? I might as well start standing up for myself now.

"Well, it's good to see you," Dad says with a grin. "How is Sedona?"

"Seattle," I say between gritted teeth. "Why can't either of you ever remember that I live in Seattle?"

"Do you want ham or turkey, dear?" Mom asks Dad.

"Turkey, please. Alecia, come sit." He gestures to the chair to his left, and I lower myself into it, set my handbag on the floor, and take a deep breath.

I wish I had a good, strong drink.

"I won't be here long," I begin, and bite my lip, mustering up courage.

"What is it, darling?" Mom asks kindly and cuts dad's sandwich in two, diagonally, just the way he likes it.

"If you didn't want me, why did you have me?"

They both still, then frown at me, flustered.

"What are you talking about?" Dad says.

"I know I wasn't planned," I continue, tracing a pattern on the table with my fingertip. "That was never a secret. But, if you didn't want me, and I was an accident, why didn't you give me up for adoption, rather than keeping me and ignoring me my whole life?"

"Ignoring you?" Mom demands, and sits at the table, the sandwich forgotten.

"Let's not mince words," I say, and look them both in the eyes. "I was never allowed to eat with you. You kept me busy in school to keep me out of your way. I hated sports. I didn't even particularly like the piano."

"Do you have any idea how much it cost to keep you in piano lessons? In sports?" Mom sits back, angry now, her brown eyes wide and frustrated. "We gave you *everything*. Sent you to the best schools. The best college."

"I had everything so *you* wouldn't have to be bothered with me," I interrupt her. "And it's the past. There's no changing it. I just want to know, why? What was it about me that was so unlovable that you couldn't bear to even eat meals with me?"

I hate that I hear the catch in my voice, but I firm my lip, refusing to back down.

"That wasn't it," Dad says softly. "You were always such a self-sufficient child, Alecia. You played well alone."

I shake my head, and can't help but laugh humorlessly.

"Dad, I learned to be self-sufficient. You two never made a secret of the fact that you'd wished it was just the two of you. I've always, *always* felt like a third wheel. You didn't want me." I shrug as Mom gasps, covering her mouth with her hand in surprise. "Really, Mom? You don't even know what city I live in."

"Maybe we could have paid more attention," Dad says thoughtfully. "But I, for one, thought we were giving you the best of everything. The best music lessons and sports programs. The school. Your mother and I worked very hard to be able to afford those things for you, Alecia."

"I worked more than full-time just to pay the tuition for the private school," Mom adds.

"I'm not saying that I did without *things*." I swallow and fist my hands, pissed that they're starting to shake. "I had plenty of things. But I didn't have affection. I didn't feel loved. And I just want to know what it is about me that is so unlovable."

"My God, Alecia!" Mom exclaims. "Of course we love you. You're our little girl!"

"I don't remember you ever saying *I love you* to me. You didn't hug me. You've never said you were proud of me."

They stare at each other in confusion, then look back to me.

"You hugged each other. I come from a very loving marriage," I continue. "But I don't come from an affectionate family."

"I guess we weren't terribly demonstrative when it came to affection," Mom says.

"Some people just aren't," Dad says with a shrug. "But we never mistreated you. We didn't hit you or yell at you or even punish you very often."

I sigh and rub my hands over my face. "Why do I feel like I'm spinning my wheels?"

"Are you saying we're shitty parents, Alecia?" Dad asks.

"Yes! And I want to know why you don't love me!" I yell and stand, my hands in fists at my sides. "I want to know why you never held me, or said kind fucking things to me! I want to know why you always sent me away rather than keeping me close to you!"

"Watch your language, daughter," Mom warns sternly, but I just shake my head and pound my fist on the table.

"I didn't deserve that!"

"We didn't do anything wrong," Mom says with a sniff, her nose in the air, and I know that they aren't going to answer me.

"Maybe," I begin thoughtfully, "you're just too self-absorbed to realize that you did anything wrong. Maybe it's easier to live in denial, in your perfect little home, your perfect little bubble, and believe that you treated me well. But I came here to tell you that you *didn't*. And that it's not okay. It's made me question myself my whole life."

I sit back in the chair and clasp my hands together. "I've always wondered why I was so unlovable. What did I do? I ran into the arms of the first man—boy then—to show me attention, and I ran as fast and as far as I could when I graduated to escape the loneliness of this house. You don't want to acknowledge that you're shitty parents? Fine."

I stand and lift my handbag. "You were shitty parents. But I love you, *because* you're my parents."

I turn to leave, but when I get to the kitchen door, I turn back to them. "If you ever want to have a relationship with your only daughter, you call me. I'm not going to chase after your love. I'm not going to beg for it. For the first time in my life, I'm at the top of someone's priority list: mine."

On shaky legs, I walk through the home of my childhood, out the door and to my car. It takes me three tries to get the key in the ignition, but I finally pull away, breathing hard, trembling, but so fucking proud of myself.

It's about time I stand up for myself.

I get to the end of the block when my phone rings.

Jules.

I send it to voice mail and shake my head. I can*not* deal with talking to any of the Montgomerys today.

Instead, I search for another contact and press send.

"Alecia?"

"Hello, Jonathan," I reply and clear my throat. "Would you be willing to meet up with me for breakfast tomorrow?"

"You're in San Francisco?"

"Yes." *No, I want you to fly your dumb ass to Seattle and meet me there.*

"Where?"

"Our diner, nine o'clock."

"I'll be there." He pauses. "Are you okay?"

"I'm going to be." I end the call and point my car toward my hotel. The phone rings again.

Unknown Number.

"Fucking telemarketers," I mumble, and send it to voice mail, and no sooner does the phone ring again.

Jules.

"What?" I snap.

"Um . . . hello." I can hear commotion in the background. People laughing.

"Sorry, Jules. What can I do for you?"

"Well, we're having a family dinner, and Jax and Logan are here, and they've decided to get married in two weeks, which I know is short notice, but we want to make sure that if you can't help plan, you can at least come to it." She pauses to take a breath and I can hear someone— *Sam?*—yell, "You better bring your sexy ass to it!"

Oh, hell no.

"I'm sorry, Jules, I'm quite sure I have an event that day."

"No, you don't. I talked to Emily."

"Then why did you just ask if I did?"

"Well, I'm polite, aren't I?"

I can't help but grin.

"If there's no event, it must be because I have something else going on. Thanks for thinking of me, but I'm going to have to decline."

I can hear movement, and the background noise lessening until it's nonexistent, and then Jules says, "Okay, cut the shit. What is going on?"

"I don't know what you mean."

"You don't sound like yourself at all. You sound . . . *sad.* Talk to me, friend."

She just had to throw friend *in there, didn't she?*

"I don't think it's a good idea for me to be at one of your family's parties right now, Jules."

"What did my idiot brother do?"

I frown and park at the hotel. "Who said he did anything?"

"I'm not stupid, Alecia. Talk to me."

I take a deep breath. My nerves are already shot from my visit with my parents, and I haven't slept in days. To my horror, I feel my eyes fill with tears.

"I just don't think it's going to work out between your brother and me."

"Why?" Jules asks in a soft voice. "I think you're perfect together."

"I need to be with someone who makes me a priority, Jules."

"Okay." She sounds confused. "What's the problem?"

"I'm not that for Dominic. And I deserve that, Jules. I *need* it."

"Everyone deserves it, but I don't understand why you think you're not a priority for Dom. Hold on." She pulls the phone away from her face and murmurs to someone quietly before returning.

"Please don't tell the family about this."

"That was my dad. He's just making sure everything is okay. He won't say anything."

"I hope you'll still think of me when events come up."

"Girl, you're doing Jax and Logan's wedding. We won't take no for an answer."

I bite my lip as longing fills me. I love working with this family. It's not just because of the money, but because they're fun and my best clients. I don't want to give them up.

And why should I have to? I didn't do anything wrong!

"Okay. I'll call you next week. I'm out of town right now."

"Where are you?"

"San Francisco. I have some demons to put to rest."

"Alecia, I'm worried about you."

"Don't be. I'll be fine. I'll talk to you next week."

She sighs in my ear. "Fine. We'll talk next week. And I mean *talk,*

Alecia."

"I'll see you soon."

WHEN I ARRIVE at the Alley Cat, the diner that Jonathan and I had Sunday morning breakfast at every week during our entire marriage, he's already sitting in our booth, near the back, looking nervous as he stares down into his coffee mug. I take a minute to soak in the sight of him. His mink-brown hair is longer than he used to wear it, almost shaggy. He's still thin, just this side of too thin, with no muscle definition on his arms. He's wearing his usual metal band T-shirt and baggy jeans.

He looks young. Carefree.

I sit opposite from him, unlike when we were married.

"You used to sit beside me," he says with a half-smile and sits back in the booth arrogantly.

I don't return it.

Instead, I sit back and say the first thing that comes to mind.

"You should be ashamed of the way you treated me."

His eyes widen, but I see I've struck him dumb, so I continue.

"The way you used to belittle my job? Not okay." My voice is perfectly calm, but my eyes are pinned to his. "The way you'd give me the silent treatment when I *disappointed* you? Definitely not okay. Making me feel small, or that your shortcomings were my fault, was not okay."

The waitress appears to take my drink order, but I simply shake my head, sending her on her way.

"You pushed me away when I tried to give you affection. You made sure I knew that I was the last person on your priority list. You had inappropriate relationships with women that *you weren't married to*." I lean forward, bracing myself on my elbows. His face has paled, but his mouth is tight, and I can see I'm pissing him off. "And making me feel like a piece of shit because my sexual appetites weren't the same as yours was not fucking okay."

He swallows hard. "Are you done?"

I tip my head back and forth, giving it some thought. "For now."

"It's good to see you too. You look beautiful, by the way."

I blink and frown at him. "I'm out of here."

"Wait." His hand covers mine before I can slide out of the booth. "Don't go. You're right. None of that was okay."

"Okay." I pull my hand out of his and watch him quietly. "Since we agree on that, now I get to ask you why."

He laughs and shakes his head. "Why was I a douche?"

"You were an asshole, Jonathan. And I want to know why. What was it about me that was so unlovable? What gave you the right to make me feel less than, especially knowing my past with my parents."

"Oh, Alecia, you are *not* unlovable. I'll apologize first and foremost if I ever made you feel that way."

My eyebrows lift in surprise.

"I was so in love with you I couldn't see straight. You were beautiful and smart and so fucking talented."

My jaw drops, and then I recover and simply scowl at him.

"If that's how you treat someone you love, I really don't want to know how you'd treat someone you can't stand."

"I was never good enough for you, Alecia. I knew that. I didn't know why you were with me. And when you started your business and it became successful, I was worried."

"Worried?"

"That you'd figure out that I wasn't good enough for you. I dumbed it down, made it seem insignificant, because I was too much of a pussy to simply be proud of you. And the rest?" He shrugs and shakes his head. "I've been going through some therapy to figure it out. I knew I was hurting you, and I hated it, but I couldn't stop."

"What's the verdict?"

"I'm a selfish jerk."

"Pretty close," I reply with a nod. "You do realize that being a complete asshole to someone that you're afraid of losing is not the way to keep them."

"Hey, no one said I was smart."

His face sobers.

"Your parents didn't deserve you, blondie. I sure as fuck didn't deserve you either. But it didn't have anything at all to do with you not being lovable."

"It seems I'm the common denominator here, J."

He shakes his head adamantly. "You had shitty luck when it came to the people who were in your life. And I've wanted to see you for a long time to say I'm sorry."

"Well, this isn't what I was expecting."

"Were you going to rail at me, throw my coffee in my lap, and stomp off all self-righteously?"

"Something like that."

"Well, before you do that, just know that I'm sorry for being a douche. You deserve someone who will love you and appreciate you in ways no one ever has before. I want that for you, blondie."

"Thanks," I whisper, and bite my lip to keep the tears at bay.

"You never came to get your piano or your other things. They're still at the house. You can come get them whenever you want."

"You didn't sell the house?"

"No."

"I don't want the piano." I sniff and shake my head, looking out the window to the waterfront.

"Seriously? But you're so damn good at it."

"I only ever played it for my parents. I won't play it again." I gaze over at my ex-husband and finally offer him a soft smile. "It was good to see you too, J."

He reaches for my hand, and for just this moment, I let him.

It feels familiar, but it's not the hand I want to hold mine. Not even close.

"I want you to shine, Alecia. And I want to tell you, right here in our place, I'm so fucking proud of you."

I lean in and kiss his hand, then smile at him. "Thank you."

And with that, I stand and walk away, not looking back.

twenty-one

Dominic

God, I'm so fucking tired. Being gone from my vineyard for ten days was too damn long. Celeste is fantastic, but I like things to be done a certain way, so I've done nothing for the past forty-eight hours but work and sleep, trying to shake this God-forsaken jet lag.

I hit send on an email, cementing a partnership with a new restaurant in the Portland area called Seduction, intrigued by the five owners, and make a mental note to take a trip down there soon to check it out.

I begin reading through an application for an event for this fall, and stumble when I see that it's Alecia who is planning the affair.

I wish she'd talk to me. I've tried to call her several times over the past few weeks, but she's not answered, and I refuse to beg her to answer the goddamn phone via text.

That's just ridiculous.

I eye my phone and wonder just how ridiculous it really is, just as there's a knock on my door, and am surprised to find Steven standing outside my office.

"Is everything okay?" I ask, as I stand and gesture for him to come inside. I close the door behind him.

"Oh, yes, I called earlier and Celeste said you were in today, so I thought I'd drop in and see how your trip went."

"It was . . . necessary," I reply and sit in my chair as he takes a seat before me. "But the issue seems to be resolved now."

I secured a loan for Gianna, without telling her that I'm the one backing it, so she can get back on her feet. And I managed to have a heart-to-heart with Marco, right after I knocked him on his ass.

Both were immensely satisfying.

"I'm glad you're home," my father replies with a smile. He steeples his hands. "Did Alecia enjoy Italy?"

I lean back in my chair and shake my head. "She didn't go."

"Why not?"

I watch my father and consider lying, but instead I simply say, "I think I fucked up, and Alecia and I are done."

He cocks a brow. "What did you do?"

I stand and turn my back to him, push my hands in my pockets and stare out the window that looks out over my land. The remnants from Will's wedding are long gone, and it's as though Alecia was never here.

Except that I see her everywhere I look.

"I thought I caught her having an affair with her best friend," I admit softly. "I was angry. Hurt, actually."

"Of course."

"But now, I'm not so sure that what I saw was what it looked like, and I can't get her to take my calls. I have a feeling she's done with me."

I sigh and turn back to him.

"So now, I need to know how I'm supposed to get her out of my system and move on."

"Well, you know what they say about getting a woman out of your head, son. Put another one in your bed."

My eyes narrow as anger shoots through me.

"I'm not interested in fucking someone else. I can't hop from the bed of the woman I'm in love with to someone else's. Maybe you can tell me how to do that, *Dad*."

Steven doesn't even flinch. "I deserve that." He nods slowly for a moment.

"Yes, you do."

"I think it's very telling that you're not interested in other women, Dom. Maybe it's not as over as you think it is. Seems a shame to give up on something you worked so hard to have in your life."

"She won't speak to me," I remind him. "And now that we're on the subject, how could you do it? How could you bounce from Gail to my mom?"

"I didn't *bounce* anywhere," he replies coldly. "I thought my marriage was over, and I was an idiot. I regretted it for a long time. I don't anymore."

"Why?" I ask with surprise.

"Because of you." He shrugs and then sighs. "You were the best part of your mother's life, Dominic. I never saw her again, but I can guarantee you that much. And now we have you in our family, and I couldn't be more thankful."

"I disrupted your life, and I'm quite sure I put undue stress on your marriage last year."

"You did neither." He waves me off and laughs ruefully. "My wife knew all about your mother not long after it happened more than thirty years ago. It wasn't a secret between us. Was it a surprise? The biggest of my life. And it was an adjustment for my other children, but I think it's obvious that you're accepted and loved, Dominic."

Loved?

I think back on the past year, at how the Montgomerys have folded me into their family, accepted me unconditionally. I am their brother, without hesitation.

Even Gail has been nothing but gracious.

Yes, they are my family and I love them back. I'd do anything for any of them.

"I'm grateful for all of you," I murmur.

"There's no need to be grateful, son." He grins at me with the smile of a man who has everything he could ever want. "Family just *is*. Now, about your Alecia."

"She's not mine."

"You're not interested in anyone else. You're trying to reach out to her." He seems to be struggling with what to say, and he finally says, "Give her some time."

"What do you know?" I ask, suspicious that he isn't telling me everything.

"I know that it's not my story to tell. Alecia has had a rough go of it lately, and maybe she just needs some space."

"Fuck that. If she needs me, I'll go take care of her."

"I didn't say she needed anyone to take care of her," he replies sternly. "I said she needs time."

"I'm not a patient man."

"Well, you come by that honestly," he says with a chuckle. "I'd like for you to show me your operation here, and then I'd like to have lunch with my son, if you're up for it."

My eyebrows climb into my hairline in surprise. "I'm definitely up for it."

"Excellent."

We walk through the grounds, the barn where the barrels are stored, the production barn, the store. He's engrossed in all of it, just as he is each time he comes out here.

"I'd like to develop a special wine for the women in our family. What do you think?"

I grin slowly, then smile widely. "I think that's an excellent idea. We could surprise them with it for Mother's Day next year."

"Perfect." Steven nods and claps his hand on my shoulder. "I'm so happy you found us, son. I should have said it months ago, but I don't think you were ready to hear it yet. I'm proud of you."

I blink hard and stare out at my vines, my heart in my throat.

"I was terrified when the P.I. gave me your information."

"I was rather nervous myself when I met you for the first time," he replies. "But just as it is with all of my children, Natalie included, you are important to our family. You are important to *me*. I'm sorry that I missed out on so many years with you, but I hope that we can have a relationship with each other going forward."

I nod, not sure what to say, knowing that anything I do say is going to sound rough.

"Good." He pats my shoulder again and walks back toward the

villa. "Let's go get lunch. I'm starving."

SHE'S AVOIDED ME all damn day.

I'm standing in Steven and Gail's backyard while children run around, my sisters laugh, and Jax and Logan are newly married.

The happy couple are feeding each other cupcakes, smashing the frosting in each other's noses.

"I've never understood the whole *let's punish the cake by smearing it all over each other* thing," Will says with a frown.

"I don't understand why you're not over there trying to snatch some cake," I reply dryly.

"Holy shit, you're right!" He runs across the lawn to the patio as if a linebacker is on his heels.

"I think he already stole one from the back earlier," Caleb says with a shake of the head. "How is he not fat?"

"Because he works out six hours a day," Leo says as he pulls his wife into his arms and kisses her head.

"This is the man section," Sam says with a frown. "Where are the girls?"

"I didn't realize we had sections," Steven says as he joins us, handing me a beer.

Alecia walks by, completely ignoring me, just as she's done all damn day.

"Excuse me," I murmur and follow her.

"Trouble in paradise?" I hear Sam ask.

"Alecia," I say and hurry to catch up to her. "Stop."

"I don't have time." She presses on her ear, and speaks into her sleeve. "I need more champagne out here, and Logan's mother is drinking out of a plastic glass, Em. That's not okay. Get her a glass flute."

"I'd really like to speak to you, *cara*."

She stops and turns to me, finally looking at me for the first time today, and she takes my damn breath away. Her hair is up in its usual knot, her brown eyes are wide, but unsmiling. She looks like she may have lost a few pounds from the way her green dress hangs on her sweet little body.

But rather than answer me, she simply shakes her head and stomps away, talking briskly to Emily in her sleeve.

What the fuck am I doing? Why am I chasing her?

"Wanna talk about it?"

Natalie has joined me, Keaton on her shoulder sleeping peacefully, watching Alecia walk away.

"Not particularly."

"She looks sad."

I haven't taken my eyes off of her. "I don't see sad."

"Then you aren't looking hard enough," Nat replies and kisses her son's head. "What did you do?"

"Why does it have to be me?"

She just raises a brow. "Because if she'd been the one to screw up, you wouldn't be chasing her the way you are."

"I'm not chasing her," I reply with frustration. "I'm simply trying to have a conversation with her."

Nat nods. "Try harder."

I glance down at her. "Thanks a lot."

"You're welcome." She smiles widely and walks away, like the smart ass that she is.

Try harder.

I sigh and then follow the way Alecia just went, into the house, and find her in the kitchen.

"Alecia," I say calmly. "I'd like a moment, please."

Emily smiles at me and nods, then hastily walks out of the room, leaving us alone.

Alecia shakes her head and turns her back on me, uncorking more champagne.

"Alecia," I try again.

"No!" She spins back to me, her eyes narrowed. "I. Don't. Have. Time. I'm working, Dominic. Just leave it be."

I study her eyes, and now I can see it. The sad. But I also see a new resolve that wasn't there a few weeks ago.

And that's what scares the fuck out of me. Is she resolved to live without me?

"I'll leave you be for now, *tesoro*." She starts to argue, but I lean in and make her look me in the eyes. "For now. But we will talk."

"Fine." She turns away again and resumes her work.

Jesus, everything in me wants to pull her into my arms and bury my nose in her hair, breathe her in, feel her against me.

I'm longing for her.

But I know I wouldn't be welcome now. Not only that, I'm not sure that *I* welcome it. Not until I know what in the hell is going on.

I turn and leave the kitchen, running into Jules as I return to the backyard.

"Hey, big brother." She smiles sweetly, and I have the distinct feeling I'm about to be set up.

"Hello, *bella*," I reply. "What do you want?"

"I just want to talk." She loops her arm through mine and walks with me to join Meg, Will, and Nate standing by Steven's newest koi pond.

"What are we talking about?" I ask.

"We'd like to do a fund raiser for the hospital," Meg says with a soft smile. "Nate thought it would be a good idea to have a dinner, dance, and silent auction, which they already do every year, but . . ."

"But rather than have it in downtown Seattle this year, we were thinking of asking if we can book the vineyard. Include packages in the silent auction of wines, and maybe a stay out there. Stuff like that."

"Of course. The vineyard is always open to you. You know that."

"Awesome!" Meg hugs me hard, then presses her hand on my chest. "You're my favorite brother-in-law."

"I was your favorite ten minutes ago when I suggested it," Nate says with a smile.

"Shh," Meg says, holding her hand over Nate's lips. "Don't ruin it."

Alecia hurries past with Meredith, talking fast and completely ignoring me.

That's the last damn time she'll pretend that I'm not here.

"She went to San Francisco, you know," Jules says quietly. My gaze jerks down to her.

"When?"

"A few weeks ago." She shrugs and takes a sip of her drink. "She won't say why. Just that she had some things to deal with."

Her family.

She went alone.

What the fuck is going on?

Jules watches me for a long minute, her usual smile gone, replaced with serious eyes.

"I need to go talk to Natalie," she says finally, and walks away.

"So the event will be in the spring," Meg says excitedly, and for the next thirty minutes, she and I bounce ideas off of each other to make the event fresh and new.

"Dom, can you help me with something?" Natalie asks as she approaches me. "I'm sorry to interrupt. This won't take long."

"Of course. What's up?"

"There's a book on the top shelf of Steven's study that I want to show Luke, and I can't reach it. Can you get it for me? I'll show you where it is."

I frown down at her. "What about Luke?"

"He's busy with the babies," she says and grabs my arm, not giving me time to look around, and practically drags me into the house, through the kitchen and down the hall to my father's study. "It's right in here—"

She looks like she's staring at the bookcase, then turns when she hears voices.

"Oh, hold on. Stay right here."

"Nat, what's going on?"

Suddenly, Jules and Alecia appear in the doorway.

"What is going on?" Alecia asks as Jules pushes her in the room, then Nat and Jules each grab a doorknob on the French doors and pull them shut.

"There!" Jules yells through the door. "Now you have to talk! So talk!"

twenty-two

Alecia

"Alecia!" Jules calls out and hurries over to where I'm talking with Jax and Logan in Steven's garden.

"Hey, Jules."

"You guys are so damn hot," Jules says as she approaches us, then hugs each of them. "Like, super hot. I love your suits."

Jax and Logan opted for grey suits, minus the jackets, with a three button vest and white button up shirts rolled on the forearms. Jax is wearing a green tie and Logan is wearing a soft pink one, in honor of his mother, who is currently battling breast cancer. They look hip and fresh and completely handsome.

"Thanks, gorgeous," Jax replies and kisses her cheek.

"Are you happy?" Jules asks them.

"Couldn't be happier," Logan says with a grin, then kisses his groom on the cheek. "This was perfect, and your family is awesome for hosting."

"Well, we were happy to do it." She sighs happily. "It's so romantic. Alecia," she turns to me. "Can I steal you for a minute? I'd like to discuss something with you."

"Of course."

"Thanks again, Alecia," Logan says and hugs me tight. "You did an awesome job."

"My pleasure." I collect my hug from the incredibly sexy Jax, then follow Jules toward the house. "What's up?"

"Oh, let's go inside and get out of the sun," she says and takes my hand in hers. "It's so hot today."

I frown over at her. "It's not that hot."

"You're not hot? Oh, I'm roasting." She fans her face and rolls her eyes. "Maybe my hormones are still out of whack from having Stella."

"She's five months old," I remind her.

"Well, either way, I'd like to go inside. Too much sun causes wrinkles." She winks at me and leads me through the kitchen. "Let's go to my dad's study. It's quiet in there."

She's up to something. One thing Jules is *not* is a good liar. Before I know it, she's planted her hand in my back and shoved me not so gently into the study, and she and Natalie pull the doors closed behind me, leaving me with an equally surprised Dominic.

"There!" Jules yells. "Now you have to talk! So talk!"

I close my eyes and sigh in defeat. *Damn them.*

"We love you!" Natalie calls in a sing song voice.

Dominic leans his hips back on Steven's desk and crosses his arms, watching me quietly. Resigned, I cross to the couch, it's back facing the desk, and lean my hips against it, facing him, mirroring his stance.

"Why aren't they talking?" Jules mutters.

Dom's lips twitch with humor.

"So, how was Italy?" I ask, breaking the silence.

He frowns and blinks. "It was fine."

I nod thoughtfully. "Good."

"How's Blake?" he asks out of the blue.

I scowl. "Fine, I guess. Why wouldn't he be?"

"Are you fucking him?" he asks quietly, and I'm struck dumb.

Am I fucking Blake?

"What did he ask?" Natalie whispers loudly.

"I don't know, they're not talking loud enough," Jules replies.

"Am I fucking *Blake*?" I repeat.

He just raises a brow and waits, but his eyes have softened as he watches me.

"You think I'm fucking *Blake*?" I hate the quiver in my voice. Hate it. How could he possibly think that?

"Let me get this straight." I push away from the couch and pace before him. "You come to my condo and walk in on something you didn't even fully understand, get angry, make accusations, and then you leave the damn *country*. I haven't seen you in *weeks*, haven't heard from you, and the first thing you ask me is if I'm fucking my best friend?"

"I saw it," he replies.

"What, exactly, do you think you saw?"

"I came to your condo to ask you to go to Italy with me, and I walked in to find Blake half naked, you coming out of the shower, and your clothes thrown all over the living room."

"You came to take me to Italy?"

My heart stops. He wanted me to go with him?

"I did."

"I was in the shower," I reply, the blood leaving my face. "Getting ready to come see you."

He tilts his head. "Excuse me?"

"Blake and I went for a run, and then he talked me into going to your place."

He swallows hard, processing my words, and I'm still stuck like stupid on *I came to take you to Italy with me.*

"And then you pissed me off so bad with your insane accusation that the reason I was going to come to your place completely left my brain."

"Why were you coming to see me?" he asks quietly.

I can't tell him this!

"I guess there's nothing left to say." I turn to walk away, but he stops me, his hand on my arm.

"Oh, there's plenty to say."

"You thought I was unfaithful to you!" I round on him, furious. "You jumped to conclusions without talking to me!"

"I've tried to call you," he replies, his voice hard and cold. "You never answered. I had to go to Italy. I had a family emergency."

"You left without me! I thought you'd just left because the going got rough! That I didn't mean enough for you to fight for me. Just like everyone else in my life."

"Alecia, no." He shakes his head in disbelief.

"I think it's obvious that this isn't going to work." I school my features and swallow hard, determined to get through this without letting him see me cry. "You obviously don't trust me, and what I need, you can't give me."

"Just tell me what you want! Tell me how you fucking feel!"

"I fell in love with you!" I yell back angrily. "I was so in love with you my heart ached. And then I find out that just like everyone else in my life, you rank me last on your priority list!"

"This is bullshit!" he exclaims. "You *are* my priority. You're my *only* priority, damn it!"

He takes my shoulders in his hands and holds me in front of him. "I was coming *to you* to take you with me."

"I was coming to you to tell you I love you," I reply before I can stop the words, and feel my eyes fill with tears. "And when I got there, I was told you'd left for Italy. And you didn't even call me to tell me your were leaving."

"Oh, baby, no." He pulls me against him, and hugs me tightly, in the special way he does. "I'm so sorry for this. For all of it. We've been hurting for weeks for no reason."

"I didn't fuck Blake," I say, the anger surging through me again as I push away from him. "I would *never* do that. How could you think that?"

"It looked really bad," he replies with a sigh. "And I've lived that before."

"The ex." I cover my mouth with my hand.

"After my mother died, I was engaged to a woman, and I walked in on her having an affair with my cousin the night before our wedding."

"Oh, my God," I whisper and glance away, covering my mouth with my hand, but then I get pissed again. "And you immediately assumed that I'd do the same?"

"I was worried about Gianna back in Italy. I was excited to see you and whisk you away on a romantic trip to my home, and when I walked unannounced into your condo, I felt like I was reliving that scene in Italy all over again."

"But nothing happened," I insist. "Nor would it ever happen. Blake is in love with Emily."

He simply nods, his eyes sad, mouth grim.

"It's been a shitty few weeks," he says quietly.

I simply nod. "One good thing came of it, though."

"What's that?"

"I went home too. To San Francisco. I confronted my parents and Jonathan."

His eyes warm. "What happened?"

I lean against the couch again and cross my arms, wanting to touch him. Aching for him to hold me again.

"My parents are my parents. They don't get it, and honestly, I don't know if they ever will, but I told them how they made me feel and I felt really proud of myself when I left."

"You should be proud of yourself. You're so fucking strong. And Jonathan?"

"That was a surprise." I frown. "He apologized to me."

"Really."

"He was actually . . . *sweet*. And it felt good to put some closure on it."

He nods and smiles softly. "I'm so happy for you, Alecia."

"So, what now?" I ask, waiting for him to make a move.

"Well, I can't unlove you, *cara*. Trust me. I've tried. The past few weeks have been a hell that I wouldn't wish on my worst enemy."

"You love me?" I ask with a whisper. Finally, *finally*, he reaches for me, crushes me to him and holds on tight.

"Loving you is like breathing, Alecia. Being apart from you, thinking that I'd never hold you like this again, was agony. I love you *so much*, and I'm so sorry that I didn't say it before."

"I'm so afraid that you'll hurt me," I whisper against his chest. "I know it sounds stupid, but I can't help it."

"Love doesn't hurt you, *tesoro*. People who don't know how to love hurt you. You have so much love to give, and trust me when I say, I'm never going to stop loving you. I'd never walk away from you and you can damn well know that I'm going to fight for you. Remember what I told you that night in your condo? It's you and me."

"I missed you," I murmur with a nod. "I missed us."

"That's the last time you'll miss me." He tips my chin up and smiles down at me softly. "I'm sorry."

"Me too."

"Here!" Jules calls from the other side of the door. "You're gonna need this!"

She slides a condom under the door, and Natalie giggles.

"Wait!" Natalie slips another with it. "Take two. You've earned it."

"They're still out there," I mutter with a laugh.

"We're not having sex in here!" Dom calls out. "And you both need to go away!"

"Killjoy!" Jules yells. "You should be thanking us!"

"Thank you!" I say. "Now go away!"

"We're not appreciated," Natalie says. "Let's go eat cupcakes."

"Will's probably already claimed them all."

"I THINK IT went well," I say, as Dominic escorts me up to my condo after the reception.

"I'm here with you, so yes, I'd say Jules and Nat's plan went well."

"The wedding, silly." I nudge him with my elbow and then laugh and wrap my arms around his waist, lean my cheek on his chest and breathe him in as we wait for the elevator. "Okay, that went well too."

"Are you tired?" he asks quietly, his lips in my hair.

"I'm fine," I reply and lead him to my door. "Are you tired?"

He shakes his head slowly, his eyes pinned to mine as he slowly stalks me through my apartment.

"Are you hungry?" I ask.

He smiles slowly, that dimple winking at me, as he shakes his head again and reaches for my hand, pulls me to him and lowers his lips to mine and kisses me gently, lightly, his mouth dancing with mine in the dark silence of my condo. My fingers find each of the buttons on his shirt and then I push it over his shoulders to the floor. He reaches for the zipper on my dress, but I quickly sink down, squatting before him, and make quick work of his belt, unfasten his pants, plant a kiss on his stomach, right between his navel and his cock as I stroke his already semi-hardness, kissing my way down to it.

"Alecia," he whispers, as I lick around the rim of the head, and grin when he sucks in a breath and his abs contract. "Fuck."

"I haven't even done anything yet," I say and grin up at him.

"You breathe and I'm hard, *cara*."

He's such a charmer.

Let's see if I can make him lose his English.

I fucking love it when he speaks Italian to me.

I plant a sweet kiss on the tip, right over the slit and then smile innocently, watching him, as I open my mouth and sink over him, pulling him all the way into my mouth.

"*Gesù hai intenzione di uccidermi,*" he whispers, and I mentally high-five myself, clench my mouth around him and pull up, swirl my tongue around the tip and repeat the motion, over and over again.

He rips the pins out of my hair impatiently, tossing them on the floor, then sinks his hands in the strands, pulling slightly, making my panties flood. I love making him crazy.

Suddenly, he's pulled me to my feet, kisses me hard, and lifts me in his arms and carries me to my bedroom. He sets me on my feet, and before I know it I'm stark ass naked and he's lain me on my back in the middle of the bed, crawling over me with blue eyes bright with pure male lust.

"I love being intimate with you," he whispers against my lips as he settles his pelvis against mine. "And I don't just mean this, although, this is fucking amazing. I mean *intimate.*" He kisses me deeply, his tongue tangling with mine, then nibbles his way down my jawline to my ear.

"Explain, please," I whisper, and then gasp when his hand journeys up my side to my breast and his thumb finds my nipple.

"Intimacy is who you wake up thinking about at three in the morning," he says, then licks up my ear lobe. "It's talking about your hopes and fears in the dark." He tweaks my nipple again, then that hand travels down my side, headed south. "It's the one person you give your undivided attention to when ten other people are fighting for it."

I gasp when his fingers find my clit and press lightly, then slip down into my folds and simply slide back and forth through the wetness.

"It's that person, always in the back of your mind, no matter how distracted you are."

"God you're good with both your mouth and your hands," I say, and bite my lip as he leans up on his elbow to stare down at me. "You say such pretty things."

"You like my mouth, *mi amore?*" he asks, making me grin.

"I know that word," I say softly.

"Which one?"

"*Amore.*"

"Do you?" he says and nuzzles my nose with his before kissing down my neck, sending electricity zinging down my limbs. Dear God, his mouth is incredible.

"I love you too," I whisper, making his head come up and his blue eyes widen.

"Say it again."

I cup his face in my hands. "I love you."

He sighs and drags his knuckles down my cheek. "One more time."

I love you I mouth silently.

He closes his eyes for a heartbeat, then opens them and smiles that naughty, you're about to have the time of your life, smile. He kisses my lips firmly, bites my lower lip, and then bites my chin softly.

"I love you, Alecia," he says and buries his face in my neck, sucking and biting the tender flesh there. "And I'm going to spend the rest of the night showing you just how much."

"This has possibilities," I reply dryly, but my breath catches in my throat when he nips at my nipple, then sucks it into his mouth, pulling back with a loud *pop*.

"Possibilities?"

"Mm." I circle my hips in invitation, but he just moves lazily to the other breast, circles it with his nose, nips at it, and watches it get hard.

"Your body is so responsive," he whispers, and blows on my wet nub, making me moan.

"Dom," I whisper.

"Yes, *amore*."

"You sure know where my buttons are."

He grins. "And yet, I find new ones all the time."

He moves down the bed, spreads me wide, and before I know it, his mouth is latched onto my clit and he's sending me over into a mind-numbing climax.

I grip onto his hair and cry out, riding the wave of the orgasm, then sigh when he moves lower, kissing me intimately. His tongue is inside me, and then he nibbles on my lips.

"You're so damn beautiful down here," he says, watching his own fingers tickle through my folds. "So pink." The tip of his finger nudges my clit, and I tense up again, my hips surge, and he chuckles "Sensitive."

"Maybe a little," I agree.

He cocks a brow and tips his head down to press a kiss to my clit, making me sigh with pleasure.

"Okay, a lot."

"I'm forever craving you," he whispers and slips two fingers inside me, slowly moving them in and out.

"Oh, my." I tip my head back, close my eyes, and grip onto the sheets. Jesus, the sensations he sends through my body should be illegal.

"Watch me," he demands. I'm a panting, quivering mess as I lift my head and watch him press his lips to me, gently at first as his fingers are still moving lightly, but then he gets rougher, more forceful, more urgent.

"Oh, sweet Jesus," I moan, unable to look away from him. "You're so damn good at that."

"It's you," he mumbles around me. "It's you."

I cry out as I come again, my hips jerking, rocking shamelessly against his face, and finally he's climbing up me and slipping inside me in one fluid motion. He braces himself over me, not moving, brushes my hair off my cheek, and lays his lips on mine.

"It's all for you."

He kisses me deeply, and I can taste myself, and him, and it's the best kiss we've ever had. It starts slow and lazy, but my hips won't stay still. I start to pulse under him, clenching, rolling, until he tears his lips from mine on a long groan and begins to fuck me in earnest, moving fast and sure, staring into my eyes.

He braces one arm on the headboard, and the sight of his toned, sexy body takes my breath away.

"You're unbelievably hot," I tell him honestly. "Seriously, your body is incredible."

He smiles arrogantly, but when I tip my hips up and clench down on him, he closes his eyes and swears under his breath in Italian, turning me on even more.

"Fuck," I agree. I reach down and press on my clit, and that's it, I tip over, coming loudly, violently.

His eyes open and he watches me raptly, and when I'm done, he pulls out, turns me over, pulls my ass in the air and slams back inside me. He smacks my ass and rides me hard and fast.

"You're mine, Alecia." He presses his lips to my shoulder, then bites me gently and groans as he comes.

"Mine."

twenty-three

Three months later...

I can hear him whistling in the bathroom, the shower running. I can picture his tight, naked body, soapy and tanned under the water.

I'm tempted to get my lazy ass up and join him, but the bed feels nice, and I'm not anxious to get this day started.

I'm nervous.

I roll over and see the photo on Dom's side of the bed of the two of us in Italy and smile. I think it's the cheesiest selfie we've ever taken, but it's his favorite of us, so he framed it and stuck it there, next to his bed.

I rest my head in my hands, and as he continues to whistle away in the bathroom, daydream happily about the day he surprised me with that trip . . .

"Close your eyes, amore," he whispers against my cheek. Summer is just beginning to give way to fall, and the air is lighter, almost crisp, here near the water. He's brought me back to the pier near my condo, with the locks of love that he still sneers at, and we are enjoying our wine in the grass.

I follow his instructions, expecting him to tell me a sexy story, but instead I feel him place something in my lap.

"If that's a puppy, you can just take it back where you got it. I don't do pets." My lips turn up in a grin as he laughs.

"Not a pet, puppy or otherwise, cara," he assures me. "Open your eyes."

In my lap is a plain white envelope, with nothing written on the outside.

"A Dear John letter?" I ask dryly.

"You're funny today," he says with a smile and tucks my hair behind my ear. I love that he is forever touching me. I'll never get tired of it. "Open it."

Inside is an itinerary, for two, to Italy.

"Holy shit," I whisper.

"I want to show you Italy. I want you to meet Gianna."

"I want to meet both," I reply, and then throw my arms around him. "We're going to Italy!"

"We are."

"When?"

"Whenever you like. The tickets are open-ended, so we can go whenever it's convenient for you to get away."

"You might be the best Italian boyfriend ever."

He laughs, lays me back in the grass, and kisses me silly, sending tingles all through me.

Charming Italian.

"You have to get out of bed," Dominic calls from the bathroom.

"I will," I reply. "This picture is cheesy."

He sticks his head out of the doorway and scowls at me. "I love that picture. You're beautiful in it."

Then he's gone again, bustling around in the bathroom. The water is running. I hear him snatch his toothbrush out of its holder.

Honestly, I love that damn picture, it's just fun to tease him about it. That was my favorite day in Italy.

"I get to crush the grapes with my feet?" I ask excitedly. "Like in 'I Love Lucy'?"

"Something like that," Dom replies and leads me into a barn with a big tub that looks like a water trough. A man dumps a bucket of grapes in it and grins at Dom.

"Tutti pronti," the man says and walks away.

"What did he say?" I ask.

"All ready," Dom replies. "Are you ready?"

"I'm going to stomp around in the grapes?"

"Yes." His eyes are full of mischief as he leads me to a bucket of warm water, and helps me rinse off my feet, then holds my hand as I climb in the large

tub and step into the grapes.

"This feels . . . weird." I stand still, facing the open doors of the barn, where I can see the rolling hills of Tuscany and lines and lines of vines. It's the most beautiful view I've ever seen.

Aside from the one in Washington, at Dominic's vineyard.

"You have to stomp on them, tesoro," he says.

"Why aren't you doing this with me?" I ask suspiciously as he aims his phone at me and snaps a picture.

"It's more fun this way."

"Uh huh." I begin to walk, scrunching up my nose at the way the grapes squish between my toes. It smells earthy and good, but feels so weird. "This is kind of gross."

"You're so funny," he says with a smile.

"I can't believe you do it this way for all of your wine," I say, as I trudge through the grapes.

"We don't," Gianna says from the doorway. "I can't believe you're making her do that."

"I knew it!"

Dominic is doubled over, laughing.

"You're such a shit," I say with a laugh. "My feet are going to be purple forever."

"Just for a few days," he says, and wipes his eyes. "You look like you're having fun."

"Please get me out of here."

He lifts me out of the tub, sets me on my feet, and holds his phone up, getting a selfie of us with Tuscany in the background, laughing, delighted with each other.

"You know," Gianna comments as she watches us. "I don't think I've ever seen you this happy, Dominic."

"I haven't been," he replies, and rests his forehead on mine. "Until I found her."

"Get your ass out of bed!" Dom calls from the bathroom.

"You're bossy," I grumble, as I roll out of bed and tug on panties and a bra, then decide, screw it, and throw his white shirt on from yesterday and join him in the bathroom. He's standing in front of the mirror, shirtless, and leans his hands on the vanity as he watches me.

"You're going to wear my dirty shirt to meet your parents?" he asks with a grin as I hop up onto the vanity next to him and swing my feet back and forth.

"You know, you don't have to go," I reply reasonably. "They're nice enough, but you shouldn't have to endure it. I can go alone."

"No," he replies simply, and combs his hair.

"I still can't believe they called," I say with a frown, watching Dom. "I mean, I told them to, if they ever wanted to have a relationship with me, but I didn't expect them to actually do it."

Big, gigantic butterflies take flight in my belly as I think about meeting up with my parents for lunch. They flew up here just to see *me*.

"I can't believe they even knew what airport to fly into." Dom snickers and pulls his shaving stuff out of a drawer. "I mean, this is kind of ridiculous."

"Alecia."

"Yeah?"

He slides me over in front of him and pins me here, his hands on the granite at my hips, and kisses my nose lightly. "Stop worrying."

"I'm not."

"You are." He kisses my forehead, then hands me his shaving cream. "Lather me up."

"This could be fun." I grin and shoot the white foam into my hands, then rub them together and begin rubbing it on his handsome face. I'm all smiles, delighted with him, as he clenches his lips closed so I can get the area between his nose and lips, then laugh when I get it up his nose. "Sorry. I don't put shaving cream on a face often."

He laughs with me as I concentrate on my task, making a complete mess of him.

"Spread it down on my neck."

I follow his directions, then lean back and take in my handiwork.

"I suck at this."

"It'll get the job done," he replies, and hands me his razor.

"I get to put a sharp instrument against your neck?" I ask incredulously.

"Don't make me regret this."

Before I can begin, he leans in and plants a kiss right on my cheek, leaving a dollop of cream on my skin, making me giggle. "You're making a mess!"

"We're even on that score."

He watches my face calmly, and holds perfectly still, as I glide the razor down his cheek, doing my best to get all of the whiskers.

When I get to his neck, I give up.

"You finish. This part makes me nervous." He grins and takes the razor, slides me aside, and leans in to the mirror to finish up.

"You did a good job, *amore*."

"I was worried that I'd cut you, my love."

He stills at my words. He always does when I call him my love.

He wipes his face off with a towel, and I lean in and kiss him on the cheek, resting against him for just a moment.

He tosses the towel aside, and slides me back in front of him.

"You can't wear this," he says and slips his shirt off of me, then to my surprise, simply wraps his arms around me and hugs me close. "Your back is so slender," he murmurs. "My hands look so big on it."

"I love the way your hands feel on my back," I reply softly, and breathe him in. "You smell good."

"Alecia, you take my breath away." He buries his face in my neck and, still holding on tightly, takes a deep breath. "You are everything good in my life."

"Are you okay?" I ask, a bit concerned. He's holding onto me almost desperately.

"I need you to know," he begins and kisses my cheek, then pulls back only far enough to look into my eyes. "I don't want to just spend my life with you. I want to spend my *only* life with you. Every day."

He swallows hard and drags his fingertips down my back, then up again, caressing me sweetly. "I know that forever is a long time, but if you tell me that I get to wake up to your sweet smile every day, it will never be long enough." He sweeps my hair back behind my ear. "A smart woman once told me that love is a daily reminder. It's saying, *I choose you. Today and every day.* Spend forever with me, Alecia."

My heart stills, then stumbles into double time.

"Did you just ask me to marry you?" I whisper.

"I need you to marry me, be my partner, my friend, my love. You're everything, *amore.* I love you more than you will ever understand."

"I love you too," I reply and kiss his lips softly.

"Is that a yes?"

"Hell yes."

epilogue

Steven Montgomery

Ten Years Later

The day is just waking up as I pad down the stairs in my son, Dominic's, home toward the kitchen. My bride of fifty years today is still sleeping like an angel upstairs, and rather than make love to her, which was my first thought, as it is every morning, I decided to let the poor woman sleep.

It's going to be a busy day.

I'm surprised to hear quiet voices in the kitchen, assuming that I'm the first up.

"Good morning, Dad," Natalie says with a grin. She and Luke are sitting at the breakfast bar, sipping coffee. It never gets old hearing this sweet girl call me Dad. I'm not the man that she comes from, but she's been mine for more than twenty years now, and I couldn't love her more. She gives me a big hug, and when I point to my cheek, she plants a kiss there as well.

"You two are up early." I pour myself a cup of coffee and lean against the counter.

"Josie and Maddie got in late, so we stayed up with Brynna and Caleb waiting for them," Luke says. "And then Haley woke up this morning with bad dreams, so we decided to just stay up. I'm still not used to the twins driving."

"Neither is Caleb," I reply. "No parent is ever ready for their kids to grow up."

"Olivia has decided that she's in love," Natalie says with a grimace, and laughs when Luke simply glares at her. "It's just hormones."

"I'll lock her in her room."

"No, you won't."

"She's twelve," Luke says adamantly.

"It's all downhill from here, son," I inform him good-naturedly. "Before you know it, it'll be *your* fiftieth wedding anniversary and you'll have seventeen grandchildren."

Luke pales and I laugh, enjoying his panic.

"We have a while before that happens," Nat reminds him, patting his face. "Of course, it doesn't help that you have three daughters."

"I'm surrounded by women," he agrees, and I smile as I think of the two littlest ones, Chelsea and Haley, who are two little spitfires, even at nine and seven. "Keaton is all boy, though, and helps balance things out."

"How's work?" I ask Luke.

"It's good."

"He's collaborating with some amazing people for his next project," Nat adds proudly. "I have a feeling he'll be nominated for the Oscar again next year."

"I don't need Oscars," Luke says with a shake of the head. "Although, it doesn't suck to have one on the mantle."

"I'm so proud of you, handsome."

She leans in to kiss him, and I refill my cup and wink at them, then head out the back door to sit on the patio before they get too carried away. The fire is already roaring, and Isaac, Stacy, Caleb and Brynna are huddled around it, drinking their own coffee, my boys cuddled up to their women.

I raised smart boys, that's for sure.

"Good morning," I greet them and sit in the single unoccupied chair. "Seems everyone is up early."

"It's a good morning for it," Isaac replies, gesturing to the sun coming up over the mountains, casting the vines in soft pink sunlight.

"It's beautiful," Stacy agrees. "And most of the kids are still sacked out in the play room, so we're taking advantage of the quiet."

"Good plan. I hear the twins got in late."

Caleb frowns and sighs. "They made curfew, I just hate that they're driving, and they came out here, so they were on the freeway late at night."

"They're good girls," Brynna says, and rubs her hand down her husband's leg. *My boys chose well when it came to their women. Strong, beautiful, smart women, all of them.*

"Is Maddie still insistent that she wants to go to New York after she graduates to dance?" Stacy asks.

"Yes," Brynna replies with a sigh. "I don't think we'll be able to talk her out of it."

"She's so good," Stacy says. "She could do great things with it."

"New York is too fucking far away," Caleb growls.

"We have time," Brynna whispers.

"A year," he says. "It'll feel like ten minutes."

You have no idea, my boy. More like the blink of an eye.

"What about Josie?" I ask.

"She has a boyfriend, you know," Brynna says and eyes her husband, who scowls again. "She'll probably go to college here in Seattle."

"If he touches her, I'll break his arms."

Brynna rolls her eyes.

"I'll help you," Isaac says casually.

"Oh good, you start in too," Stacy says.

"Sophie's a teenager now. I may need his help before long."

"I'll be there, brother." Caleb salutes Isaac with his mug, making us laugh.

"Liam and Michael were up until the wee hours of the morning playing video games. We may not see them until the dinner tonight," Isaac says, referring to both of their youngest boys.

"We're here to celebrate, so why shouldn't they get to do what they enjoy?" I ask with a shrug.

"I'm so happy that you and Mom wanted to do this," Isaac says. "Of all the things you could have done for your fiftieth, you chose to have all of us come here for the weekend."

"We would have sent you on a cruise, or to Europe, or somewhere quiet and fun," Caleb adds.

"There is nowhere your mother and I would rather be than with our children."

And that's the God's truth.

"You hate me!" A high voice shrieks and a small blonde girl runs outside in a sprint, crying.

"Erin! Get back here!" Meg yells, running after her older daughter.

"Hate us!" the youngest, Zoey, agrees and runs behind her sister, giggling.

"Stop being dramatic and get back here!" Meg stops, with her hands on her hips and glares at her daughters. "Why do they have to have their father's speed?"

"It's okay, lazy bones, I got this." Will jogs past her and runs into the backyard after his daughters. "When your mother calls you, you come! Do you hear me?"

"They're not children," Meg says. "They're aliens."

"That's why I didn't have any," Sam says with a yawn as she comes out back, Leo by her side. She wraps her arm around me and kisses my cheek. "Thanks for including us this weekend."

"You and Mark are a part of this family, sweet girl. We wouldn't have it any other way. Here, have a seat." I stand and shake Leo's hand. "I'm going to go wake my wife up."

Leo drops into the chair, smiling when it rocks, then pulls Sam into his lap. "Rock with me for a while, sunshine."

"When does the new album come out, Leo?" Will asks as he carries his girls, one under each arm, back to the house.

"Next month," Leo says with a grin.

I walk inside, and in the short time since I left the kitchen, it's become a war zone.

"Mommy, I'm not hungry!" Abigail cries to Nic, who is holding her youngest, Finn, on her hip.

"You need to eat anyway," Nic says patiently. "Breakfast is the most important meal of the day."

"Listen to your mama," Matt says, boosts Abbi onto his lap, and offers her a bite of waffle on her fork. "She knows these things."

It does my heart good to see Nic and Matt with their children. Thank God for adoption. They share a smile, the kind that also makes my heart warm.

They love each other. And at the end of the day, what more can you ask for?

"Did you seriously just drink out of my glass, you little brat?" Lucy, Mark and Meredith's oldest, demands of her little brother, Hudson. "You are *disgusting!*"

"Hud," Mark says and ruffles his son's hair, "don't be disgusting."

"I want you to dance with me," Emma demands of her aunt Meredith.

"Emma." Alecia gives her daughter a stern look as Dominic strolls into the kitchen and sweeps his lovely wife up in a hug. "Aunt Meredith just woke up. Let's give her some time, okay?"

"Okay," Emma says, defeated.

"Good morning," Dominic says, as he takes in the chaos, then erupts into laughter. "Never a dull moment when the family gets together."

"I love it," I reply and pull my son into a hug. "Thank you for this."

"Nonsense," Dom replies. "We don't get together as often as we should."

"Where's Grandma?" Lucy asks.

"She's still in bed," I reply with a wink. "You all tuckered her out yesterday when we played football."

"Grandma's good at football," Liam says as he walks in the room, looking for food.

"That she is," I agree, and suddenly want to go cuddle her. "I'll go see how she is."

"Hey, Dad," Dominic says, and the automatic smile that comes when he calls me *Dad*, slides across my face. "Happy anniversary."

"Happy anniversary!" The others echo and clap.

"Thank you. I think I'll go give your grandmother her anniversary present," I say, just as Jules and Nate walk in the room with their daughter, Stella.

"Dad," Jules says with a scowl. "Ew."

"Nate," I say with a laugh as I pass by them. "I'm going to let you handle your wife."

"I've been trying to *handle* her for more than a decade, Steven. I've learned that's just not possible."

"That's right." Jules smiles and kisses my cheek. "Love you, Daddy."

"Love you, baby girl."

"Oh, for the love of all that's holy," she says as she sees Luke and Natalie kissing by the refrigerator. "Do you not know *how* you got four kids?"

I laugh as I climb the stairs to the bedroom. My family is big and chaotic and sometimes overwhelming, but they are perfect.

I slip inside the room and smile softly at the woman sleeping quietly. This person, right here, is the center of my universe.

I lie beside her and just stare at her sweet face. After fifty years of marriage, she still takes my breath away. There may be a few more lines on her face, and a few gray strands in her hair, but I love her with the love of a young man. She gave me all of those beautiful people downstairs.

She gave me a life. The best life a man could ever hope for.

As we are in the winter of our lives, I realize how rich we are. The money is nothing; it's our children, our grandchildren, our friends, who fulfill us.

And most of all, each other.

I drag my knuckles down her soft cheek and smile when her eyes flutter open and she presses her lips to my hand.

"Good morning, my love."

"Thank you," I whisper.

"Whatever for? I haven't even left the bed yet today."

"For loving me. For our children." I press my lips to her forehead. "For being mine."

"I've been yours for a very long time."

"Not nearly long enough."

The End

Introducing the Boudreaux series! Here is a sneak peek at book one in the Boudreaux Series, EASY LOVE, available now!

easy LOVE
SNEAK PEEK

prologue

Eli

"**Y**ou work too hard." The voice comes from behind me. I'm standing behind my desk, gazing out over the French Quarter and Mississippi River from my fifty-fourth floor office windows in New Orleans. The sun is blazing already. It's only eight in the morning, but it's a stifling eighty-six humid-filled degrees out there, much hotter than the cool comfort of my office.

It seems all I do is watch the world from this office window.

And where the fuck did that thought come from?

"Earth to Eli," Savannah says dryly from behind me.

"I heard you." I shove my hands in my pockets, fingering the silver half-dollar that my father gave me when I took this position, and turn to find my sister standing before my desk in her usual crisp suit, blue today, her thick dark hair pinned up and worry in her hazel gaze. "And hello pot, I'm kettle."

"You're tired."

"I'm fine." She narrows her eyes at me and takes a deep breath, making my lips twitch into a half smile. I love getting her riled up.

It's ridiculously easy.

"Did you even go home last night?"

"I don't have time for this, Van." I lower into my chair and motion for her to do the same, which she does after shoving a banana under my nose.

"But you have time to stare out the window?"

"Are you trying to pick a fight today? Because I'll oblige you, but first tell me what the fuck we're fighting about." I peel the banana and take a bite, realizing that I'm starving.

Savannah blows out a deep breath and shakes her head while mumbling something about pigheaded men.

I smile brightly now.

"Lance giving you problems?" My hands flex in and out of fists at the idea of finally laying that fucker flat. Savannah's husband is not one of my favorite people.

"No." Her cheeks redden, but she won't look me in the eye.

"Van."

"Oh good, you're both here," Beau says as he marches in my office, shuts the door behind him, takes the seat next to Savannah, steals my half-eaten banana out of my hand, and proceeds to eat the rest of it in two bites.

"That was mine." My stomach gives a low growl, not satisfied in the least, and I give a brief thought to asking my assistant to run out for beignets.

"God, you're a baby," Beau replies and tosses the peel in my garbage. My older brother is taller than my six-foot-four by one inch and as lean as he was in high school. But I can still take him.

"Why the fuck are you two in my office?" I sit back and run my hand over my mouth. "I'm quite sure you both have plenty to do."

"Maybe we missed you," Savannah says with a fake grin and bats her eyelashes at me.

"You're a smart ass."

She just nods knowingly, but then she and Beau exchange a look that has the hairs on the back of my neck standing up.

"What's going on?"

"Someone is stealing from us." Beau tosses a file full of spreadsheets in my direction. His jaw ticks as I open it and see columns of numbers.

"Where?"

"That's what we don't know," Savannah adds quietly, but her voice is full of steel. "Whoever's doing it is hiding it well."

"How did you find it?"

"By accident, actually," she replies crisply, all business now. "We know it has to be happening in accounting, but it's buried so deep, the who and how is a mystery."

"Fire the whole department and start over." I shut the file and lean back, just as Beau laughs.

"We can't fire more than forty people, most of whom are innocent, Eli. It doesn't work like that."

"There has to be a paper trail," I begin, but Savannah cuts me off with a shake of her head.

"We're paperless, remember?"

"Oh yeah, saving the fucking trees. Are you telling me that no one knows what the fuck is going on?"

"It's not a huge amount of money, but it's big enough to piss me off," Beau says quietly.

"How much?"

"Just over one hundred G's. That we've found so far."

"Yeah, that's enough to piss me off too. They're not just stealing post-its out of the supply closet."

"And it's not predictable. If it was a regular amount, on a routine, we could find it no problem. But I don't want to cause mass hysteria in the company. I don't want everyone to think that we're looking over all of their shoulders every damn minute."

"Someone is stealing and you're worried about the employees feelings?" I ask with a raised brow. "Who the fuck are you?"

"He's right," Savannah adds. "Having the co-CEO's of the company on everyone's asses isn't good for morale."

"What about having the CFO do it?" I ask, referring to Savannah, who shakes her head and laughs.

"No, I don't think so."

"So we just sit back and let whoever the fucker is use us as his own private ATM?"

"Nope." Savannah smiles brightly, her pretty face lighting up. "I want to bring Kate O'Shaughnessy in."

"Your college friend?" I glance at Beau, who has no expression on his face whatsoever. Typical.

"This is what she does for a living."

"She looks over people's shoulders for a living? She must be everyone's favorite person."

"You're on a roll today," Beau says quietly.

"Kate works with companies who are dealing with embezzlement. She comes in as a regular employee and blends in, investigating on the down-low."

"Can she actually do the job? It won't work if she doesn't know what she's doing."

"She has an MBA, Eli. But I want to put her in as an administrative assistant. They see and know everything, and they talk to each other. She's likable."

"Okay, works for me." I glance at Beau. "You?"

"I think it's the way to go," he agrees. "None of us have time to do it ourselves, and I don't trust handing this off to anyone else. Like Van said, people talk. I'd like to keep this quiet. Kate will sign all the necessary non-disclosure agreements, and from what I've heard, she's excellent at her job."

"One thing," Van says and leans forward to stare at me, the way she does when I'm about to be in deep trouble. "You're not allowed to mess around with her."

"I'm not an asshole, Van . . ."

"No, you're not allowed to get your man-whore hands on her."

"Hey! I am not—"

"Yeah, you are," Beau says with a grin.

I sigh and roll my shoulders. "Not having the same date twice doesn't make me a whore."

Van simply raises a brow. "Leave her be."

"I'm a professional, Van. I don't sleep with the employees."

"Is that what you said to that assistant that sued us a few years back?"

"Anymore."

"God." Van shakes her head as Beau laughs. "She's a nice woman, Eli."

Instead of replying, I simply narrow my eyes at my sister and swivel in my chair. Kate's a grown woman, one I'm most likely not attracted to anyway.

It's been a few years since much of anything has held my interest for long. That would require feeling something.

"Call her."

chapter one

Kate

"Hello?" I ask breathlessly as the cab I'm in whizzes down the interstate, heading directly for the heart of New Orleans.

"Where are you?" Savannah asks with a smile in her voice.

"In the cab on the way from the airport. Are you sure I shouldn't check into a hotel room?"

"No way, Bayou Industries owns a beautiful loft that we'll pretend you're renting while you're here. Come directly to the office. I have a meeting, so I won't be able to greet you, I'm sorry."

"It's okay," I reply and bite my lip as the cabbie cuts off another motorist and my stomach rolls. "I'm hoping to make it alive. I might not survive the cab ride."

Savannah chuckles in my ear and then I hear her murmuring to someone else in her office. "I have to go. Eli will meet you."

"Eli? I thought I'd meet with Beau—"

"Eli's not as scary as we've all led you to believe. I promise." And then she's gone. The cab swerves again, and I send up a prayer of thanks that I didn't eat breakfast this morning as I use my hand to fan my face.

It's darn hot in the Big Easy.

During all the years I went to college with Savannah and her twin brother, Declan, I never did make it down here to visit them, and I can't wait to explore the French Quarter, eat beignets, have my tarot cards read, and soak it all in.

Of course, I'd rather soak it all in while not wearing so many clothes. Who knew it would be so hot in May? I shimmy out of my suit jacket, fold the sleeves over so they don't wrinkle, and watch as above ground cemeteries, old buildings, and lots of people zoom by.

Eli is the one Boudreaux sibling I've never met. I've seen photos of the handsome brother, and heard many stories about his stoic, tough, playboy ways. Van says the stories are exaggerated. I guess I'll find out for myself.

Well, not the playboy part. That's just none of my business.

Finally, we come to an abrupt stop. There's a red cable-car on one side and mountains of concrete on the other. I stumble out into the hot Monday afternoon, and sweat immediately beads on my forehead.

It's not just hot. It's sticky.

But I smile despite the discomfort, tip the reckless cabbie and roll my suitcase behind me into the blessedly cool building, where a woman sits behind a long, ornate desk, typing furiously on a computer while speaking in the phone.

"Mr. Boudreaux is unavailable at this time, but I'll put you through to his assistant, one moment." She quickly pushes a series of keys, then smiles up at me.

She's very smiley.

"I'm Kate O'Shaughnessy."

"Welcome, Ms. O'Shaughnessy," she says, holding that smile in place. "Mr. Boudreaux is expecting you." She types furiously and begins speaking into her phone again. "Hello, Miss Carter, Ms. O'Shaughnessy is here for Mr. Boudreaux. Yes ma'am." She clicks off efficiently. "Please have a seat. Can I get you some water?"

"No, thank you."

Miss Efficient simply nods and returns to her ringing phones. Before I have a chance to sit, a tall woman in black slacks and a red sleeveless blouse walks out of the elevator and straight to me.

"Ms. O'Shaughnessy?"

"Kate, please."

"Hello, Kate. Mr. Boudreaux is in his office. Follow me." She smiles and offers to take my suitcase, but I shake my head and follow her into the elevator. She doesn't ask me any questions, and I'm thankful. I've learned to lie well in this business, but I don't know what she's already been told. I'm led past an office area and into the largest office I've ever seen. The massive black desk sits before a wall of floor-to-ceiling windows. The furniture is big and expensive. Comfortable. There are two doors, each on opposite sides of the room, and I can't help but wonder what they lead to.

"Ms. O'Shaughnessy is here, sir."

"Kate," I add without thinking, and then any hope of being able to think at all is tossed right out of those spectacular windows when the tall man standing before them turns to look at me. The photos didn't do him justice.

Yum.

The door closes behind me and I take a deep breath and walk toward him, hiding the fact that my knees have officially turned to mush.

"Kate," I repeat and hold my hand out to shake his over his desk. His lips twitch as he watches me, his whiskey-colored eyes sharp and assessing as they take a slow stroll down my body, then back up to my face. Jeez, he's taller than I expected. And broader. And he wears a suit like he was born to it.

Which, I suppose he was. Bayou Enterprises has been around for five generations, and Eli Boudreaux is the sharpest CEO it's seen in years.

He moves around his desk and takes my hand in his, but rather than shake it, he raises it to his lips and places a soft kiss on my knuckles.

"Pleasure," he says in a slow New Orleans drawl. Dear God, I might explode right here. "I'm Eli."

"I know." He raises a brow in question. "I've seen photos over the years."

He nods once, but doesn't let go. His thumb is circling softly over the back of my hand, sending my body into a tailspin. My nipples have tightened, pressing against my white blouse, and now I wish with all my might that I hadn't taken off my jacket.

"Please, have a seat," he says and motions to the black chair behind me. Rather than sit behind his desk, he sits in the chair next to mine and watches me with those amazing eyes of his.

A lock of dark hair has fallen over his forehead and my fingers itch to brush it back for him.

Calm the eff down, Mary Katherine. You'd think I'd never seen a hot man before.

Because I have.

Declan, the youngest of the Boudreaux brothers, is no slouch in the looks department, and is one of my best friends. But being near him never made my knees weak or made me yearn for a tall glass of ice water. Or a bed. Or to rip his clothes off his body.

Whoa.

"Did Savannah fill you in on what's happening?" Eli asks calmly, his face revealing nothing. He crosses an ankle over the opposite knee and steeples his fingers, watching me.

"Yes, she and I have talked extensively, and she's emailed me all of the new-hire paperwork, as well as the NDA's, which I've printed and signed." I pull the papers out of my briefcase and pass them to Eli. Our fingers brush, making my thighs clench, but he seems unaffected.

Typical. I don't usually inspire hot lust from the opposite sex. Especially not men who look like Eli. Which is fine, because he's my boss and my best friends' brother and I'm here to work.

I clear my throat and push my auburn hair behind my ear. With all of this humidity, it's going to be a curly mess in no time.

"That's a beautiful ring," he says unexpectedly, nodding toward my right hand, still raised near my ear.

"Thank you."

"Gift?"

He's a man of few words.

"Yes, from my grandmother," I reply and tuck my hands in my lap. He simply nods once and glances down at the papers in his hand. He frowns and glances up at me, but before he can say anything, his office door swings open and Declan walks in with a wide smile on his handsome face.

"There's my superstar." I squeal and leap up and into his arms, and Dec squeezes me tight and turns a circle in the middle of the wide office. He finally sets me on my feet, cups my face in his hands and kisses me square on the mouth, then hugs me again, more gently this time. "You okay?" he whispers in my ear.

"I'm great." I gaze up into Dec's sweet face and years of memories and emotion fall around me. Laughter and tears, love, sadness, affection. "It's so good to see you."

"Have you done anything fun since you got to town?"

"I almost lost my life in a cab," I reply with a laugh. "I came straight here."

"I'll take you out tonight. Show you the French Quarter. I know this great restaurant—"

"That won't be necessary," Eli interrupts. His voice is calm. He's standing now, his hands shoved in his pockets, his wide shoulders making the large office feel small. "You have a gig tonight," he reminds Declan.

"I can take you out before."

"Don't worry about Kate this evening," Eli replies, still perfectly calmly, but his jaw ticks.

I feel like I'm watching a tennis match as my head swivels back and forth, watching them both with curiosity.

"You know what Savannah told you," Declan says softly to Eli.

No response.

Declan glances back down to me. "I really don't mind calling the gig off tonight and settling you in."

"I'll be fine, Dec." I grin and pat his chest. "Where will you be playing?"

"The Voodoo Lounge."

"I might just show up." I push up onto my tiptoes and kiss his cheek.

"I don't want you wandering around the French Quarter after dark."

"I'll take her," Eli offers, earning a speculative look from Declan who then gazes down at me and kisses my forehead softly.

"I'll save a seat for both of you then," he replies with a happy smile.

"Have a good afternoon. Don't let the boss man run you ragged." He winks at me and grins at Eli, then slips back out the door.

"You and Declan are close," Eli says when I turn back around. His hands are still in his pockets as he rocks back on his heels.

"Yes. He, Savannah, and I were sort of the three amigos in college."

"Are you planning on fucking him?"

"Excuse me?" I feel my jaw drop as I stare at the formidable man before me. I prop my hands on my hips and glare at him. "That's none of your darn business."

He purses his lips as though he's trying not to laugh. "It's none of my *darn* business?"

"That's what I said."

He tilts his head and looks like he's about to say more, but then he saunters to my suitcase and pulls it behind him as he gestures for me to follow him.

He's kicking me out?

"Miss Carter, I'll be out the rest of the day. Reschedule my appointments."

His assistant gapes at him and then sputters, "But, Mr. Freemont has been waiting . . ."

"I don't care. Reschedule. I'll see you tomorrow." Eli calls the elevator, his eyes never leaving me as we wait for the car to arrive. "Do you have a change of casual clothes in here?"

"Yes. The rest of my things are being shipped down and should arrive tomorrow afternoon."

He nods and motions for me to lead him into the elevator.

"Eli?"

The air literally crackles around us as he glances down at me and raises a brow. He's barely touched me and my body is on high alert and my mind is empty.

"Where are we going?"

"To your place."

"You know where my place is?"

"I own it, *cher.*" He sighs and finally reaches over and tucks my hair behind my ear, making me shiver. "Are you cold?"

"No." I clear my throat and step away from him. "If you'll just give me the address, I'll take a cab to my place."

"I wouldn't dream of endangering your life again," he replies with a half-smile, and every hair on my body stands on end. Good lord, what this man can do with a smile.

I need to get my hormones under control. It's simply been too long since I got laid, that's all. And I'm not going to scratch this particular itch with this particular man. He's my boss. My best friends' brother.

No way, no how.

"You coming?" he asks.

Yes, please.

I realize the elevator has opened and he's standing next to me, waiting for me to go first.

"Of course."

"Of course," he chuckles. "We can walk it, it's not far, but it's hot out, so we'll drive."

I nod and follow him to his sleek, black Mercedes, which he expertly drives down the narrow streets of the French Quarter. I can't help but practically press my face to the window, trying to take in everything I see at once.

"It's so beautiful," I murmur.

"Have you been here before?"

"No. I can't wait to walk around and soak it all in."

He parks less than three minutes after we set off, and kills the engine. "We're here."

"Already?"

"I told you, it's not far."

"I could have walked that, even with the heat."

"It's not necessary to make you uncomfortable," he replies simply and climbs out of the car, gathers my bag, and with his hand on the small of my back, leads me up to a loft that sits above an herb shop called Bayou Botanicals. I can smell sage and lavender as Eli unlocks the front door and ushers me inside where I stop on a dime and take in the beautiful.

The outside of the building is well kept and beautiful with worn red bricks and green iron railings, but the inside is brand new and simply opulent.

"I'm staying *here?*"

"That you are," he confirms, his accent sliding along my skin like honey. "You'll consider this your home while you're with us. Here are your keys." He passes the keys to me, then turns his back and leads me to the kitchen, which boasts brand new appliances, dark oak cabinets and matching granite countertops. "The bedroom is through there," he continues and leads me into a beautiful room with a four-poster bed. "The linens are clean and fresh. The bathroom is there." He points to this left, but my eyes are stuck on the doors that lead out to the balcony, which offers a beautiful view of the street below and Jackson Square just a block away.

"There are times that it gets noisy with music and people, but there's never a dull moment in the French Quarter."

I nod and turn back to him. "Thank you. Shall we go back to the office?"

"It's mid-afternoon, Kate. Take the rest of the day to settle in."

"Oh, but, I'm here to work. Surely, I could—"

"It would look odd to bring on a new hire in the middle of the day, don't you think?"

Of course it would.

I smile sheepishly and nod. "You're right. I'll work from here." I toss my jacket onto the bed, pull my laptop out of my briefcase and walk briskly into the kitchen. "It's going to be a process."

"Kate, I don't want—"

"I'm not going to be able to just dig in and start investigating. Van's right to give me an assistant position, but that's going to be even tougher." I tie my hair back off my face and lower into a kitchen chair as I talk briskly. If I talk about work, I won't be ogling him and thus losing more brain cells.

"Kate."

"I'm going to have to play by the rules for a while, a couple weeks at least. I need people to trust me, so they'll open up to me."

"Kate."

"I—"

"Enough!"